It Rained in Dallas

It Rained in Dallas

By Robert Rienzi

Four Seasons Publishers
Titusville, FL

It Rained in Dallas

This is a work of fiction.
All characters and events portrayed in this book are fictional, and any resemblance to real people is purely coincidental.

For information contact: Four Seasons Publishers
P.O.Box 51, Titusville, FL 32781

PRINTING HISTORY
First Printing 2002

ISBN 1-891929-76-3

PRINTED IN THE UNITED STATES OF AMERICA
1 2 3 4 5 6 7 8 9 10

Always kind, caring and when needed, the modest provider of worldly advice. This unrivaled being will always have all of my love.

Thanks mom.

My thanks to the following:

To Jan Mello and Drew Ingenito for their interest in their endeavor and assistance in editing.

To Professor Iatrides and Professor House of S.C.S.U. for the stimulating lectures and encouraging words.

To Kathleen Ahern for reading each chapter as it was written and offering valuable suggestions.

To all my friends who allowed their names to appear on these pages. Some became heroes and others were eliminated, please forgive me for the latter.

And finally to my brother Bill, for giving up his time to listen to my ideas, even when he had had enough.

I

"What do you mean stand down?" He knew exactly what 'stand down' meant.

"Don't concern yourself, we have everything covered. Besides, your superiors have a vacation planned for you."

"A vacation!"

"Yes, the General will fill you in on your assignment." Just as the Colonel was about to speak, the phone went dead.

Colonel L. Fletcher Prouty had now been discharged from his duties as head of security for the President's campaign swing through Texas. He wondered why. For the past three years whenever President Kennedy left the White House, the Colonel was in charge of arranging for security and he handled every detail with a professionalism that all had admired in the Pentagon. For the President's motorcade through Dallas, Prouty was excluded.

As he sat in his Pentagon office wondering why the change in plans, Prouty's secretary strolled in, clicking her Juicy Fruit and a pencil neatly tucked in her beehive hairdo. The Colonel always found her amusing.

"Yes Darlene."

"Colonel, the General would like to see you – like pronto!" she replied.

"Is he in his office?"

"Yes, he's got LeMay and Smith in there with him and he asked – no he insisted – that when you returned – like I said, pronto." And Darlene swaggered out, clicking not only her Juicy Fruit but also her high heels that accentuated her well defined legs to the delight of all the inhabitants of the Pentagon.

"I'm on my way." He would much rather have continued with the show that Darlene was putting on, but there was no time for that now. The General was waiting.

Along the way to the General's office, Prouty knew that in a few moments he would find out just what this vacation and assignment were all about, removing him from his duties in Dallas.

"General, you sent for me sir?'

"Yes Prouty. You're going to New Zealand."

"New Zealand sir?" Prouty was in shock.

"Yes, the convention on International Security. You'll bring back all the information needed to complete the reports that Kennedy's been up and down my ass about." It was always clear to Prouty that after the Bay of Pigs and the missile crisis, there was little love between the Joint Chiefs and their Commander in Chief.

"So, let's see..." the General continued, "You'll have that report on my desk no later than November 27. You'll be leaving on Wednesday the 20th."

"But sir, who will be handling the President's trip to Dallas?"

"That's all taken care of. Enjoy New Zealand and we'll meet when you return on Monday, uh... the 25th."

"But sir, again......"

"Colonel, enjoy New Zealand!" The General was now a bit testy and Prouty recognized this immediately.

"Yes sir." As Prouty saluted and exited, he could not help

wondering what all this secrecy was about.

In the Oval Office, President John F. Kennedy sat at his desk smoking his favorite Cuban cigar while conversing with his friend, Senator George Smathers.

"You know George, I'm really not looking forward to this Texas trip."

The President knew that he needed Vice-President Johnson's help in Texas in his bid for re-election. To most, it appeared that Kennedy would have little difficulty in winning a second term. Still, a trip to Texas was in order. The unity of the Democratic Party was the chief objective of the trip. Governor John Connally and Senator Ralph Yarborough were at odds on a number of issues. In addition, the conservatives of the Lone Star state were making lots of noises concerning Kennedy's liberal stance on civil rights, the Nuclear Test Ban Treaty, the President's refusal to decimate Cuba and his plan regarding the oil depletion allowance. Despite the importance of the visit, the President was not looking forward to going.

"I've got to go Texas – it's just a real pain in the rear end and I just don't want to go. I wish I could get out of it."

"What's the problem?"

"George, you know how Lyndon is...Lyndon is Vice-President and he wants to ride with me. But John Connally is the Governor and he wants to ride with me...and I think that protocol says that he's supposed to ride...and now Lyndon wants Jackie to ride with him, which I really don't understand. And you know that Connally is a little bit jealous of Lyndon and Lyndon is jealous of him. So, all this silly fighting is going on...I wish I could think of a way to get out of it. The thing that really bothers me is why would Lyndon insist on Jackie riding with him?"

"Well, John..." Just as the Senator was about to answer, the President's secretary entered the Oval Office.

"Please excuse the interruption Mr. President..."

"For you, anytime Miss Lincoln." And the President meant it.

He always felt deeply indebted to her three years of faithful service. "What can I do for you?"

"Mr. President, Colonel Prouty from the Pentagon is on line three. I told him you were in conference with Senator Smathers but he insists it's urgent. I'm sorry Senator." The Senator smiled and nodded.

"George, do you mind? This will only take a moment."

"Go right ahead John, I think I'll take you up on that cigar."

"Thank you Evelyn, and uh put him through."

"Colonel, good to hear from you. Let me guess…must be about my cigars, my supply is getting low. You know all these Senators are always popping in to see their President about this or about that, when the truth of the matter is all they want are my Cuban cigars. As a matter of fact Senator Smathers is sitting here right now puffing away with a big smile on his face. Did you get my order?"

"No sir, Mr. President. I'm still working on that one. I'm hoping that I'll have them tomorrow. The reason I called sir, and I apologize for interrupting your meeting with the Senator, is that on your trip to Texas I won't be handling the security and I just wanted to let you know. The General informed me this morning that everything has been taken care of. But sir, for the life of me I can't figure this one out. They're sending me to New Zealand for the preparation on your International Security report that you requested and they won't tell me who's handling the security arrangements for Dallas. Sir, this is highly unusual."

"What's there to figure Colonel?"

"Well sir, everything seems so secretive."

"Colonel, I wouldn't give it a second thought. Uh, when are you leaving?"

"Wednesday the 20th."

"That only gives you two days to hunt down my favorite smoke." The President always referred to his Cuban cigars as his favorite smoke.

"I'll do my best sir. But you know how difficult it's becoming."

"Perhaps it's time to open a dialogue with our friend down there, Mr. Castro, to insure a steady flow."

"Not a bad idea sir. However, it may not be too popular, especially where you're going this week."

"Right. Well Colonel, New Zealand will be I'm sure, entertaining. Let me know how things are going on that other matter."

"You bet sir. Mr. President this security thing really bothers me. I don't know, I just have a strange feeling."

"Colonel, if it would make you feel better, I'm meeting with Hilsman late this afternoon and I'll run it by him and have Evelyn let you know with a memo in the morning. Does that help?"

"Yes it does. Thank you and goodbye sir."

"Enjoy New Zealand." And the President hung up.

"That's odd."

"Wanna let me in on it?" Replied Smathers.

"Well it seems that Colonel Prouty, who always handled all security on every trip I've made is being sent to some sort of convention in New Zealand for work on this International Security Report. Something that he says I asked for. On top of that they won't tell him who's making the arrangements for Dallas. George, I never requested any such report from the Pentagon."

"Who won't tell him?"

"You know. The guys with all the fruit salad on their hats who think that just because they're military men, their opinions on military matters were worth a damn."

"Do you see a problem here John?"

"Oh no. It's just that Prouty…there was something in his voice…oh it's probably nothing. Getting back to our earlier conversation George, that's exactly how I feel about this whole Texas thing."

"Before you know it, it'll be Friday night and Air Force One will be touching down at Dulles and you'll never have to set foot in the Lone Star state again. That is of course unless you and Jackie decide to spend your next vacation on the prairie!"

"Very funny George. What vacation? How's the cigar?"

"Not bad. I think I'll be back tomorrow for more consultations with my President."

The President smiled as he puffed on his favorite but his mind was now adrift. Why did Prouty say that the President requested the report and why didn't anyone inform the Colonel about the arrangements for Dallas? And most important, why did Lyndon want Jackie to ride with him?

II

That afternoon in the briefing room, the President met with Roger Hilsman, the head of intelligence at the State Department, Attorney General Robert F. Kennedy, General Maxwell Taylor, Foreign Security Advisor McGeorge Bundy and John Scali, the ABC-TV news correspondent to the State Department. Scali's covert meetings with KGB agent Feklisov during the Cuban missile crisis had earned this seat at special meetings with the President when the State Department was involved.

The President got things underway.

"Gentlemen, thank you for coming on such short notice. I believe that what I'm about to run by you will be of interest, affecting the security of the United States and of course hopefully, in a way that will benefit the future of all Americans. Please feel free to make comments and suggestions."

"As you all know since my visit and speech last June at American University, the results were fruitful. The signing of the Nuclear Test Ban Treaty and the installation of a hot-line between Moscow and Washington and most important here is that relations with the Soviet Union are truly moving in a very positive direction. Mind you, I'm not jumping the gun here, as we are all aware… the irascible Chairman Khrushchev could turn at any time. However, things are looking up – for now. That is precisely why Cuba deserves a shot." The President stopped and looked around at the surprised expressions. The only one who was not taken by the President's remarks was the Attorney General. He already knew.

"Just how much of a shot, Mr. President?" asked Hilsman.

"Well Roger, how about the whole nine yards. The way I see it is if were going to make an honest attempt at and set the example for all to witness, and if in fact we are successful with all who oppose our ideals, then world peace will cease to be merely a hope, but rather a very tangible entity. As far as Mr. Castro is concerned, there are those in the Western Hemisphere who would benefit from his sudden departure, but in order to meet the goals of our chosen path, a friendly dialogue with the Cuban leader just may serve our interests in maintaining a peace with the Soviets. The added bonus of course is that if we lift the embargo American business will benefit, placing positive effects on the domestic home-front."

"I see the benefits involved Mr. President. However, I'm not sure that they'll outweigh the opposition you are certain to receive from fanatical groups…groups that may become even more troublesome," replied Hilsman.

"Well, I guess we'll just have to weather that storm when it hits. And my good friend General Taylor?" The President had a great deal of respect for Maxwell Taylor, dating back to the reasons for the General's retirement from service in the late 1950s.

"John, unfortunately there are those in the Pentagon that already sense a pacifism in the government due to the handling of all operations in Cuba. They're military and as a result, they think in those terms. Any opening with Castro will only serve to fuel the fires of discord between yourself Mr. President, and your

Chiefs."

"Thank you General. Perhaps if I meet with the Generals staff, some type of understanding may be reached. Otherwise, I believe they'll just have to live with it." The President was clearly irritated with the Pentagon's position, which was nothing new.

"Bobby, have you anything to add?"

"On the issue of the lifting of the embargo, let me say this about that....if we instituted this measure in steps...testing Mr. Castro's dedication to an agreement...sort of on a timetable...over an extended period...but then this all hinges on whether Mr. Castro is willing to tie into trade agreements with the United States. If he does I believe he will be very guarded in his steps...in effect testing our commitment. It won't be easy, I'll tell you that."

"Well, the seed will be planted this week while I'm in Texas. Tomorrow morning I'll be meeting with Jean Daniel from the socialist magazine *L'Observateur* and it just so happens that he'll be in Cuba for an interview with Castro on Friday. I will mention to Daniel that the United States is interested in opening talks with Castro and I'm sure that it will create a new slant in his questioning when he gets to Cuba. If all goes well, when I return from Texas I'll begin the process with a letter and if Mr. Castro responds in a positive way....then arrangements will be made for a visit to Cuba."

"You'll go sir?" replied a startled Bundy.

"Of course Mac...that's the plan."

"Wouldn't you think that Lyndon or Rusk could handle all negotiations, keeping you out of harms way sir?"

"If someone is going to try to assassinate me, there isn't a thing I or anyone else can do to stop it. Besides, Jackie has been wanting a trip to a warm climate and this may present the perfect opportunity. Also you're all aware of the effect she has on leaders everywhere I take her. Sometimes I feel like they all show up for her and I'm merely her escort. It kind of takes the heat off." The President's remarks had all in attendance laughing.

"All kidding aside gentleman, on this one I believe it is my duty to clear up matters with Mr. Castro…personally."

"If there's nothing else, I thank you all for coming and please do send me your thoughts concerning the issue discussed here today."

The President turned to his left, "Roger can you stay behind?..I won't keep you long." Hilsman nodded.

"In the Oval Office sir?"

"Yes," and the two walked together down the hall to the Oval Office.

"Cigar Roger?"

"Don't mind if I do sir," and they both lit up. The President relaxed in his chair and took a long drag.

"Roger, who's handling the security arrangements for Dallas?" The President came right to the point.

"Why…Prouty of course. He handles everything…certainly no one better. Why do you ask?"

The President then filled him in on New Zealand and the report that he never requested and the fact that Prouty was not privy to the present arrangements.

"That's odd."

"My exact words Roger. I was hoping that you might be able to shed some light here."

"Afraid not, but I'll put out some feelers….tonight….maybe I'll have something for you in the morning."

"Good, you're help on this is appreciated." Roger Hilsman would do anything for his President, his devotion had no limits – the President need just ask.

"Keep in mind Roger, my only concern here is who is tending to security in Dallas. The rest I'll deal with when I return from my trip."

They talked for another forty-five minutes on unrelated topics as they enjoyed their smokes, at least the President gave that impression.

After Hilsman left, the President stood at a window in the Oval Office and stared out into the night. The questions were digging deeper now…Why New Zealand?……What report?……Who's handling security?……Why the secrets?…Why Lyndon?…Why Dallas?…..

III

The intercom buzzed.

"Mr. President, Roger Hilsman on line two."

"I'll take it....thanks."

"Good morning Roger!"

"I don't know how good it is Mr. President. We need to talk sir." There was an urgency in Hilsman's voice.

"I'm all ears...shoot!"

"I'm afraid the information is far too sensitive sir...I prefer that we meet in person, if that's okay with you."

"Certainly.....I'm meeting with the writer Daniel at 10:00am...can you make it here say ...noon?"

"Good, see you then sir." Click.

Sensitive, the President's mind was now racing. Just what the hell is going on here...the Pentagon is up to something.

The President pressed the call button for his secretary.

"Yes Mr. President?"

"Evelyn, would you be a sweetheart and get me all the information you can on some sort of convention in New Zealand, it's an international thing. Supposedly begins on Wednesday or Thursday. Oh, and also contact Colonel Prouty at the Pentagon, see if he's available to meet here sometime this afternoon."

"Anything else sir?"

"I think that's enough to keep you busy for now, don't you Miss Lincoln?"

"Yes sir."

As he squirmed in his chair for a more comfortable position, he felt the pain. It reminded him of the 1961 Vienna summit after the nightmare of the Bay of Pigs. There, the back pain was excruciating while he tried in vain to reason with Khrushchev. It always returned in times of stress. He had a feeling it would only worsen after his noon meeting with Hilsman.

The voice on the intercom broke the silence: "Mr. President, Mr. Jean Daniel here to see you."

"Send him right in Miss Lincoln."

"Mr. President, it is an absolute pleasure to finally meet you!"

"Welcome to the White House Mr. Daniel. I've kept abreast of your articles and I find your views are most interesting."

"May I ask in what way Mr. President?"

"Well specifically, your recent commentary on the merging of ideas through the Nuclear Test Ban Treaty and the overall easing of tensions between the United States and the Soviet Union, has assisted in driving home the point that our ideologies need not be opposed, but rather a way can be found to focus on our common interests.....on the earth's natural resources, a bright future for American and Soviet children and of course a lasting peace. Please have a seat Mr. Daniel. Coffee or tea?"

"Tea would be fine."

The President reached for the intercom, "Evelyn, would you be so kind as to have Barbara prepare a pot of tea?"

"Right away sir."

"Mr. Daniel, as you probably already know, I'm leaving for Texas tomorrow...sort of a campaign kickoff for next years election….." The President seemed to be setting the tone for the interview when Daniel interrupted –"Do you perceive any pitfalls that could jeopardize your reelection?"

"There are always pitfalls and mountains to climb, nothing is a given. For instance, the unity of the Democratic Party is in need of attention, nothing serious, but that is precisely the reason for my visit. You know it's been said that a sound foreign policy has its roots in a solid domestic policy. Our achievements and goals outside our borders will, we hope, closely resemble the steps we are taking here at home. Also, we……" Just as the President was about to open the Cuban issue, Barbara entered with tea and small pastries exquisitely presented on the Presidential tea service.

"Thank you Barbara."

"Your very welcome Mr. President." Barbara was a real piece of work and the President had a very different fondness for her than he had for Miss Lincoln.

"Please help yourself Mr.Daniel." As Daniel saw to his tea, Barbara turned on her way out, long blond hair falling across one side of her face, tight sweater and short tight skirt revealing a figure that most men would give up some part of their anatomy for, looked at the President with a smile, winked and disappeared. The President just smiled.

"As I was saying," the President was about to find the most direct route to open the Cuban issue, "as we strengthen our domestic policy, we hope to improve foreign relations with all…and most important, with those whose beliefs are directly opposed to ours, on the surface. I have to tell you Mr. Daniel, I've given a great deal of thought to the Cuban situation and I believe that the United States and the Soviet Union can work in conjunction to assist not only Cuba, but also all third world nations, with the goal that in time…they will reach the point of self-sufficiency. This can be achieved with the onset of trade agreements and foreign aid. The backing for this kind of endeavor….or getting right to the point, let me say that a great deal of money is spent and wasted on nuclear research and stockpiling, which the United States and the Soviet Union are equally guilty of. I'm speaking of a great deal of money here that can be better channeled through domestic and foreign policies, with the goal of helping those in need. We feel a good starting point would be Cuba. There, the Soviets are already assisting Mr. Castro and I firmly believe that a joint effort on the island of Cuba will begin the process of unifying our countries, putting our differences aside in our shared quest of friendly relations and world peace. It can be done and it is our goal."

"Mr. President, do you believe that after all the turmoil between Cuba and your country, that Fidel Castro would even consider opening a Cuban-American dialogue?"

"My hope is that yes he will. That is why I have chosen to personally attend to the matter with Mr. Castro."

"Personally, as in face to face?"

"Yes. I feel it is my duty and obligation to bring about a peace with Cuba. If Mr. Castro would like, I'd be willing to arrange for a visit to Cuba, in the very near future."

"I don't know if you're aware of this, but I'll be in Havana for an interview with Castro on Friday. I would very much like to get his reaction to your proposal. Would you mind if I tested the waters?"

"Feel free Mr. Daniel."

"Good, this adds an entirely different dimension to Friday's visit." The President's plan had succeeded and the journalist had a story of world proportions. Both sides had been served.

As the interview went on, they discussed a variety of issues between the Soviets and the Americans. At 11:30am, Daniel closed the interview.

"Mr. President, I thank you for your time....it was an absolute pleasure listening to your views. I admire your strength and vision, and I wish you well in your goals."

As they walked to the door, the President's final words to the journalist – "Well Mr. Daniel, the time has arrived when somebody had to pick up the ball and do something constructive with it. Perhaps Chairman Khrushchev, Mr. Castro and I can score a touchdown for mankind. God willing, that goal will be achieved."

"Amen, Mr. President. Thank you and goodbye."

They shook hands and Daniel left the Oval Office.

As the President relaxed in his favorite chair, he reflected on the importance of the interview and that it could not have gone better. The seed was planted and Daniel would now do his part. He then realized that the back pain had eased. However, he still had Hilsman's findings to deal with.

He pressed the intercom.

"Evelyn, anything on New Zealand and were you able to contact Prouty?"

"Mr. President, if you could give me another 5 or 10 minutes, I'll have a complete file on New Zealand ready for you."

"You're a peach!" The President was clearly in a good mood.

"As far as the Colonel is concerned, he's nowhere to be found....excuse me, that's not quite true...he just walked in!"

"Who Prouty?"

"Yes, shall I send him in?"

"Yes my dear and when the file is ready, just come in and leave it on my desk. Thank you Miss Lincoln."

"You're welcome sir. I'm here to serve while you protect."

Just then the Colonel entered the Oval Office.

"Colonel, it's good to see you. We need to talk."

"We certainly do Mr. President."

Prouty was carrying a wrapped bundle under his arm.

"Sir, I apologize for popping in without an appointment...but I was able to come up with your favorite panatellas." The President smiled as Prouty handed over the package containing three boxes of Cubans.

"I don't know how to thank you Colonel....but I'll think of a way."

"Sir, something is up at headquarters and I do not like it!"

The President sat and stared pensively at Prouty.

"Please, have a seat Colonel."

The Colonel was clearly on edge as he began – "This morning as I passed the boardroom, I overheard a part of a conversation that was very unsettling." He paused.

"Do go on."

"Well…General Lemnitzer, LeMay and Smith were…I believe it was LeMay who said" and the Colonel's speech was slow – "Kennedy is going to get the shock of his short life. He'll never know what…..and just then an announcement came over the PA drowning out the conversation. You know how the halls of the Pentagon echo from the announcements….then one of them closed the door to the boardroom. I don't like it sir…I'm afraid…can you cancel your trip to Dallas?"

"Well Colonel, this certainly sheds a new light on things." The President thought…the enemy within. It reminded him of the novel *Seven Days in May*, where a pacifist president was threatened with elimination by the military.

"Colonel you mustn't breathe a word of this to anyone – is that clear!"

"Yes sir, but………"

"Hilsman is due here in about…let's see…" the President looked at his watch, "…ten minutes. He's got something on this very matter."

"Hilsman is involved?"

"After our last conversation, if you'll recall, I told you I'd run it by Roger and the results of that request….will be here……….."

Just then the intercom buzzed.

"Sorry to interrupt Mr. President, Roger Hilsman is here to see you."

"Send him in Evelyn."

As Hilsman entered the Oval Office, Miss Lincoln whisked by and placed the New Zealand file on the President's desk, quickly exiting.

"Thank you Evelyn."

"You're welcome, Mr. President."

Hilsman, Prouty and the President exchanged greetings.

"Well gentlemen, I believe that we, or I, have a problem in need of immediate attention."

Hilsman stared at the President with a puzzled look, then at Prouty so that the President could see him.

"It's okay Roger, we're all in this together."

IV

The red light flashed on the General's gray phone. It was the ZR line, untappable, connected directly to an office in downtown D.C. It could only be one person – the former head of the CIA, Allen Dulles.

"Allen, I was just about to call you, we have a slight problem."

"I'm listening," replied Dulles.

"This morning in a meeting with LeMay and Smith, Lemay made a belligerent remark.....you know how Curtis can get...well, he said something like 'Kennedy won't know what hit him' and...I believe our good Colonel Prouty overheard it."

"I'd say that this is more than a slight problem. Where is Prouty now?"

"Don't know. Can't find him."

"I suggest you look a little harder, you know what it means if this thing were to surface. Find him and you know what to do with him."

"Yeah, I'll take care of it. Why did you call?"

"Just checking in to make sure everything is in place and I see that it isn't. Take care of Prouty and do it quickly – am I making myself clear?"

"Yeah it's clear, who's running this operation anyway?"

"General, let's not go there. The plan is to stay calm and focused."

"You're right. How about the garlic eaters, are they ready or are they gonna fuck this up like they did with the last two Cuban operations – Pluto and Mongoose?" The General clearly had little patience for the underworld.

"Giancana and Trafficante have their men in position. Everything is set. By the way, I'm meeting with General Cabell tonight…dinner at the Hyatt, 7:30, join us, and please General, see to this Prouty thing!"

"Prouty's history. I think I'll take you up on that dinner."

"Good, Cabell will be filling us in on arrangements with his brother in Dallas. Like I said, it's all set – Operation Crossfire is a go. Later." Click and the red light went out on the General's phone.

"Mr. President, there are no security arrangements for Dallas!" A grave look took over Hilsman face as he continued, "my contact in the Pentagon tells me that Dulles, as in the fired head of the CIA, has been meeting with your favorite Generals on a regular basis and here's the kicker…General Cabell, the other pink slipped member from the Bay of Pigs mess, just returned from Dallas. I know you're thinking that it was probably just a family visit…after all, his brother Earl is the Mayor down there. Coincidence…I'm afraid I don't think so. Something's abrew and please Mr. President, consider canceling your trip."

"Well Roger, this all may be just coincidence but….I am inclined to agree with you. You know I always felt that firing Dulles and Cabell for their inept participation in the Cuba project, would someday come back to bite me on the ass. This may be jumping the gun here, but Colonel I want you in Dallas this week. We'll arrange for a stand-in for your flight to New Zealand. Your superiors must be led to believe – business as usual. Roger, put a tail on Dulles as quickly as possible. There isn't much time, Air Force One leaves tomorrow morning at 10:00 and I plan to be on it. Until then we have a lot of work gentleman. Colonel, please fill Roger in on the conversation you overheard...I want to take a look at this file."

After the Colonel finished his story, Hilsman jumped to his feet.

"John! Excuse me, Mr. President! You mustn't go! You can't! As your friend I won't allow it!"

"Thank you for your deep concern Roger. Your service and your friendship are very important to me....However, like I said – business as usual. If in fact there is a planned coup underway and we are not misreading this whole thing, we'll put together a few surprises of our own."

The President went to the intercom.

"Miss Lincoln, great work on the file and uh...get my brother over here as quickly as possible. I believe he's in a meeting in his office...take him out of whatever he's doing...my orders. Thank you dear." The President had a way of maintaining his charm under the most dire situations.

"Right away Mr. President."

"Gentlemen, it's going to be like O'Neil said – a long days journey into night."

V

"When you arrange for the alert, just make sure that Tippit is the only patrol in Oak Cliff. I want every other patrol car in Dealey. He doesn't want to participate, so he'll probably be trouble. We'll roast his ass and pin it on the patsy." Chief Curry was as red in the neck as they come.

"Right. Who'll do the job?"

"Ruby sent this greasy Cuban exile, says he's reliable."

"How reliable is Ruby?"

"Earl seems to think that we can't go wrong with the guy. The way it's set, Ruby will take out the patsy at the assigned spot…the Texas Theater. Then he'll escape…we arrive and find the patsy Oswald, dead in the theater, pin Kennedy's murder on him along with Tippits, our old boy Johnson takes over the White House and us boys down here in Texas reap the rewards. We're home free!"

His belligerence was beginning to show as he threw down two

shots of Jack Daniels and then proceeded to slosh down a pint of ale.

"I love this town during Mardi-Gras. Broads everywhere. Dime a dozen blow-jobs." He then pulled out his .44 Magnum and placed it on the bar. Everyone backed off. Guy Bannister was drunk and dangerous. He then began uttering unintelligibles about Kennedy and how he would love to introduce the business end of his revolver, to the President's mouth.

"Soon," and he looked around to see who was listening, "it'll all be over and we'll have a real President in the White House. One that won't take any shit from the commies and that other one, the Cuban prick. Boy, things are sure gonna change in this country and it's about fucking time." Everyone in the bar figured Bannister was talking about Kennedy losing the next election. They had no idea of the planned events in Dallas.

Jim Flannery sat in the corner booth sipping on a coke while awaiting his late lunch. He could not help but overhear Bannister's remarks. It sickened him, freedom of speech was one thing but this was going too far. He got up, approached the bar and within moments he was standing beside Bannister. He stared at the source of the acid tongued remarks and then looked down at the revolver on the bar.

"What's your problem skinny?" Flannery was a tall good looking lanky man, with nothing approaching the physical attributes of the big boned, muscular Bannister.

"I'd appreciate it if you would keep your views on the President to yourself."

"Oh you would, would you!" With that, in a lightning movement, Bannister grabbed the revolver and with a backhand, slashed across Flannery's bony face. The tall man went down, his face quickly covered in crimson. A deep gash had opened between his cheekbone and the bridge of his nose. The nose was also broken.

Three men got up and rushed to Flannery's aid. As they helped him up, a crowd quickly gathered at the bar.

"Who's next?" Bannister was ready to take on everyone. Luckily, the bartender knew the big man and convinced him to leave.

"Are you alright? Looks like your gonna need stitches."

"I'm okay." He really wasn't. "Who was that guy?"

"No one you wanna know. You're not from around here are you?"

"No, up north." The truth was that Flannery was on assignment from the *Washington Post*, investigating a lead on subversive activities in New Orleans and their possible link to the local Mafia boss, Carlos Marcello.

"What's his name?"

"Who?"

"The guy who majored in pistol whipping!"

"Guy Bannister," answered a young lady in the crowd as she approached Flannery.

"Bannister! Isn't he involved with the Save America group?"

"That's the one. He runs it. Right wing, clan crazy, NRA gun toters. Scary bunch."

Just then, the bartender handed Flannery a clean towel for his wound.

"By the way my name is Jim Flannery…ouch!" as he pressed the towel to the wound to stop the bleeding.

"Pleased to meet you, I'm Susan McNeil, *New Orleans Sun*…seems to me Jim Flannery, you require some attention. That cut needs stitches. Have you got a car?"

"No I don't. My rental is back at the hotel."

"Good place for it. Come on, Nurse McNeil to the rescue…New Orleans General is about a half mile…I'll take you."

"Are you sure?"

"Anything for a fellow journalist." She said demurely.

"How did you know?"

"On special occasions I do read the newspapers Mr. Flannery. The *Washington Post* is one of my favorites, when I can get it!" She smiled as they walked out the door and headed for her car.

Susan's medium length auburn hair in a pageboy cut, framed a cute face with just the right amount of make-up. Slender, well dressed....Jim liked what he saw. She did too.

The ride to New Orleans General was filled with rush hour traffic.

"Just what did you say to provoke the big bully? Not that it takes much."

"I didn't care to listen to his comments about the President and I told him. I really wasn't expecting the reaction I got. You know I get a little tired of people criticizing Kennedy...if they would take the time to consider what he did one year ago with the missile crisis, they'd feel differently. Without his and his brother's vision, we probably wouldn't be here right now...nuclear war would have seen to that."

"I read your work on the crisis and I was very impressed...a real Kennedy man..huh?" She turned and smiled.

He couldn't help but notice as her skirt pulled up revealing her shapely nylon clad legs. She knew he was looking and she liked it.

As they inched their way through traffic, a marquee caught Flannery's eye – *Bannister's Military Books and Memorabilia.* As they passed, he pointed at the shop.

"Is that the same Bannister...?"

"You got it. The one and only."

"After we finish at the hospital, I'd like to pay that shop a little visit."

"Do we have a death wish, Mr. Flannery?"

"Oh no, nothing like that. Strictly business...perhaps I should tell you the reason for my visit to New Orleans." He then told her about his assignment and how the chance meeting with Bannister might prove to be the link he was looking for.

"Well, let's talk about it after we get you taken care of."

They pulled into the emergency entrance of New Orleans General and to their surprise, it was relatively quiet. It was Tuesday, 4:55pm and there wasn't a soul in the emergency room. Flannery was signed in and taken to a room for repairs. While Susan waited, she went to the payphone to call her boss at *The New Orleans*

Sun.

"Lane here."

"Mark, its Susan!"

"Where have you been? I needed you to cover the Mayor's emergency press conference…I wanted you to handle it. Christ! I had to give it to Byrd."

"Jeff is very capable and I'm sure he'll do a good job…but I'm onto something…I'm not quite sure at this point where it's going…but I need a little time. Please Mark!"

"You could charm the stripes off a Zebra. Okay, in twenty-four hours I want something…as in Wednesday at 5:00…got it?'

"Aye aye Captain!" And she hung up.

Mark Lane sat at his desk knowing full well that Susan always delivered. He had a soft spot for her, no it was more than that…he wanted her. He sat back in his chair and stared at the pictures on his desk…a lovely wife and two beautiful daughters. For Mark Lane, they always served as a reality check.

At 5:45, Jim Flannery emerged.

"You look like the Mummy!"

"Thanks. I think they got a little carried away with these bandages but they just might serve a purpose." She knew where he was headed. "Susan, what's on your agenda for tonight?"

"Well, I thought I'd go with this friend of mine to check out some military books and war memorabilia, something I've always wanted to do!" Susan was good at this.

"Well, after you get your fill of the history of warfare, perhaps you'd like to join me for dinner at my hotel? Would a couple of filet mignons and a bottle of Dom Perignon interest you?"

"That's some expense account Jim Flannery. I'd love to."

As if by instinct, she tenderly placed her hand in his and they stood motionless for what seemed like an eternity. Jim placed his free hand on her shoulder and drew her closer. They kissed. The guard at the door and two RN's watched as the couple embraced. The moment was then broken by a siren entering the emergency gate.

"We'd better go if we're going to catch Bannister before he closes…if he hasn't already. When we drove by earlier, did you happen to notice if he was open?" When she finished, Susan clutched his hand and pulled him to the exit.

"Yeah, the door was propped open and there was a woman inside behind the counter. Maybe we'll get lucky."

They got into the car and sped off. It was almost six o'clock now and the traffic had eased.

"In case our friend is there, you'd better take off that jacket." Flannery's khaki suit jacket had bloodstains covering one lapel.

"Oh,……yeah."

"Now get rid of the tie and unbutton your collar."

"Shall I continue Miss McNeil?"

"Later…you just might get lucky."

"Is that a promise?"

"I said might."

When they pulled up in front of the shop, they found the lights were on and the door was still propped open. There was one difference, the woman was gone and in her place was the burley Bannister talking on the phone.

"I was afraid of this."

"Don't worry Susan, he'll never recognize me with these bandages. Let me initiate the conversation…I have a plan."

"I wish you'd let me in on it!"

"Just follow my cue…you're real good at this."

"Oh God!" She was in a panic as they entered the shop.

VI

From the Oval Office Hilsman made the arrangements for the tail on Dulles.

"Listen Cappetta, use whatever equipment is needed. If you can get sound, all the better. And keep in mind, this is a matter of utmost security. It's 12:45pm now, if you come up with anything, call the number I just gave you...I'll be here for most of the night."

"Right." Click.

"Mr. President, the tail is set."

"Roger, this character Cappetta, you're sure he's reliable...you know he may see or hear something of vital interest...can he be trusted?"

"You have my word on this sir, he's the best."

"Good."

The President walked slowly toward a window in the Oval Office. He was deep in thought. The mid afternoon sun was cutting diagonal patterns through the windowpanes and across his face. It felt good. He just stared out onto the West lawn.

There was silence in the room. Colonel Prouty sat on the couch and watched the President while Hilsman quietly paced the sun-drenched floor.

The Attorney General's car pulled up along the West lawn. He got out and made the short hike. When he approached the glass doors to the Oval Office, he saw the President staring out the window, arm's folded and clearly in deep thought. He entered.

"John, is everything okay? Did something happen? Colonel...Roger?"

The President turned toward his brother.

"Bobby...we have a problem...we uhhh...Roger, Colonel would you please fill in the Attorney General?"

"Yes sir."

Hilsman took a seat on the couch next to the Colonel while the Attorney General sat in the President's favorite chair facing them. The President remained at the window, pensive.

Hilsman began.

When he hung up the phone, Susan approached the shop owner. The place had a musty smell, typical of an old book shop.

"Hi, I wonder if you could help us?" Along with the mustiness, Susan sensed the distinct smell of liquor.

Bannister looked her up and down, then Flannery.

"Looks like you ran into a brick wall."

"Something like that." Flannery suddenly got the urge to return the favor. He thought better of it. "You probably heard...up on the Interstate...two days ago...eleven car pile-up...I was one of the unfortunate...hit the passenger side windshield...a real mess!"

"Well, you're still alive and kickin! How can I help you two?"

"Mussolini's speeches...there's a volume I've been looking for, hard to find...do you have it?" Susan looked at Flannery in disbelief. Where the hell did he ever come up with this one.

"Christ what a speaker! Send goose bumps up your spine. Yeah, I've got it…gonna cost ya…rare volume!"

"Can I see it?"

"I keep all the rare stuff locked in a cabinet in the basement. You two make yourself at home…I'll get it." Bannister came out from behind the counter, went to the back of the shop and down the stairs to the basement.

"How did you…Mussolini?"

"Took a chance…never mind that…You watch the basement door, I'm gonna look over his desk here."

"What do you expect to find?"

"I'll tell you when I find it…now go watch that door!"

Bannister shouted up from the basement – "You know my wife is always rearranging…I'll find it!"

Just then the phone rang. They both stared at it on the counter.

Another shout from the basement - "Would you be a honey and answer it? Take a message, tell them I'll call them back, I gotta find this thing!"

Susan picked up the receiver.

"Hello, Bannisters."

"Rhoda, it's Billy-Bob in Dallas. Just tell your husband that Friday is all set. Operation Crossfire is a go. Tell him the positions are the Dal-Tex building, the School Book Depository and the picket fence at the rail yards. Did ya get all that?"

"Yup." Susan answered in her best southern drawl and Billy-Bob hung up.

As she hung up the phone, Susan thought… Crossfire, positions, what was that all about?

Bannisters heavy steps could be heard as he made his way from the basement.

"I knew I'd find it. Rhoda's always changing things." He handed the book to Flannery. The burley man turned to Susan – "Who called?"

"They hung up." Susan's mind was adrift and Flannery sensed it.

"This is just what I've been looking for. How much?"

"You already know how rare that is…say seventy-five dollars, or if I can interest you in coming to one of our Save America meetings, cause I think you're the kind of material we're looking for, then you'll get the Bannister discount,… Mister?"

"Dawson, Bill Dawson, yes I am interested." Flannery gave the name of one his fraternity brothers from his days at Boston University.

"Our next meeting is Friday night, right here, back room, 8 o'clock, can you make it?" Bannister was really selling now.

"I'll be here. Now how about that discount?"

"Twenty-five and not a penny less."

Flannery handed him the money and shook his hand. "See ya Friday night." As they exited the shop, Bannister could not help but think that the man who called himself Dawson, looked very familiar. If it weren't for those bandages?

As they closed the car doors, Susan turned to Flannery – "You're not really going Friday night…are you!"

"Never mind about that…what was that phone call all about…you seemed shaken?"

"Something about a crossfire and Dallas and positions…I don't know…I'm starved, can we eat now? What hotel are we…I mean you staying at?" Flannery smiled – "The Marriott."

VII

He couldn't help but think that he knew this guy Dawson from somewhere. The phone rang.

"Bannister's."

"Guy, it's Billy Bob. Did you get my message?"

"What message?"

"Well, it wasn't but fifteen minutes ago that I spoke to Rhoda and gave her the rundown on Friday's activities. Didn't she tell you?"

"What did you tell her?" Bannister thought about the young lady with Dawson.

"I told her that Friday's operation and the positions were all set. Why? Rhoda's been in on this since day one."

"What else?"

"That we'd be using the Dal-Tex, the Depository and the rail yards. What gives?"

"So why the fuck are you calling now?" Bannister was clearly upset with himself for letting a stranger answer his phone at such a crucial time and Billy-Bob was used to the volatility of Bannister's temper. He figured he was drinking.

"The reason I called was that I forgot to mention that in the event of rain, an alternate plan is in the making. He'll be taken out at the Trade Mart, you know...where he's supposed to give his speech. Rain or shine, he's gonna get it!"

"Yeah...anything else?"

"That's it for now. I'll ring you when I get all the details."

"Good." Bannister banged down the phone. He mumbled to himself – "Jesus Christ, that woman...she knows but will she put it together. No, she couldn't. I can't take that chance." Suddenly it came to him, the bar, the tall skinny guy, the guy defending Kennedy...Dawson! "I've got to find them." He sat down and tried to compose his thoughts, the alcohol didn't help. But how...he knew. He grabbed a book off one of the shelves, turned out the lights and locked the shop. He headed for the hospital.

It made no sense to get his car from the lot, it was only a couple of blocks, he'd walk. Besides, the night air might help to clear his head of the day's drinking.

When he arrived at New Orleans General, he went directly to the emergency room. He approached the desk.

"Could you help me please?"

"I'll try." Came the reply from the nurse behind the desk.

"This afternoon I was having lunch at the Bourbon Street Grill and there was a terrible fight. One of the men was injured badly." He ran his hand across his face where he had pistol whipped Dawson. "And I was wondering...well, the injured man left this book at his table and I would really like to get it to him. I had talked to him while we were waiting for our tables, he was such a nice guy." Bannister could lay it on thick when he had to. "Did he check in here?'

"Why...yes he did. I believe his name was Flannery. Quite a gash. You say you have his book?"

"Yes and I'd like to get it to him...If that's possible?"

"Let me see..." The nurse dug through the files on the desk.

"You know this is against Hospital policy, but seeing that you want to return the man's property…here it is Flannery, Jim Flannery. The only address he gave is the Marriott Hotel."

"Thank you so much." Bannister quickly turned and headed for the door. Jim Flannery he thought. Why did he tell me his name was Dawson? The big man's heart was now racing. This was trouble. What else did the couple know?

He walked to the lot, got in his car and headed straight for the Marriott. He checked his belt. The .44 Magnum was tucked neatly in its holster. As he drove, he pulled it out and checked the chambers – full. He'd use it if he had to and his feeling was that he would.

"Will you hurry up, I could eat a horse!"

"I'll be right out!" Came Jim's voice from the bathroom. He removed most of the bandages, leaving only a small strip covering the stitches. He cleaned up, changed his clothing and he felt better.

"Well Mr. Flannery, that's a big improvement. The Mummy's been returned to his crypt I see!"

"Come my dear, dinner awaits." He took her in his arms and planted a wet kiss on her neck as they left the room and walked to the elevator.

"Ohhh Jim, that feels so good!"

"I know, I thought you needed that. Can I do it all night long?"

"Maybe. Depends on your behavior at dinner."

As he pressed the down button for the elevator, he placed his arm around her waist and kissed her deeply with his tongue. She returned the favor.

Susan whispered, "Mr. Flannery, we are making progress aren't we?" Susan was receptive to Jim's advances, to say the least.

The moment was broken by two rings. Both elevators had arrived at the same time.

"Your choice my dear?"

Susan pointed to her left and as the doors opened, they both stepped in. Jim pressed the Lobby button and as the doors slowly closed, he continued his advances. They were locked in an embrace when a strapping figure passed…it was Bannister and he was heading in the direction of Jim's room. They never saw him.

VIII

It was unusual for a Tuesday night, the Hyatt dining room was nearly filled to capacity.

"All systems are go thanks to my brother Earl and the boys down in Big D." General Cabell enjoyed his role in the operation. He desperately wanted to get even with Kennedy.

As Dulles and General Lemnitzer listened to Cabell, a man brushed by Dulles and tripped, landing on the floor by their table. The man got up, he grabbed the table by the edge and cleverly pressed a sticky device the size of a quarter on the underside of the table. He apologized profusely for his clumsiness and made his way to the barroom. Sitting at the bar he placed another device, this one smaller than a dime in his ear, all connected to a neat little tape recorder. Cappetta ordered a drink and listened to the plan that could uproot America and forever change history.

"I like your taste in champagne Mr. Flannery." They clicked their glasses, locked eyes for a brief moment and the waiter interrupted.

"Are you ready to order sir?"

"Yes." Jim ordered for both. Susan liked that, a man who took charge.

Jim approached the subject of the phone call. "Now that we're relaxed and our dinner is ordered, it seems a good time to tell me about that call at the bookshop."

"Okay, from the beginning. This character Billy-Bob thought I was Bannister's wife Rhoda and..." Susan went on to describe the conversation word for word.

"Dallas, Friday, Operation Crossfire, three positions...sounds like some type of secret mission. Maybe it's CIA stuff or something like that. I don't know." Jim was perplexed.

"Isn't President Kennedy going to be in Dallas on Friday?" Asked Susan.

"Yeah, Presidential motorcade through the city, then he's giving a speech...I wonder if the route they're taking through the city..." Jim stopped and put his glass down. He was deep in thought.

"Crossfire, Jim do you think that someone or some group is planning to kill our..."

"No it couldn't be, or could it? Susan, we have to find out if the three positions are on the motorcade route. How can I...excuse me just for a minute." Jim got up and went directly to the front desk.

"Pardon me, but would it be at all possible for you to get me a map of Dallas, Texas, preferably a street map?" Jim placed a twenty dollar bill on the counter. The man behind the desk quickly palmed it.

"I don't see why not sir, you're Mr. Flannery in room 680...Is that correct?"

"Yes and I'll be in the dining room for awhile and then my room."

"I'll see to that right away sir."

"Thank you." As Jim returned to the table he caught a glimpse of the big burley man passing through the lobby. The glimpse was enough to know that it was Bannister.

He sat down and silently stared straight ahead.

"You look like you saw a ghost!"

"Uh…no, the concierge is digging up a street map of Dallas, we should have it soon." He forced a smile as he lifted his glass and toasted with Susan. There was no way he was going to tell her about Bannister.

Susan sensed something amiss all through dinner. When the waiter delivered their coffee, he placed a large manila envelope on the table in front of Jim.

Jim thanked the waiter, opened the envelope and spread the map out on the table.

"Here's the Depository and over here is the Dal-Tex building and let's see…here are the rail yards. Susan, these three positions surround Dealey Plaza. A perfect triangle…a crossfire…MY GOD!"

"Jim, we need to find out if Dealey Plaza is on the motorcade route. Is there someone in D.C. you can call?"

"I could call Scali from ABC. We worked together after the missile crisis. How's this: We finish our coffee, go to the room and make some calls?"

"Is that all?" Susan purred seductively.

"Uhhh..no, of course not. But Susan, we could be onto something of major importance!"

"Okay, so you think Scali may help?"

"Yeah, he's got an in at the State Department. Hilsman, Roger Hilsman, I think he heads up the intelligence team.

"Well let's get crackin Flannery!"

Jim called for the check.

IX

Cappetta couldn't believe his ears. He asked the bartender for a phone.

"Yes, Roger Hilsman."

"Mr. Hilsman, it's Cappetta. I've got some tape that you've got to hear right away sir. All I can say is that this is big!"

"Where are you?"

"I'm at the bar in the Hyatt Hotel, Dulles is here with two Generals. Like I said, this is big."

"Get a cab and have him take you to the West lawn of the White House. Walk up a short incline to the glass doors…that's the Oval Office. I'll be waiting. Oh, and you will be cleared at the main gate."

"Got it." Cappetta hung up. The White House, the Oval Office, the President, he couldn't believe it.

At 9:45pm the cab pulled up along the West lawn. Cappetta got out and walked the short distance to the glass doors. He tapped on the glass. Hilsman appeared and held open the door while the two men shook hands.

"Hello Roger." Cappetta said almost grimly. "I wish we were meeting under different circumstances."

"Believe me, so do I." Hilsman introduced him to the Colonel and the Attorney General, and then steered Cappetta toward the President.

"Sir, I would like you to meet Mr. Cappetta, he has something for us to hear."

Cappetta, a medium sized well-built man had hands like a vise. He shook the President's hand. The President winced. "It's a pleasure to meet you sir and I admire the work you've done over the last two years. But I have to tell you sir…I voted for Nixon. Although I will say that whoever it is that you run against in '64 you are my choice!" Cappetta's delivery and candidness broke the tension in the room. Everyone laughed.

"Well uhh…Mr. Cappetta, I appreciate your candor and I wish I had been able to convince you in 1960. However, it seems as if we have made considerable strides…haven't we?" They all laughed again. The President had an immediate liking for Cappetta. "Well Mr. Cappetta, now that you've joined our ranks, about that tape."

"Yes sir. Can I place this on your desk?" Cappetta had taken the silver reel to reel tape recorder out of his pocket. The President nodded as the five men stood around the President's desk in silence. He then pressed a black button.

"General, you say Earl has everything in order, how about Curry? Is he tending to the rebel cop…what's his name?"

"Tippet. He'll get his in Oak Cliff while all the attention is focused on Dealey. Chief Curry made all of the arrangements."

"What about the snipers? We don't want any mess-ups." This was a voice the President recognized immediately. It was Allen Dulles.

"Trafficante supplied one and the others came from Bannister down in New Orleans, all top-notch men. Kennedy's gonna get blasted, I can tell you that!"

For the next twenty minutes the conversation shifted to sports, girlfriends and the food they were eating. Then Dulles asked:

"General, has anyone in Dallas considered the possibility of rain? You know that rain will place everyone in the motorcade in hardtops or bubbletops, which as you know are bulletproof."

"Good point Allen. And yes we do have an alternate plan in the event of rain and that is to..." Just then the recorder shut off. It ran out of tape.

Cappetta looked at everyone as they stared at the little machine in disbelief. He apologized, stating that although this was the latest technology in portable surveillance equipment, the machine had to be running in order for the receiver in his ear to pick up any sound. As a result, by the time he changed the spool, the conversation had shifted again to unrelated topics and never returned to the operation in Dallas. He offered to play the second tape, which was of no importance, but no one was interested. They had had enough.

"Bobby, Roger, Colonel...if at all possible I would think that catching the conspirators in the act...red-handed so to speak, is the only way here. We have to find out where these snipers' nests are being set-up. If you'll recall from Mr. Cappetta's tape, I believe it was General Cabell who had mentioned Dealey. That may be the setting for my... where I'm...I'm to be killed." The President tried valiantly to remain calm. "We've got the goods on some pretty important people at the top, now we need to find the mechanics. If I can survive this ordeal, and I have every intention of doing just that, our country gentlemen, will be shaken for some time. If we persevere, we'll get through it...are you all with me?" The first one to answer was his brother Bobby. "You are my President, but foremost to that, you are my brother and we will see this through together."

Then Hilsman and the Colonel assured the President that they had no intention of abandoning ship. Even Cappetta chipped in:

"Mr. President sir, I hope you won't hold it against me for

voting for Nixon. We all make mistakes sir and if you'll have me, I'd like to stay on and offer my services in any way that will help in getting you out of this mess." Once again, Cappetta brought a smile to all their faces with his honesty.

"Thank you Mr. Cappetta and welcome to the front lines!"

The Attorney General interrupted – "John, I'll call for some food. Every man is this room has to be starved by now, including our new friend Mr. Cappetta!" The somber mood had changed to an alliance against the enemy within. The Attorney General picked up the house phone:

"This is Bobby Kennedy."

"Yes Mr. Bobby! Rochester here. What can I do for you sir?"

"Hi Rochester, we've got five very hungry men here, do you think you can help us?"

"Of course, you've always been my man, sir. You say the word!"

"How about some sandwiches... say for twice the number we've got here and coffee, lots of coffee and maybe some sodas and you know Rochester if you've got something hanging around for dessert...that would do just fine!"

"Comin' right up Mr. Bobby, where shall have I this extravaganza delivered?"

"The Oval Office and I owe you big time Mr. Rochester!"

"Anytime sir, anytime." Rochester loved the Kennedy boys.

X

"Before we left the dining room, I asked the waiter to send up another bottle of champagne. I hope that meets with your approval."

"You devil Mr. Flannery." Susan smiled, but Jim was preoccupied.

"I think I'll make that call now."

Jim got Scali's number through information.

"Hello." A voice grumbled as if awakened out of a deep sleep.

"John! Jim Flannery, did I wake you?"

"Jim Flannery! How are ya buddy it's been awhile? Knowing you this is no social call…not at this hour."

"John I need some help."

"Anything for you, but I was just trying to fall…"

Jim tried to cut to the quick.

"I'm here in New Orleans on assignment and I…"

"Wrong time of year old buddy. You know when you're supposed to arrange your New Orleans assignments – Mardi Gras!"

"Yeah, all kidding aside, on the President's trip to Dallas...the motorcade...does it pass through Dealey Plaza?"

"Geez, you got me on that one! But I do know someone who might be able to help. Can this wait 'til morning?"

"John, this is urgent!"

"Look, give me your number...where are you staying?"

"I'm at the Marriott in New Orleans." Jim gave him the number. "If you come up with anything tonight call anytime, like I said, this is urgent."

"I'll see what I can do." Scali hung up and thought...What's Flannery up to at this hour?...Who knows?...I'll call Hilsman in the morning...No I'd better do it now." He dialed Hilsman's home number.

"Hilsman residence."

"Yes, may I speak with Roger please?"

"Mr. Hilsman isn't available at the moment, may I take a message?"

"Yes, Miss Perkins this is John Scali..."

"Oh! Mr. Scali, Mr. Hilsman is in a meeting with the President, says he'll be at the White House most of the night...shall I get him a message?"

"No, that won't be necessary. Thank you very much." He hung up and looked at the clock – 11:00pm. He dialed the Oval Office number that Hilsman had given him in the event of an emergency. As it rang he thought, "Boy this better be an emergency!"

"Yes." The Attorney General's voice was loud and clear.

"Mr. Kennedy this is John Scali, how are you sir?"

"I've been better John, what can I do for you?"

"Well, I'm trying to locate Roger, this may be important."

"Your in luck John, I'll put him on."

"Hilsman."

"Roger, it's Scali, I'm awfully sorry to bother you but I just got a call from Jim Flannery, you know the *Post* reporter?

"Yeah."

"He's in New Orleans on some assignment and he wanted to

know if the President's motorcade in Dallas would be passing through Dealey Plaza. I have no idea what he's up to but believe me, it sounded urgent."

"Yes, Dealey is on the route. Will you be in touch with him tonight?"

"Yeah, I told him I'd get back to him as soon as I got something."

"Listen John, I'd like you to come here…right away! You can call Flannery from here."

"But Roger, I was just about to…"

"John, all I'll say to you at this point is that your President needs you."

"Needs…You can count…West lawn entrance?"

"Right."

"Twenty-minutes." And Scali hung up. He quickly dressed, got in his car and sped off to the White House.

He pulled up to the main gate and hoped that Hilsman called ahead.

"Good evening Mr. Scali. You're cleared to the West lawn sir."

Scali parked at the designated spot and made his way to the Oval Office. He was shaking. When he peered through the glass and saw the President, the Attorney General, Colonel Prouty, Hilsman and an unidentifiable man, he began to perspire. Whenever he felt a big story was in the making, his nerves got the best of him. He tapped on the glass and entered.

After greetings were exchanged, Scali was introduced to Cappetta. The vise had Scali wishing he had never extended his right hand.

The ABC newsman then informed the group of his conversation with Flannery and the subsequent call to Hilsman.

The President addressed Scali - "Did Mr. Flannery offer any reason for his request?"

"No sir, he did not. His only concern was Dealey Plaza and like I said, there was an urgency in his voice."

The President's curiosity was peaking – "Mr. Scali, please make that call to New Orleans and Roger..." He looked at Hilsman, "hit the button for the speaker phone." The President began pacing. "I think we all need to hear this."

The Oval Office went silent. All that could be heard was the line ringing...waiting for the connection to New Orleans.

Susan was in the washroom freshening herself in front of the mirror when the phone rang.

"Yes?" Flannery answered.

"Jim, John Scali here and yes, Dealey is on the motorcade route. Does that help you?"

"I don't believe it! This is ...John I have some information that you must get to your contact at the State Department." Everyone looked at Hilsman except Cappetta. "And more important John, President Kennedy has got to know what I'm about to tell you."

"My good friend, you have the opportunity now to inform him yourself."

"What are you talking about?"

"The President of the United States. Tell him directly what you've uncovered."

Hilsman broke in – "This is Roger Hilsman Mr. Flannery. We have a situation here and we need all of your input. Can we count on you?"

"Of course, yes! What can I do!"

"The President is listening on the speaker phone...address him directly and please tell him anything you know. This is of extreme importance Mr. Flannery."

Jim then told them of how he and Susan arrived at this point - of his assignment, about Bannister, the phone call in the bookshop and the street map.

"This is the President Mr. Flannery." Jim would know the voice anywhere.

"Yes, how do you do sir?"

"Oh, I've had better days…uh Mr. Flannery, I want to commend you on your investigation." The President went on "the information that you've supplied is of great importance and as you know a matter of the utmost security. I'd like to place you and the lady on my payroll now…can I count on you Mr. Flannery?"

"Why of course Mr. President! Anything for you sir…What would you like me to do?"

"In a moment Mr. Hilsman will give you a number here at the Oval Office. He'll be here all week while I'm in Texas, keep in touch with him. At some point we'll arrange for you to meet Colonel Prouty in Dallas. Good luck Jim!"

"You too sir…you too."

Hilsman cleaned up the loose ends with Flannery and hung up.

The President then addressed the group, "Gentlemen, the information that has been uncovered to this point will hopefully assist us in squashing any opposition to this administration's achievements and goals. There remains one stumbling block…if it rains gentlemen, I'm fair game."

XI

Jim slowly put down the phone. "Susan! Come in here, you're not going to believe this!"

"What is it good looking?"

Jim sat on the edge of the bed and told her the story.

"The President! So, we're on the government payroll…huh!"

Before Jim could answer there was a knock at the door.

"Room service."

"Here," Jim handed Susan his wallet, "That's our champagne, pay the man…I need to use the boy's room."

"Just a minute!" Susan answered.

When she opened the door Bannister quickly stepped in, spinning her around as he placed his huge paw over her mouth and whispered in her ear, "Okay beautiful, where's boy wonder?" He then stuck the .44 into her ribcage and released his grip on her mouth just enough so that she could talk, "He went to get ice," she whimpered.

"Well, we'll just have to wait, won't we." Bannister's back

was to the hallway, which wrapped around to the bathroom. The bathroom door, even if he were facing the hallway could not be seen from where he stood.

"Hmmm, you feel good, little lady." Bannister was getting aroused.

Just then a sharp pain traveled through his neck forcing him to release his grip on Susan. His knees buckled under a second blow to the neck. The .44 Magnum fell to the floor and Bannister's burley torso followed with a thud. The big man lay there snorting in pain. Jim applied the *piece de resistance* with his right foot to Bannister's cheekbone. "There, now we're even." He never thought he would have this chance to settle the score. Susan then threw her arms around him and began sobbing on his shoulder.

"There, there, it's okay. I won't let anything happen to you…that's a promise!" Where they were going, he wasn't so sure that he could keep his word.

"Oh Jim! That big smelly…he touched me…can't we get out of here…PLEASE!"

"Let me grab my bag." He quickly packed his things and ripped the top page off the pad with Hilsman number. Bannister was still out when they left the room. As he closed the door, Jim noticed the tray with the champagne on the floor. He grabbed the bottle, "Wherever we're going this may come in handy!"

"My place is only ten minutes from here…shall we?"

"I thought you'd never ask," as he pressed the button for the lobby.

Allen Dulles and the General hailed a cab outside the Hyatt.

"You know General, I purposely avoided the subject of Prouty in front of Cabell."

"I know and I'm glad you did. Cabell would have thrown a fit. Anyway, everything will be taken care of tomorrow."

"Would you like to fill me in?"

"Prouty's taking a commuter flight to Idlewild where he picks up his connection to New Zealand. There will be a…a specialist waiting at the airport in New York…Icepick Ivan, an Eastern European defector…hates Kennedy…our kind of guy."

"Excellent General! I think this calls for a nightcap. Driver, the Jockey Club." The two settled in for the ride.

Bannister came to. His neck and face both throbbed with pain. He had trouble opening his jaw.

"Son of a bitch!" He mumbled and went to the bathroom and put his head under the running water. He looked in the mirror. A stream of blood ran from his cheekbone to his neck. Not as bad as Flannery's but…I'll get that bastard he thought. He grabbed a towel and walked around the room. Everything was gone with exception of a pad on the night table. He picked it up and placed it under the lamp. Noticing the indentation of numbers, he pulled a pencil from his jacket pocket and lightly rubbed the graphite tip along the pad. Two numbers appeared both with the same area code, which he recognized immediately. He grumbled out loud, "They called someone in D.C.…but who?" He picked up the phone and dialed. No answer. He then dialed the second number. "Yes, Hilsman." After a short pause, "Who's calling?" And the phone went dead.

"Hilsman," he mumbled. "The State Department guy, Kennedy's right hand man. Oh Christ! Now what! I gotta get those two!" He bolted for the door. As he exited the hotel, the cool November night air felt good on his throbbing cheek. "Now what?" he mumbled, "Now what?"

"But there are so few people with access to this number…I don't like it!" Hilsman's suspicious mind was at work. After all that is what he got paid for.

"Roger, anyone can dial a wrong number?"

"Yes Mr. President but…"

The President cut him off, "Let's forget about the call…we have much more important things to deal with…okay Roger?"

"Yes sir." But Hilsman wasn't buying it.

Hilsman then went over plans with Prouty and Cappetta while the President and his brother made some final decisions on the motorcade.

"Roger, tomorrow my brother will arrange for you to use Lyndon's plane for your team."

"Mr. President, I would much prefer to use the Department's smaller plane...I don't want to draw any undo attention...if you know what I mean sir?"

"I like the way you think Mr. Hilsman."

During all this Scali wondered what his role would be, he really didn't care he just listened. When the time came this would be the story of the century.

XII

"What do you think he'll do when he comes to?"

"Who Bannister?" Jim knew exactly who she was referring to.

"No, Rip Van Winkle…of course Bannister. Do you think he might be dead?"

"He's alive and he'll be looking for us. In order for him to show up at the hotel, he must have done some quick digging and found out something. I'll bet anything that he knows that we're on to him. He may have talked with his buddy Billy-Bob."

"I knew we should have stayed away from that book shop." Susan was just about to finish her thought when she pulled into the lot and parked.

"Well, here we are…it's only a small apartment but it is home."

Jim grabbed his suitcase and champagne and they walked a short distance to the building. "In the morning I'll go back to the hotel and take care of my bill and the rental car."

"Do you really think that's necessary? You know he may be waiting there."

"That's a chance I'll have to take. It'll be okay, trust me."

When they entered her apartment, Jim put down his bag and immediately Susan threw her arms around him. She then looked over at the couch. "My cat owns that couch so you'll have to make other accommodations…Mr. Flannery." Susan wasn't too eager.

"I'm sure we'll come up with something agreeable to both of us…now how about icing that champagne Miss McNeil."

"Right away and take the phone off the hook. We've had enough interruptions for one night." She then excused herself to freshen up. Ten minutes later she returned in a very short and very revealing nightie. Jim was sitting on the couch opening the champagne as she sat next to him and sensually placed her legs across his lap. He stroked her calves and then her thighs as they sipped their wine. They were aroused.

Rochester's extravaganza was just that. Everyone had eaten and they were about to wrap it up for the night.

The Attorney General addressed the President – "John, it's uhh…going on two o'clock and if we're going to remain sharp we should all get some sleep and…uhh…you have that flight. You know we can cancel Texas and go after the bastards with what we have!"

"I really don't think that we have enough Bobby. Besides, we have to give them the opportunity to expose themselves…if we don't, then they'll just go after me somewhere else…somewhere, sometime when I least expect it. So, it's business as usual. Colonel, tomorrow call the U.S. Sheriff's office…what's his name?"

"Malinsky, Chief Deputy Paul Malinsky." Offered the Colonel.

"Right. Get him over here…my orders and have him hand select a group to take to Dallas, no more than ten men. He'll need warrants…Bobby you take care of that…and get Bundy to…"

"Bundy left for Honolulu this morning" came the Attorney General's response.

"Honolulu?"

"Yes sir, Bundy, McNamara, Taylor, Lodge and two Generals…you know…the Vietnam talks."

"Why wasn't I informed of…well I'll approach that subject later." The President was shocked to learn that some of the most important members of his cabinet were away without his knowledge. His mind was in a spin. "Could the men that I hand picked and placed so much trust in be a part of this…this?"

"Sir, I'd like to be in Dallas…with you."

"Roger, I need to have you run things from this office. You'll also have to have your men poised to round up the brass here in D.C. Bobby more warrants."

"Right."

"Well gentlemen, I wish you all well and please do get some rest." The President then shook each man's hand as if he were never to see them again and exited the Oval Office.

Climbing the stairs to the Presidential quarters he thought of the plans that lie ahead and the plans against him. He had tried so hard he thought and it all came down to this. He decided that Jackie would be told at the appropriate time, perhaps when he told her that she would be riding with Lyndon.

As he settled into bed, Jackie turned and placed her arms around the President's neck and purred in his ear – "Now that your meeting is over, how about some of that Kennedy charm for the First Lady?" It was more of a demand rather than a request. The President wanted nothing more than to close his eyes and fall asleep, however, her warm touch and the sweet smell of her presence aroused his manliness. He placed his arms around her tiny waist and fell deeply into the dream of passion. They were one.

XIII

"Paul Malinsky please."

"May I ask who's calling?"

"Yes, Roger Hilsman, State Department."

"One moment please."

After a brief pause, "Chief Malinsky here, Mr. Hilsman what can I do for you sir?"

"Chief, a matter of extreme importance has surfaced and I...and the President need your services. Can you get to the Oval Office" Hilsman glanced at his watch "it's now 8:45am…say 10:00am?"

"The Oval Office…as in the White House?" Came the startled response of Chief Malinsky.

"It's the only Oval Office in town…we'll be waiting."

"But I have a full agenda for the day!"

"I'm afraid you'll have to cancel all of it…the President's orders. And Chief Malinsky?"

"Yes?"

"You are to tell no one that you're coming here…am I clear?"

"Yes, I'll be there, ten sharp."

"Good." Hilsman then hung up.

The Colonel was glad that Hilsman decided to make the call, he could be very persuasive when necessary.

"Well Colonel, the gears are just beginning to mesh and your stand-in should be arriving at Idlewild for his connection to New Zealand."

"You never told me Roger, what does this guy Merriam, Larry Merriam look like?"

"I'd say he's about your height and weight...same hair and eye color...no twin but he could easily pass for your brother. Don't worry, with the uniform and the nametag, no one will suspect."

He matched the description perfectly. He found his man. Merriam checked in at Air New Zealand and the nametag confirmed it...Colonel L. F. Prouty.

After the clerk handed Merriam his documents, he found a seat and opened the morning paper. He had a little less than an hour to kill before boarding his flight. He read of the President's trip to Texas and then got up, grabbed his briefcase and headed toward the men's room. The man followed. As Merriam entered the men's room the man stopped, looked around and went in. There was one other occupant and he was in the far stall. Merriam stood at the sink and splashed cold water on his face, reached for a paper towel and as he turned he noticed a man at the urinal. He turned back toward the sink and the man left the urinal and approached. Merriam saw him in the mirror but thought little of it. As he fixed his uniform, the man grabbed Merriam from behind, placed his left forearm around Merriam's face and with his right hand drove an 8 inch icepick through his cervical spine, exiting about an inch above his Adams apple. Merriam shook violently and fell to the floor. Icepick Ivan quickly exited and disappeared in the crowd.

XIV

"Get up sleepy head…breakfast will be served!" Susan was a fireball in the morning. "Yeah, yeah…what time is it?" Jim pulled the sheets up not wanting to face the morning light.

"It's 8:15 and we've got a big day ahead of us." Playfully, Susan jumped on the bed. "You certainly were a tiger last night…Mr. Flannery…or should I say a wolf?"

"I don't recall hearing any complaints…come on get under the covers, there's something I have to show you!"

"Not now. Besides, I've seen it already. Right now I have to feed you so you'll be strong. Remember, we've got a lot to do."

"Yeah, okay." Jim grudgingly lifted himself out of bed and Susan directed him to the shower. "Go on, get in the shower and I'll have breakfast ready when you're done."

As he stood under the hot shower, his thoughts shifted to Dallas, the President, Hilsman, Scali and the crossfire.

Bannister sent Rhoda to open the shop. It was Wednesday,

8:30am and he made his way to the Bourbon Street Grill. They'd be serving breakfast but that wasn't the reason for his visit. "Morning!"

"How ya feelin' today Guy?" Came the bartenders reply.

"Beautiful day...how about a coffee and some of that danish?" Bannister sat at the bar and engaged the bartender in conversation.

"Ya know that guy that I hit yesterday...well I feel real awful about the whole thing. He really didn't do anything...I guess I was a little hard on him." Bannister was good at showing remorse when he wanted something and right now he wanted information on the woman.

"Yeah, you sure gave him a good one, a souvenir for life. Wouldn't be a bit surprised if that reporter he left with makes a case of it."

"What reporter?" Bannister almost choked.

"Susan McNeil from the *New Orleans Sun*. She always comes in here for lunch...they left together. She volunteered to take him to the hospital. Like I said Guy, you did a pretty good job on the man's face."

Bannister downed his coffee and threw a five down on the bar. "Gotta go, you know open the shop, get ready for the day...thanks!" On the way out, Bannister stopped at the payphone. Searching the phone book he checked all the spellings. He mumbled out loud- "Here it is...Susan McNeil, 2213 Gen. Sherman Drive." He wrote down the address and number and then placed a dime in the slot and dialed.

"Hello!" Came Susan's voice.

After a pause, the line went dead.

Susan continued, "Hello! Hello!" Nothing and just as she hung up Jim entered the kitchen.

"Hang up?"

"Yeah...let's eat and go. I've got a strange feeling."

"What's the matter?"

"I'll tell you later. Come on, let's eat."

When they finished their breakfast, Susan grabbed her jacket and pushed Jim to the door.

"What's the hurry?" Jim protested reaching for his own jacket.

"Please Jim, just call it woman's intuition." They left the apartment and walked to the stairwell where it was only one flight to the lobby. Descending the stairs, Susan saw the big man through the glass doors in the lobby. He was looking over the apartment listings.

"He's here…I knew it. I knew it was him…the hang up."

Jim stopped dead in his tracks right behind Susan. "Christ! This guy's like a bad penny…come on." They went back up the stairs through the hall and past Susan's apartment. "Is there another exit?" Jim asked.

"Yeah, this way!" They ran down the hall to the rear of the building with Susan leading the way. Exiting the building at the rear, they ran to Susan's car.

Jim took the keys from Susan and he quickly wheeled the car to an exit in the rear of the building, only to find it blocked by a garbage truck. They waited what seemed an eternity. Jim watched the rearview mirror,nothing. Then he appeared. "There he is! Get down!" Susan ducked under the dash.

Bannister stood by his car staring at their car. He was far enough away so that he could not make out the driver.

Jim nervously tapped on the wheel – "He's watching…just standing there…watching. He's trying to decide if his prey is in this car!" Just then the garbage truck moved. Jim drove slowly by the truck and out of the lot. "I don't think he'll follow."

"Can I get up now?" Susan moaned.

"Oh! Yeah, which way to the Marriott?"

"Take the back roads…go left."

Idlewild was alive with New York police. The murdered man was an officer in the United States military.

"What did you hear?" Detective Calarco asked.

"Nothing! I left the stall and there he was on the floor...with that thing in his neck. Boy, what a grizzly sight." Pete Wilson, an airport security guard feared they would pin the murder on him.

"Go on Mr. Wilson, you're free to leave. We'll be in touch." Calarco couldn't figure this one. He mumbled out loud – " A dead United States Colonel...no robbery...appears to be a professional job...an icepick...this doesn't make sense...but murder never does."

XV

The Attorney General busily worked in his office preparing the warrants for Dallas, New Orleans and D.C. When finished he would have Chief Justice Marshall sign them.

Over at the Oval Office, Hilsman and Prouty awaited the arrival of Chief Malinsky.

"Yes Miss Lincoln?"

"Chief Malinsky is here to see you Mr. Hilsman."

"Send him in."

Malinsky, an imposing figure at 6'5", good build and chiseled features, entered the Oval Office. Hilsman got up and extended his hand in greeting.

"Good to see you Chief, it's been awhile."

Malinsky's record in the department was flawless and Hilsman had great respect for the man. Malinsky felt the same for Hilsman.

"It's good to see you too Roger." Hilsman then introduced the Chief to Prouty.

"Now Roger how can I be of assistance to you?"

"Well, let me start by saying that our President is facing a most unusual situation and I can't stress this point enough, that everything I'm about to tell you, must be held in the strictest confidence...even your men mustn't know all the facts. So far is this agreeable to you?"

"Why yes of course Roger, please continue."

Hilsman, with Prouty's assistance then filled Malinsky in on all the information to date.

Without batting an eye Malinsky offered - "Has anyone been sent to Dallas to check the three sites for any unusual activity, characters, etc?" Malinsky was quickly on track and Hilsman knew he had the right man.

"No, we haven't gotten that far yet. The plan is to send you and a small group, say...ten men armed with warrants to quietly round up the mechanics, shortly before the motorcade enters Dealey Plaza." Hilsman waited for Malinsky's response.

"Why wait until then! Why not slap the brass here in D.C. with warrants...NOW...and the hell with the mechanics. Once we have the conspirators in custody the operation will crumble. Besides, the mechanics will surface through interrogation. Roger, I really don't like the idea of placing the President so close to disaster. If for any reason the leaders of this coup should decide to change positions and my men are left with no takers at the Depository, the Dal-Tex and the rail yards, then I would say that it's a pretty fair assumption that Lyndon Johnson becomes the 36th President and that is precisely what we are trying to avoid." Malinsky made some good points, exactly what Hilsman was looking for.

"Yes Chief, I see your point, but the President insists on 'business as usual' and that no one here in D.C. will be taken into custody until after the crossfire positions are secured by your men. I know we'll be cutting it close, but his wishes are to catch them in the act so there can be no question of guilt. He wants to crack this thing and sometimes I wonder if he's being a little foolish or...is he just a very brave man. I don't like the scenario anymore than you do, but I believe if we work together and think this thing through…and with a little luck, we can avoid disaster." After stating the Presidential position, Hilsman then turned to Prouty – "Colonel, what time is your flight to San Antonio?"

"This afternoon…4:00pm, commercial flight. I'll be wearing a disguise…goatee and a wig…" As Prouty was about to continue, Miss Lincoln entered.

"Excuse me gentlemen, but I think you all need to hear the latest news from Idlewild Airport." She turned on the radio behind the President's desk.

The report stated that a United States military officer was murdered at Idlewild Airport. Prouty and Hilsman stared at one another in disbelief. Prouty spoke first – "Could it?" Hilsman – "No. Of course not." Chief Malinsky had his own view – "Why yes of course, it makes sense. You Colonel, became the weak link in their diabolical plans. Regardless of whether they knew of your eavesdropping at the Pentagon or not, you had to be eliminated because of your association with President Kennedy. In the unlikely event that their plan had succeeded and then you return from New Zealand with a million questions, probing the lack of security…you become a threat…so, they eliminate you beforehand. Sort of tying up loose ends before the fact. This is a clever group and that cleverness will eventually cause their downfall. Okay Roger, let's do it the President's way…I've got seven good men that I can place absolute trust in. We'll leave for Dallas tonight. I'll need those warrants real quick. Is anybody working on them?"

"The President's brother Bobby is taking care of that. We should have them before noon."

"Good and…" A bulletin interrupted Malinsky – "We just received confirmation from the New York Police that the murdered man at Idlewild Airport has been identified as Colonel L.F. Prouty, President Kennedy's personal advisor on security. Details at this time are sketchy, but sources at the scene are stating that the murder took place in the men's room of the international wing and that the murder weapon was an icepick. As more information becomes available, we will cut in on the regularly scheduled broadcast."

"Well Colonel, Chief, that confirms it…and now we have to move fast to get Merriam's body in our hands before an ID is made."

"This guy Merriam, rings a bell. That name may have passed through the Sheriff's Department. How did you settle on him?"

"A con-man who was involved in a huge tax scam. He was a repeat federal offender and faced time in the big house. I offered him immunity if he would don the uniform and spend a few days quietly vacationing in New Zealand. He jumped at it…poor guy." Hilsman knew this meant trouble if pictures of Merriam were to find their way to the papers. "Miss Lincoln, please call the NYPD and find out where the body is being taken. Use your influence…you know…President's orders…and mention that no pictures of the deceased…use the excuse that he's a United States officer and that the body will have to be shipped immediately to Bethesda. And Miss Lincoln?"

"Yes Mr. Hilsman?"

"You can work here from the President's desk. You are a part of this and I think it would be best if we keep this from others in your office. Okay?"

"Yes sir, thank you for including me Mr. Hilsman." Miss Lincoln immediately went to work at the President's desk.

"Gentlemen, the Colonel's body is uh…" Miss Lincoln paused and looked at the Colonel and then continued "is now being taken to the morgue in Queens. I've been told that there have been no pictures taken… and that the body will be flown as quickly as possible to Bethesda as per the President's orders. Anything else sir?"

"Yes. Contact Dan Corsi in Administration at Bethesda. Have him keep the body under wraps until the President returns from Texas. He's a good man…he'll work with us." Hilsman turned to Prouty – "Colonel, your family and friends…I know it's a huge imposition…they have to believe this story. They can't be told…not yet. If we're to succeed in cracking this operation, they have to believe that you're dead. I'm sorry Colonel, but there is no other way."

"I understand Roger. You're absolutely right…business as usual."

XVI

Air Force One touched down in San Antonio at 12:30pm, CST. The President and the First Lady along with Vice-President Lyndon Johnson and his wife Lady-Bird, were driven to the Aerospace Medical Center where President Kennedy delivered the dedication. After a luncheon, the Presidential entourage spent considerable time touring the new facility where the President and First Lady met and talked with the Center's staff. At 4:30pm, they were driven to the San Antonio Sheraton where they would spend the night.

The Presidential suite was lavishly prepared for the President's arrival. In the sitting parlor, there were vases with fresh cut flowers and wreaths of red and white carnations, welcoming the Commander in Chief. The President sat in a chair by the window and pensively stared out over the San Antonio skyline. The First Lady could not help but feel that her husband was troubled by something. "Jack, are you okay?"

"Uh...yes...I mean no Jackie. Please dear, sit down

here...there's something I must tell you, it's time." The President searched for the right words to begin the story.

"What's time? Darling, you seem so preoccupied. You've been this way all day!" Jackie nervously sat on the edge of her chair directly opposite her husband. He continued to stare out over the skyline and then decided to come right to the point: "There is a plan underway, right now, as we speak, by a group in Washington, to uh...to eliminate me." The President's voice tailed off to almost a whisper.

"Did you say eliminate, as in MURDER!" Jackie was already in shock.

"Yes." The President then went on to relate the entire story to his wife. He left nothing out.

"Well, you know we ARE canceling the remainder of this trip...and for that matter we are not leaving this hotel until Colonel Prouty and whoever get down here and provide some protection to get you back to Washington...SAFELY!" The President knew this would be difficult.

"Jackie, I understand your concerns...they're no different than my own, however, our plan is I believe...a good one. Please trust me...we must catch them in the act...so that there will be no doubt of their guilt...and uh...when we get to Dallas...you will be riding with Lyndon."

"What? Why with Lyndon? Who's to say that this group isn't going after him too?"

"It's the safest place...you see my dear...Lyndon is uh...we believe...one of them." The President then told her of Lyndon's earlier request to have her ride with him, removing her from harm's way.

The First Lady was speechless. She began trembling. Tears filled her eyes. The President got up from his chair and knelt beside her. They grasped each other's hands. "Oh Jack, I'm so afraid. What if something goes wrong and they..."

"Please Jackie, trust me." As they embraced, the President felt the pain return, shooting through his back. The tenderness of the moment was shattered by the phone. The President rose to his feet and slowly walked to the desk where the phone sat.

"Yes, this is President Kennedy." He tried desperately to stretch out the pain in his back.

"Mr. President, it's Roger."

"Yes Roger, it is good to hear your voice. Are we on schedule?"

"Well sir, everything is set with Malinsky, but we did have one problem." Hilsman then related the plans with Malinsky and of the incident at Idlewild.

"Oh dear, I'm very sorry to hear that. We'll have to do something for the man's family. I'll see to that when I return." The President was beginning to feel more certain that he would be returning to Washington. Perhaps it had something to do with his conversation with Jackie.

"Also Mr. President, the Colonel will be arriving in San Antonio early this evening. He has a 4:00pm flight and he'll be staying at the Central Hotel. He'll be in touch with you and Mr. President...he'll be wearing a disguise...dark brown full wig, goatee, string tie and cowboy boots...you know, a little local flavor. He'll fit right in."

"Good Roger. I'll call you tonight after the dinner here for Senator Yarborough. We can talk about Malinsky's plans then."

"Right." And they both hung up.

The President turned to face the First Lady. She spoke first. "Can you tell me what you were sorry to hear?"

"A man died trying to serve his country. When we return to Washington, I'd like to do something for his family." The President quickly changed the subject: "You know it's already 5:45 and we have that dinner at 7:00...I think I'll shower...would you call for cocktails delivered for say...6:30?" The President was searching for a way to get the First Lady's mind off the events ahead.

"Sounds good." She forced a smile as she got up and approached her husband. As they embraced, she placed her head on his shoulder.

"Jack, I'm so afraid. Please tell me that nothing will go wrong. This whole thing scares me."

Again searching for the right words, he whispered in her ear: "Please my love, trust me…just trust me."

"Well done General, very precise." Allen Dulles would like people to think that he was a man of precision. However, his careless planning at the Bay of Pigs told the true story of his character. "And without any clues…the New York Police are baffled. At least now the Colonel will be of no concern when this operation is completed."

"The only concern that I have Allen is whether or not the Colonel told anyone what he overheard."

"General, I believe that if he had told anyone in the White House, Kennedy would have canceled his trip. It's on the news, he dedicated the Aerospace Medical Center in San Antonio this afternoon and he's headed to Houston in the morning. Somehow I don't believe that Prouty heard anything."

"So then we eliminated him for nothing!"

"General, you're not getting the point. After Kennedy is taken care of, the Colonel would return from New Zealand with plenty of questions concerning security measures that were ignored, which would have placed your office in a difficult position. Who knows, he may have been able to uncover the whole plan and then what? You know General, I was going to insist on his elimination the day you informed me of his possible eavesdropping. As it turned out, his big ears provided the perfect excuse. But, like I said I don't believe for a second that he heard anything."

"Yeah, you're probably right Allen, nothing to worry about. Kennedy's on schedule and so are we. What's the forecast for Friday?"

"So far they're saying partly sunny for the remainder of the week. That'll put them all in their convertibles."

"Good. I really don't like the rain plan. And Allen?"

"Yeah?"

"I spoke to the driver of Kennedy's car…you know the Secret Service guy Greer and instructed him to slow the pace when they arrive in Dealey. He was a bit hesitant but I convinced him that the Mayor of Dallas wanted his picture taken as his limo passed through the square…local political bullshit…you know. Anyway, Greer knows nothing but he agreed. This should give the sharp-shooters ample time for direct hits."

"Very good General, your planning is perfect. Oh, and one other thing, have you spoken to Lyndon about the transition?"

"Yes. He's ready to take control before Air Force One arrives in D.C. But he is acting a little anxious. He told me that he doesn't want to know any of the details and to just get the job done – period, and this is a direct quote – 'Do it right and you'll get your war'- he doesn't want the office too bad does he?"

"General, just the thought of power can do strange things to a man. But in this case he'll be merely a puppet for the Pentagon. He'll find out who's pulling the strings. You know Kennedy did me a great favor when he fired me. Had I remained as the head of the CIA, my involvement with the holdings at General Dynamics and Bell Helicopter would have been impossible. Now with the present plans underway, you and I along with a select group of your Generals are in a position to not only control the economy through the envisioned war effort in Vietnam, but also General we will become very wealthy men…very wealthy."

"Allen, I can't help but think that Kennedy should have been on his way to burying himself after the Bay of Pigs, but the missile crisis really bailed him out with the country and the world for that matter. The guy really became a statesman of world stature. And then all the bullshit with the Nuclear Test Ban Treaty and the hot-line to Moscow and the final straw was his Vietnam pullout plans. It's just too bad that we can't count on next years election to get rid of him…that we have to resort to this."

"General, are we feeling throes of regret with the present plan? Spare me the fucking guilt and tears. The man has to go and you said it yourself shortly after he took office. So cut the bullshit and stay focused. You know this thing doesn't end with Kennedy lying in a pool of blood in Texas, USA – no it doesn't end there. They'll be a great deal of time and effort spent to keep the lid on this thing for years to come. It won't be easy but we have all the right people working in the right places, so please, no more speeches about conscience and remorse. Am I clear General?"

"Yeah, yeah." Dulles heard a click and the line went dead.

XVII

"Mark, it's Susan."

"Susan, where are you? You know its 6:00 and we had a deal. Remember? Something on my desk 5:00 Wednesday? So far you're only an hour late, where the hell are you Susan?" Mark Lane was irritated.

"I know I'm late Mark, but what I'm working on will be the story of our lives. This is so big Mark that I'm unable to tell you anything until Friday afternoon. All I can say at this point is that I've been instructed by the President to keep this quiet. Please Mark, don't press me now!"

"The President? Susan what are you involved in? Isn't he in Texas?" At this point Lane had no idea how to respond.

"Listen Mark I'm giving more than I should. I'm in a motel just outside Baton Rouge and we're headed to Lafayette where we'll pick up route 90 to Lake Charles and then south to the Charles Airport. We have a charter waiting to take us to Dallas. That's it, that's all I can tell and that's probably too much!"

"Okay Susan, I'm taking the bait…when will I hear from you and whose we?"

"Soon Mark, I promise." And she hung up.

"You told him too much."

"Oh Jim I'm sorry. He is my boss and I had to tell him something. It'll be okay."

"Yeah, I guess you're right. I think its time that I call Hilsman and let him know where we are."

"Good, and after I'd like to get something to eat. I'm starved."

"You're always hungry."

Susan did not respond, she just stared out the window and watched the sun setting over Baton Rouge.

"Mr. Hilsman, Jim Flannery here."

"Yes Jim, where are you?"

"We're in Baton Rouge on our way to the Charles Airport to pick up a flight to Dallas."

"When do you get in?"

"We expect to arrive very early Thursday morning."

"Good. Call me when you arrive and I'll have further instructions for you. I think it'll be a good idea for you to meet up with Chief Deputy Malinsky and his men. And Jim, I want you and your partner to record every detail as it happens…leave nothing out. This is critical and we're counting on you…do you understand?"

"Why yes, of course."

"And Jim?"

"Yes?"

"The woman, Miss McNeil, she understands that she mustn't talk to anyone at her paper about any of this?"

"Oh, yeah, she knows…I'll call you from Dallas in the morning." Both men hung up.

"Now, let's see about some food." Jim grabbed Susan's hand and they left the motel.

As they pulled out of the lot, Jim noticed a car parked across the road that looked familiar. It was the same light blue Pontiac that he saw this morning in his rearview mirror while waiting for the garbage truck to move. Again he watched his rearview mirror as he drove away. The Pontiac didn't move. He breathed a sigh of relief. "Good." He thought, "a false alarm."

They found what looked like a decent diner advertising real down home Cajun cooking. Jim pulled into the lot.

"This looks okay…what do you think?"

"Yeah, I love Cajun…you might find it a little hard on the stomach…are you ready for that?"

"I can handle…" Just as Jim was about to finish, he caught the sight of the blue Pontiac pass slowly by and Bannister was behind the wheel. It disappeared in the lot on the opposite side of the diner.

"Well good looking are we getting out or are we…?"

Jim quickly cut her off – "Listen Susan, what do you think about heading straight to Dallas…right now?"

"What on earth are you talking about? We have a flight scheduled for 7:00am and right now I am very hungry!"

"Susan, our friend just pulled in the lot over there." Jim pointed in the direction.

"Not Bannister again. Are you sure?"

"As sure as my name is Jim Flannery!"

"Geez, this guy just won't quit! I really thought we lost him in New Orleans."

"Well he's here and we didn't. Look, he's probably sitting in his car waiting for us to go in that main entrance. Let's do exactly what he expects us to do. We'll go in so that he sees us, walk directly to the back door…get back in the car and leave. Come on!"

As they approached the entrance, "Susan, don't look at his car…just look straight ahead."

"Does this really mean that we can't eat now? You know, we haven't had anything since breakfast!"

"Later."

When Jim opened the door he couldn't help but notice out of the corner of his eye, the big man watching as they entered the diner.

"Perfect! He saw us and he'll be waiting!"

As they passed through the diner, Susan stopped at the counter and lifted the cover of the pastry holder and grabbed two large danish. She noticed that they were very stale – "If this is any indication of the food here, I'm glad we're not staying!"

Jim left three ones on the counter, "That should cover it!" as he smiled at the waitress. She did not return the favor after hearing Susan's remarks.

They quickly walked to the rear of the diner, through the kitchen and before anyone could question them, out the back door. They found themselves in the lot just as Jim had planned and got in the car. Jim slowly pulled out in the opposite direction so that Bannister could not see their movements.

As they drove down the highway toward Lafayette, the blue Pontiac slowly pulled out of the lot across the road from the diner. Bannister had changed position when the couple entered the diner, so as to get a better view of their car when they left. They had no idea that he was behind them.

"Well, we've got to make some minor changes." Jim offered.

"What do you mean?"

"He knows where we're staying so we can't go back there tonight…let's drive to Lake Charles, get a room and pick up our flight in the morning. The only thing that's changed is the motel." Jim thought he had everything figured out.

"Can we stop at the motel and get our things?" Susan was munching on her stale danish.

"Yeah, why not." Jim pulled up to the motel. "I'll stay in the car. You go in and get your things and grab my bag, I never even opened it."

"Aye aye Commander!"

Two minutes later Susan placed the bags in the back seat and got in.

"Do you think we can stop on the way to eat?"

"I don't see why not. We finally lost the fat man." Jim entered the traffic and began the 100 mile drive to Lake Charles.

"We can relax now." Jim was feeling confident that they were alone.

"Yeah, are you sure?" Came Susan's response.

"I told you that I won't let anything happen to you and I meant it!"

Susan slid across the bench seat of her 1962 Impala, placed her head on Jim's shoulder and whispered in his ear – "Don't forget to stop at the first restaurant."

"You're so romantic!"

"Later, if you're lucky." And they both settled in for the drive.

Behind a black pick-up truck and a light duty delivery truck sat the blue Pontiac, patiently moving through the darkness.

XVIII

The First Lady didn't have much of an appetite, but she managed to maintain her usual charm and had all the local politicians eating out of her hand. The President marveled at her grace and magnetism. It gave him a chance to step back from the limelight and wonder which of those present were involved in the plans against him. He reasoned to himself that the locals at this dinner party were probably all innocent and that the only conspirator present was his, what he thought, "good friend and partner", the Vice-President.

The President watched as Lyndon sat conversing with Senator Yarborough, mending the damaged political fences or he thought "Were they discussing plans that would take place in my absence?"

It was 9:20pm and the President had enough. The sight of the Vice-President not only sickened him but also evoked feelings of sadness. Lyndon's years as a great politician would come to a screeching halt with a swing through downtown Dallas. He even considered telling Lyndon that he knew of the plans to take over the White House and grant him some kind of Presidential immunity, but then he thought that Lyndon would just have to take his punishment like the others. He was a conspirator and had to be dealt with accordingly.

The President motioned to the First Lady and after saying their good-byes, they retired to the Presidential suite. The First Lady held the President's hand tightly all the way.

"Jackie, you were wonderful tonight, thank you sweetheart." As they entered the suite, the First Lady answered:

"Oh Jack, are you sure about all of this? It just seems so...completely unbelievable. Tonight I saw you staring at Lyndon...could there be some mistake?"

"It's like a bad dream...but we do have information linking the Vice-President to the people I told you about earlier...you know...the Generals and the Mayor of Dallas. Thank God for the work of Roger and the Colonel...without them we'd be in the midst of a hornet's nest...without a clue. We are ready for them providing that it doesn't rain on Friday."

"What does rain have to do with it?"

"Well, remember I told you about the man who taped the conversation between the Generals and Dulles?"

"Yes, you said his name is Cappetta."

"That's right. However, Mr. Cappetta's recorder ran out of tape just as General Cabell was relating the plans in the event of rain."

"But Jack, if it rains we will be in hardtops and I know that they are bulletproof. So I guess that leaves two places where you'll be out in the open."

"Yes and where might that be?" The President was enjoying the First Lady's participation. It helped relieve some of the anxiety that both were feeling.

"Well, it really doesn't take one of your nuclear physicists to figure this one out!"

The President sat in the Queen Ann chair smiling, as he watched his wife pace the bedroom floor.

"As we exit the plane at Love Field and the luncheon at the Trade-Mart." She stopped her pacing and stood staring at the President.

"Excellent! You're a regular Sherlock Holmes!"

"Oh Jack, this is no time for tomfoolery…let's be serious."

"I'm sorry dear. I was just looking for a little levity." He got up and approached his wife and attempted to place his arms around her. She jumped on the bed, grabbing a pillow and in a lightning movement, threw it, hitting the President square in the face. "How about that for levity, Mr. President?" He quickly returned the favor and soon they were laughing and wrestling on the bed in their underwear.

The playfulness ended when the two locked in an embrace. They kissed deeply and lovingly. For a long moment they held onto one another. Jackie broke the silence.

"What is the airport in Dallas…Love Field like?"

The President, lying on his stomach across the bed, propped his hand under his chin and spoke – "It's completely out in the open…no large buildings to speak of…be kind of difficult I would think for a sniper in that situation. It's the Trade-Mart that bothers me…very closed in…lots of buildings for them to set up in…let's just hope it doesn't rain and that Roger has a plan if it does. That reminds me, he's expecting my call."

"How about letting me call downstairs for a nightcap first?" Tenderly she bit his ear.

"And then…?"

"You know, Mr. President."

The First Lady made her call then the President, in his robe went to the desk in the sitting room and dialed the Oval Office.

"Hilsman."

"Roger, sorry it's so late but things went a little longer than I expected."

"Oh, that's perfectly all right sir…how are you holding up?"

"Better than can be expected…the First Lady…I told her everything."

"Everything sir?" Hilsman voice went up a couple of octaves.

"No need to worry Roger, at first it was very difficult for her...but she seems to have accepted it now. We've been hashing over the possibilities in the event of rain."

"And sir, what did you come up with?"

"Well, we haven't totally ruled out Love Field...it's the Trade-Mart that seems to be a smarter move on their part...more buildings...easier for snipers. And Roger?"

"Yes sir?"

"Tell me how things went with Chief Malinsky."

"His response to our plans surprised me. He's a sharp mind...excellent choice sir!"

"Good. I kind of thought he'd be. Please continue Roger."

"He's taking seven of his best men and I've sent fourteen of mine, they should be there now. They'll cover Love Field, Dealey and the Trade-Mart."

"Well done Roger, you're way ahead of me. Speaking of getting ahead of oneself, what do you think of the Attorney General's position?"

"I think your brother is a fine man...doing an excellent job! Why sir?"

"That's not what I meant Roger. YOU my good friend, how do you feel about moving up in the administration? The Colonel will be a natural for your present position at the State Department." There was a short pause. "So, do I take it that no response means that you'll accept?"

"But sir, your brother...I don't want to..."

"Roger, I have big plans for my very dedicated brother. Remember, Lyndon will be a memory and a bad one at that."

"I understand sir...YES, of course!" Hilsman understood the President's plans completely.

"Good. Congratulations Roger!"

"Thank you John...uh Mr. President."

"Now, the rain plan...what does the Chief have up his sleeve?"

There was a knock at the door. Jackie quickly appeared from the bedroom dressed in a very elegant housecoat and answered it.

She took the tray with the President's favorite port – Warre's 1952 – over to the desk and poured for both. The President smiled – "Thank you dear." She kissed him on the top of his head and disappeared to the bedroom. The First Lady never interfered in his phone conversations. She knew he would share everything later, he always did.

"Malinsky's plans are in complete agreement with your assessment sir. Aside from the heavy coverage at Dealey, he's preparing intense security for the Trade-Mart area and a lighter coverage at Love Field. I know we're gambling at the airport, but considering that we can't use any Dallas police because of their involvement, we are limited in the number of men that we can call on without alerting anyone to our counterplans. Because of Dulles I just don't trust anyone in the CIA or the FBI right now. I believe we'll just have to persevere with what we have."

Just as the President was about to respond, line two blinked on his phone.

"Roger, I'm sorry I have another call, would you hold?"

"Yes of course sir."

The President pressed line two. "Yes?"

"Mr. President sir, it's the Colonel."

"Yes Colonel, where are you?"

"Here sir, in San Antonio! I'll make this quick sir. I'm at the Central Hotel, just three blocks from you. I'll be at the breakfast tomorrow morning…in a disguise…Roger told you?"

"Yes."

"And I'll be at your side the entire way and you'll never even know it. I'll be watching everything and everybody and should I spot any danger, you'll know it immediately sir."

"Thank you Colonel, that's very comforting. I look forward to seeing you at breakfast…goodnight Tex!"

"Goodnight sir."

The President smiled and pressed line one.

"Roger, that was the Colonel."

"Good, he's there. He'll stick to you like glue. I feel better knowing that one of us is there with you."

"Me too Roger and uh... about Malinsky's plan...I have to agree with you...our trust level in the departments you spoke of is at a low right now. We'll address that problem when this thing is over. I have to believe that we're in pretty decent shape with what we have."

"There is one other matter sir...without your knowledge I sent Cappetta to Honolulu to find out what THEY were up to."

"And?" The President was eager. This issue was another of major concern to him.

"You're not going to like this sir but they're rewriting your Vietnam plans...you know NSAM 263?"

"Yes, and?" An uncharacteristic trace of anger found it's way into the President's voice.

"Well, Cappetta informs me that the rewrite calls for a gradual increase in troops, setting up a protracted war effort and after the '64 elections all hell breaks loose with concentrated bombings in the North."

"My God! They want war badly enough to murder the President! Our country and I owe you and the Colonel more than we will ever be able to repay. Roger, if this conflict in Vietnam comes to fruition, it will not only destroy our efforts toward peace with the Soviets, but also it could take years to reach any satisfactory conclusion for both sides. It can be nothing but a blood bath. So now we're getting to the truth. Their reasons to eliminate me revolve around this administrations desire for a world peace and peace does not fit in with their sinister plan. That plan may have been hatched when I refused to abide by the Pentagon's wishes to decimate Cuba during the missile crisis. These men must be stopped before they destroy our country."

"Yes...I'm in complete agreement sir and whatever it takes...we will stop them!"

"And uh.." The President tried to maintain his calm. He then changed the subject and focused on the events. "When does Mr. Cappetta return from Honolulu?"

"He's expected here in about an hour or so...he's reporting directly to me on his return."

"Good. I just had a thought about Mr. Cappetta. Let's use his special talents...tomorrow night I have that testimonial dinner in Fort Worth at the Texas Hotel...all the honchos will be there. Perhaps we could have Mr. Cappetta get some tape...you know...dinner conversations...the Dallas Mayor Earl Cabell will be present with all of his cohorts. Is that a possibility?"

"Not only is it a possibility but consider it done. Mr. Cappetta will be there, you have my word." The President's ability to move through a crisis situation with flexibility and strength always amazed Hilsman.

"Good. And Roger?"

"Yes sir?"

"Think of a position for Mr. Cappetta in intelligence. I'd like to have this man with us in the years to come."

"Right. Anything else sir?"

"I think we've covered all the bases. Oh, we leave for Houston after the breakfast tomorrow morning...then do the luncheon with Governor Connally...after we fly to Fort Worth for the testimonial. Busy schedule...I'll call you when we get into Fort Worth. Goodnight Roger."

"Goodnight Mr. President."

The President sipped his port and reflected on his conversation with Hilsman. Everything seemed to be in order. When he thought of Cappetta's findings, he got a sick feeling in his stomach. It made him more determined than ever to put an end to their diabolical plans.

His thoughts then shifted to the aftermath and the effects on the country. He whispered to himself – "America will be wounded when this thing is over...for some time...but her strength and greatness will enable her to survive. These men...if they're allowed to be successful...could spell disaster for our great country…for all Americans. I will not let that happen. God be with us."

The President rose from the desk, turned out the light and retired to the bedroom and the waiting First Lady.

XIX

"I decided to stay late and do a little cleaning up."

"Yeah, look, I'm in a phone booth, any calls?"

"Yes Guy, CM called. He wanted to know how things were moving. I think you should call him right away, he seemed a little upset. Will you be home tonight?" Rhoda learned to never question her husband's whereabouts or motives. She was tired of the beatings.

"Don't think. Listen, on my desk there's a small black notebook. Get me CM's number."

Rhoda dutifully found the book and gave him the number.

"Thanks. I got a slight problem here…I'll see you when I iron things out." Click. Bannister showed just enough respect to keep Rhoda. To him, she was merely a servant.

He put all of his change on the counter in the phone booth and then dialed CM.

"Yes, how can I help you?"

"Mr. Marcello please."

"May I ask who's calling?"

"Yes, Guy Bannister and I'm returning Mr. Marcello's call."

"Just a moment Mr. Bannister."

Bannister thought of how polite she was and how Marcello could take a lesson from his help.

After a pause, "Yeah, Guy what the hell is going on?"

"Mr. Marcello, everything is on schedule. What do you mean?" Bannister was now on his best behavior.

"Look, don't bullshit me you fucking Nazi, I got a call from the Texan, Billy-Bob, he tells me that someone knows about our program. What gives?......Well, I'm waiting?" Carlos Marcello did not like to wait.

"Mr. Marcello, I don't know what you're getting at?"

"Look, if you wanna continue with this line of bullshit your next meal will be your own balls! Now for the last time what gives?"

Bannister began sweating. He knew that an angry Carlos Marcello was more dangerous than ten crocodiles in the Louisiana swamps.

"Oh that! Now I know what you're talking about." Bannister was trying to summon up the courage to tell him.

"Yeah, well?" Marcello was growing even more impatient, if that was possible.

Bannister swallowed hard and began – "Earlier this week a couple came into the shop looking for a rare volume. I went to the basement to get it and the phone rang. I yelled up to them to answer it and the woman did. Later I found out it was Billy-Bob and I guess he thought the woman was Rhoda. He gave her all the information on the positions in Dealey. When I returned from the basement, she told me that it was a hang-up. I didn't think anything of it until...about 15 or 20 minutes later when Billy-Bob called back to see if I got the message. He told me what he said to her and I never mentioned that it wasn't Rhoda."

"He knows now because he talked to Rhoda today. He said you acted like you had your head up your ass. Maybe that's where it belongs, you fucking moron. So where are those two…Jesus Christ?" Marcello was beside himself.

At this point, Bannister didn't see any advantage in telling Marcello about the Washington phone numbers that he found in Flannery's room or for that matter, the fact that she was a reporter. "I'm on their trail right now and I promise you they won't make it through the night."

"That's the most intelligent thing I heard you say yet. Where are you?"

"Lake Charles, down the road from their motel…The Sunset Inn…just a few minutes from the Charles Airport."

"Okay, listen closely. All I'm gonna say now is that this is a multi-million dollar fucking operation and if it goes sour because of your stupidity, there won't be a rock you can hide under you shithead and I promise it won't be pleasant. And you can include Rhoda in that. Get those two and get them tonight. Am I crystal fucking clear?"

"Yes…yes Mr. Marcello…" Click. And the line went dead.

Carlos Marcello paced his study, picked up the phone and dialed a Baton Rouge number.

"Hello?"

"Frankie, it's Carlos…I need a job done tonight. Can you handle it?"

Frankie "The Onion Head" Ingenito was the best hit man in the south. He earned his endearing nickname by placing a large Bermuda onion in the mouth of each of his victims.

"Depends…how much?" He was also very greedy.

"Blank check, you name it. This has to be done tonight."

"Fifty thousand and not a fucking dime less!" The Onion Head was probably the only man on earth that could get away with that kind of talk to Carlos Marcello. Also, Marcello knew that Frankie was the best and he always delivered.

"Deal. There may be three of them…one for sure. The other two may be taken out before you arrive."

"Three! That's gonna cost."
"Listen you little prick…"
"Okay, okay, I'll do it. Where are they?"
Marcello read off the details and hung-up.

XX

"God, I'm so full." Susan moaned.

"Well my dear, you ate enough to satisfy a small regiment. Let's take a walk, it's only 10:15 and the night air might help."

"Yeah, that sounds good, let's go."

They left the Sunset Inn and walked with the traffic south toward the Charles Airport. After about ten minutes, the motel was out of sight. They decided to sit on the fender of an abandon car that sat in a field about ten yards from the road. The night air was crisp and all the stars shone brightly.

Susan looked up – "You see that over there," and she pointed to the sky, "that's the big dipper. When I was a little girl my father and I would sit in the yard and he would point out all the constellations. He was some guy. He worked the farm for years to make a good life for my mother and me and to send me to college. I miss him more than ever now. I think he'd be proud of his daughter. You know, the farm girl becomes the big time reporter." Susan chuckled.

"I'm sure he would be very proud. What happened to him?"

"Heart attack. He was tending to the fields one day and didn't return for dinner. We found him slumped over the wheel of his tractor." Susan's voice tailed off to a whisper. Jim noticed her eyes welling up with tears.

"I'm sorry Susan."

"Thanks. Me too. As I grow older I miss him more. I still see my mother. We have lunch together every weekend, sometimes dinner. She finally sold the farm and moved into an apartment on the outskirts of New Orleans. Then she got a job in an office as a file clerk. She kind of likes the city life now. She's doing fine…a real survivor. How about you and your family?"

"Are you sure you want to know?"

"Yes, of course!"

"I grew up in Newton, just outside of Boston. Family's still intact, two brothers and a sister. I spent most of my life there…went to Boston University, got a job with the *Boston Globe* as an assistant reporter and wrote some political stuff on Kennedy as a senator…then I got lucky and landed a job with the *Washington Post* just as Kennedy entered the White House and here I am…with you in God knows where and…" Just then the light blue Pontiac drove by, heading in the direction of their motel. They both saw it and looked at each other in disbelief.

"Look Susan, this guy really wants us dead and I'm getting a little sick of it."

"So what do you propose we do? You know we can't go back for my car…damn, that was my first new car."

"Don't worry, your car will be fine. Now we just have to figure out how to get to the airport."

"It's only about ten to fifteen minutes by car which should make it less than an hour by foot. So let's start walking Mr. Flannery." Susan got down from the fender of the car and reached for Jim's hand. Jim stopped, pulled out his wallet and checked for Hilsman's number.

"Good, I have the number for the Oval Office. I guess everything else in that motel room is expendable, for now. When we get to wherever were going, I'll call the motel...I'll make up something. Come on, let's get going, if were lucky we'll find a place to sleep."

"Hey Flannery?"

"Yeah?"

"I really like being with you on this...this adventure. You're not only a fun guy but you're also pretty smart...for a man!"

"Very funny Susan." Jim drew her hand up to his lips and kissed it. "I like being with you too, but let's not lose sight of the fact that a lot is expected of us. The President, as Mr. Hilsman told me, wants us to record all the details in Dallas. They want everything on paper. It probably won't be easy...are you ready for this?"

"I think so Jim." Susan paused. "I would like very much to help President Kennedy in anyway that I can. I'm just a southern girl who didn't spend her life in Boston writing about the Kennedys, but I do have my convictions and believe that he is a rare talent in politics and I'll do whatever it takes to help him."

Jim gripped her hand tightly. "I know Susan, I guess I knew that about you all along. That's why we're together."

"That's only part of it Mr. Flannery." Susan said demurely.

They put their arms around each other's shoulders and walked down the desolate road. Their silhouettes disappeared in the darkness.

XXI

Bannister got out of his car and walked the short distance to the Sunset Inn parking lot. The lot was less than half full. He spotted the 1962 Impala parked in front of unit 9. The blinds were drawn and the lights were out. He knocked…no answer. He figured they were sleeping. He then went around the building to the office where he saw through the window, a middle aged man sitting at the counter reading a book. There was a television set on behind him with an episode of *The Fugitive* playing. He entered the office.

"Good evening!"

"Hi there, what can I do for ya?" The man closed the book, turned down the volume on the TV and smiled at Bannister.

Bannister approached the counter.

"My son and his wife are staying here…Mr. and Mrs. Flannery."

"Yup, the Flannerys are in room nine. Funny thing."

"Yeah, what's that?"

"You're the second gentleman tonight that inquired about them.

The other gentleman left just ten minutes ago.

"Is that so. Did he leave a name?"

"No. Said he'd come back in the morning, didn't want to disturb them tonight. Very nice man. Real considerate ya know!"

"Yeah. What did this man look like?"

"Uh Mr. Flannery, are you the police or something?"

"Yeah something like that." Bannister lost his patience and placed the .44 on the counter. "Anyone in that room?" Bannister pointed to a door marked PRIVATE.

"Just my wife an she be sleepin' like a baby. Look mister, I don't want no trouble, you can put that thing away…I'll give ya all the money in the cash drawer!"

Bannister walked quickly around the counter and pushed the man to the door marked PRIVATE. "Shut up and open it, NOW!"

Just as the man opened the door and walked into a well lit room, Bannister hit him with the butt end of the .44 on the back of the head. The man stumbled and fell to the floor. The man's wife jumped from the couch and began screaming. Bannister ran to the couch and grabbed the woman by the neck with his left hand. His strength cut off her breathing as he shoved her face into a pillow on the couch. He covered her head with another pillow and held it while she fought for her life. His bulk was too much for her to overcome. Her body then went still. She was dead.

He turned to see the man on the floor beginning to move. He let out a groan as he struggled to get to his feet. Bannister grabbed a large pillow from the couch, ran across the room and pushed the man to the floor, placing the pillow over the man's head. He then shoved the .44 into the pillow and squeezed the trigger. The report from the .44 was muffled, producing a dull thud. The man's body went lifeless.

The burley Bannister was now sweating. His brow dripped perspiration. He looked over his two victims, turned off the lights and exited, closing the door behind him. He searched the key rack and found the spare for room nine.

Quickly he made his way to the room. His adrenaline was

pumping. He slowly and quietly inserted the key and opened the door. As he entered the dark room, he felt the cold hard steel smashing into his neck, forcing him to lose his balance as he barreled across the room, falling to the floor at the foot of the bed. The door slammed shut in the darkness. Bannister looked up and saw the man's outline against the dimly lit window. He got up and charged the figure like a linebacker. The force of his weight propelled the two men into the wall and to the floor where they wrestled in the dark. Bannister groped for his knife that he carried strapped to his ankle. With his massive strength he shoved the dagger into the man's stomach and turned the knife mercilessly, tearing at the man's stomach until there was no movement.

After a minute passed, Bannister slowly lumbered to his feet in the darkness. He searched for the light switch. As he turned it on, he expected to see Jim Flannery's body, but to his surprise it wasn't.

He mumbled out loud – "I know this guy…Frankie… what's his name? What the hell is he doing here?" Then he remembered – "He's a hit man for the mob! Christ!"

He then noticed bulges in Frankie's jacket pockets. He felt the bulges and then placed his hands in the pockets and pulled out three Bermuda onions. "Frankie The Onion Head…that's right…but why?…Marcello…Marcello sent him…that bastard. Three onions, one for me and the other two for Flannery and the girl!"

Bannister then looked around the room and saw two suitcases by the closet. They were unopened.

"Where the hell are those two? They must have seen me and bolted…I know Frankie didn't get them…he still had his trademark in his pockets…the airport…that's it they must be walking. Yeah, they couldn't have gotten too far."

Bannister walked to the door, again looked around, flicked off the lights and opened the door. He quickly closed it, turning the lights back on. He bent down and forced Frankie's mouth open breaking his jaw. He then picked up one of the onions and jammed it into the gaping recess. He slammed the lower jaw shut on the onion – "There you little prick!" He then exited the room. He thought about how to deal with Marcello when the time came. He had no idea what he would say. Right now he didn't care. He had just killed three people and he was desperate to up the count to five.

He got in the blue Pontiac and made his way to the Charles Airport.

XXII

They could see the lights and the sign announcing their arrival at the Charles Airport. It was 11:30pm and with no motels along the way, Jim wondered how would they spend over seven hours waiting for their flight.

"I can see the hanger, maybe somebody there can help us."

As they entered the hangar, a friendly voice called out from behind a twin engine Cessna – "Can I help you folks?"

"Yes you can. My wife and I here have a bit of a problem. Our car broke down just a few miles back. We're from Washington D.C. on our way to Dallas…death in the family."

"Sorry about your loss. Geez, you young folks are a long way from home to break down in the middle of nowhere. How can I help?"

"Is that your plane?…sure is a beauty!" Jim walked around the aircraft pretending to admire it. He despised flying.

"Yeah, she is at that." Men who loved their cars, planes, boats and their country, always used the feminine gender. "Just got her...brand new...two weeks now. Only spent a few hours up in the air with her...you know with all the rain we've been having up until a couple of days ago."

Susan quickly caught on to Jim. "Sure is a beautiful night." She walked to the hanger door and looked up at the sky. "Be a great night to fly!"

The man followed her, looked up and repeated what Susan said, almost word for word – "Yeah, sure is a beautiful night...great night to fly!"

"Hey, I just might be able to help you two. You say you need to get to Dallas, right?"

Jim couldn't believe his ears. Susan crossed her fingers.

Susan and Jim spoke in unison – "Yes, that's right!"

"Well, I could take you two fine young people and all it would cost ya is the gas!"

"Are you sure, we don't want to put you to any trouble?"

"It's no trouble. I'd like to kinda take her for an extended spin and I'd have company to boot. What do ya say?"

"Well, you're generosity is overwhelming...we just can't resist, Mister?" Jim extended his hand to the man.

"Ferguson, Arly Ferguson and you're?" The two men shook hands.

"Jim and Susan Flannery."

"Well Mr. and Mrs. Flannery, let me do a little math here." He estimated the miles and flight time while busily scratching away on his pad.

Two minutes later, Arly Ferguson tore the page out of his little notebook and handed it to Jim. "How does that figure look young man?"

Jim stared at the numbers in disbelief - $38.25. It was a fraction of what their charter would have cost. He paid Arly Ferguson and added a crisp one hundred dollar bill.

"There's no need for that young man!"

"I insist Mr. Ferguson, you're a very kind man."

"Well thank you Mr. Flannery...and you too, Mrs. Flannery!"

Susan smiled – "You're very welcome. Like my husband said you're a very kind man."

"Thank you…now she's all gassed up, so why don't you two just hop on board……watch your step there young lady." Jim and Susan settled into their seats while Arly Ferguson went to a desk, wrote something down and climbed into the cockpit. He then flicked on the interior lights and within moments they were out of the hangar and headed for the runway.

"Mr. Flannery, please don't touch any of the controls."

"Oh you don't have to worry about me Mr. Ferguson."

"Nothing incoming tonight, checked the roster so we have the runway to ourselves."

"That's just great!" Jim braced himself. He hated takeoffs and landings. And for that matter, everything in between.

As the twin engine aircraft lined up for takeoff, the blue Pontiac screeched to a halt on the tarmac outside the hangar. Bannister watched and easily made out the well-lit figures in the cabin of the Cessna. He drew the .44 and carefully aimed. Susan glanced to her right and saw Bannister. "Jim! Look, it's him!" The Cessna was at takeoff speed and lifted gracefully when the big man squeezed off a shot. The bullet entered the cabin striking Arly Ferguson in the temple. He fell back and to the left. "Jim!" Susan yelled from the back seat, "Pull the yoke back, pull it easy!"

Jim looked around, "What's the yoke?"

"The thing between your legs!" As Jim pulled back on the control, the Cessna steadily climbed while Susan tried to move Arly Ferguson's body so that she could get behind the controls. She dragged his body to the back and climbed into the vacated seat.

"There, I've got it…Jim you can let go of the stick now!"

"Susan, you know how to fly this thing?"

"I've had a little experience in single engine aircraft. I guess with a twin you just double everything."

"Susan, that doesn't sound quite right."

"I know. I'm making this up as we go along."

"Oh great."

"Jim why don't you check on Mr. Ferguson? See if there's a pulse. Maybe we can get him to a hospital or something."

"Right."

"Yeah, thank God, there is a pulse, pretty strong. The bullet didn't penetrate. Looks like a sort of glancing blow that ripped part of the skull on the surface. He's not bleeding very much, but he is out like a light. How long are we going to be up here?"

"I think it's a little over an hour. We've got about fifty minutes left to mayday."

Jim took off his jacket and ripped the sleeve from his shirt and proceeded to tie it around Arly Ferguson's head. "There, that should help stop what little bleeding he has."

Jim got back in his seat and stared at Susan. "Did you say MAYDAY?"

"Yes I did."

"Whatever for. It seems to me that you're doing a pretty good job flying this thing?"

"Yeah, I'm pretty good at takeoffs and keeping it afloat, but the reason they wouldn't give me my license…well…I failed the part that brings you back to earth."

"You mean landing!!"

"Yes sir."

"Did you ever crash?"

"No silly, I'm here aren't I! The instructor would always take over and get us out of trouble."

"Trouble…oh Christ Susan!"

"Don't worry. I'll try a few different things this time. After all we have two engines and a lot more controls. It'll be fine, you'll see."

"Yeah, where's the parachutes?"

"Oh Jim, just relax. It's a beautiful night, enjoy the ride."

"How can I enjoy the ride when we don't have an instructor with us to bail you out when we get into the deep stuff?"

"In my purse you'll find a small pillbox, please take two. You'll enjoy the flight more."

"Yeah, very funny."

Susan watched the compass reading, "West-Northwest. We're right on course," as the Cessna hummed through the night.

XXIII

Bannister watched as the Cessna disappeared in the distance. It looked as if something was wrong with the little plane as it increased altitude at such a rapid pace. He thought – "Maybe I hit one of them…good! But they got away again…how the hell did they get out of that motel without me seeing? Must have been when I called Marcello…but why didn't they take the car? They left it to fool me into thinking they were still there! Then they walked to the airport. Christ, if I didn't meet up with Onion Head, they'd be dead now. Pretty smart those two… I'll bet anything they're on their way to Dallas…and I'll never find them. Christ! And Marcello…I may have been able to smooth things over with the Mafia if they were out of the picture…but now…? And he wanted ME capped too! Fucking dago bastard! What a mess."

He then turned to the hangar. One of the large doors was open but there wasn't a soul to be found. He walked to a glass partition with a desk behind it. Checking the desk he found a clipboard with a roster sheet marked – FLIGHT SCHEDULE November 20, 1963. His eyes went directly to the last entry – Arly Ferguson, Cessna 200G Twin, 2 passengers – Mr. & Mrs. Flannery, Tof D – 11:35pm., Dest. – Dallas.

"Oh shit! I was right! Now what?"

He threw the clipboard on the desk and walked to his car. As he was about to get in he saw two headlights coming up the road from the airport entrance. The car pulled up along side the blue Pontiac. An older man with a beard got out and walked over to Bannister.

"Hi there!"

"Good evening. My name is Flannery."

"Owen's the name, Emmitt Owen. Pleased to meet you Mr. Flannery. Just got back from a late supper. I'm the watchman here, although I do a little flying myself. That's my little sweetheart just over there." Emmitt Owen pointed toward a well-used single engine aircraft in the back of the hangar. "What brings you here at this hour Mr. Flannery?"

"I was suppose to meet my son and his wife here for a flight to Dallas. A charter with a…" Bannister searched his mind for the name on the flight schedule. "…Mr. Ferguson, I believe that was his name."

Emmitt Owen looked around the hangar – "Arly's plane, it's not here! That's strange!"

"What's strange Mr. Owen?" Bannister knew.

"Arly Ferguson was here, kinda watching the place when I left for supper. Now he's gone and his plane too. He didn't tell me he had a flight! Excuse me Mr. Flannery, I've gotta check that roster."

Bannister watched as Emmitt Owen looked over the flight schedule. He was trying to make up his mind – "Do I use force or do I pay the man?" Bannister checked his wallet - $126 in cash.

"Well, here it is," Emmitt Owen pointed to the roster, "he took your son and his wife to Dallas…just about twenty minutes ago. Can't understand why he didn't tell me? But I gotta remember that Arly forgets just about everything. Geez Mister, I'm sorry about all this!"

Bannister had his strategy planned – "That plane of yours, does it fly?"

"Sure does! She's a little long in the tooth, as long as I keep her tuned she does just fine."

"I'd like to hire you Mr. Owen. I've got $50 here for a quick flight to Dallas…what do you say?"

"That's very kind of you my friend, but I really can't leave...somebody's got to be here. Ya know, they give me free room and board for my sweetheart over there for three nights work. I'd really like to help you but…"

Bannister cut him off, upping the ante – "Would say…$100 change your mind?" Bannister waved the money as he spoke.

"That's awfully generous and very tempting Mr. Flannery…but I'm just gonna have to say no. You do understand my predicament, don't you?"

"Of course Mr. Owen. Now understand mine." Bannister pulled the .44 from his waist and pointed it at the bewildered man. "Is that thing fueled up?" He pointed to Owen's plane.

"Yes it is…but…"

"Look, from here on in keep your mouth shut and do exactly as I say and you won't get hurt. If you're a good little pilot you'll get the C-note" He lied. The man was making the last flight of his life. With his gun pointed at Owen, Bannister walked over to the desk, picked up the phone and dialed.

"Hello?" Rhoda sounded a little tired. She just returned from a night of cleaning at the shop.

"Rhoda, I have an emergency."

"Guy! Are you okay?" One would think that Rhoda would cherish the thought of Guy Bannister falling off the end of the earth, never to return.

"Yeah, now listen: Call Hank and get him to drive you to the Charles Airport…it's just south of Lake Charles. When you get here, my car is in front of the hangar…keys are in the visor…take it back to New Orleans. This has to be done before…" Bannister put the phone on his shoulder and addressed Owen – "What time does life show up around here?"

"Well, Charlie usually takes over at 6:00am."

"Okay Rhoda, you've got to get here and leave with my car before 5:00am. Got it?"

"But Guy, what do I do if I can't get Hank?"

"Listen Rhoda, we've got trouble. Just get Hank and get down here! Is that clear?"

"Yes dear, of course..I'll be there."

"Good. I'll call you from Dallas."

"Dallas! But you're not supposed to be…" Bannister slammed down the phone, cutting Rhoda off. He hated answering to her.

"Okay Ace, let's get moving!" The two men walked to the back of the hangar and boarded Owen's sweetheart. After a series of tries, the single engine kicked to life.

"Are you sure this thing will make it?"

"Positive! She hasn't let me down yet. Hey Mister?"

"Yeah, what is it Ace?"

"That C-note…did ya really mean it?"

"Of course! It's the least I can do."

"I guess this won't be so bad after all. I just wish you'd put that gun away!"

"Makes you nervous, doesn't it?"

"You bet!" Just as Emmitt Owen answered, he pulled back and the single engine lifted the plane into the darkness.

"Good. That's the whole idea. It kind of uh…keeps you honest."

"Whatever you say Mister. I'll just set this course…let's see Love Field…that would be West-Northwest and…"

"Look Ace, we won't be landing at Love. About twenty-five miles south of Dallas there's an abandoned airstrip…old military installation…that's where we're going."

"But if it's abandoned, what about lights? I don't know if I can land my baby in complete darkness!"

"Maybe an extra C-note will help your night vision?"

"Three C-notes just might give me the vision of a Texas Grey Horned Owl!" Emmitt Owen howled with laughter.

"You got it Ace!"

"Thank you mister!"

Bannister thought – "Too bad, he's not such a bad old guy, but he's got to go. No traces……none."

"I think I see the lights…there!" Jim pointed to the Love Field runway.

"Love Field?" Susan repeated in the mike, "Love Field are you there?"

"Loud and clear!"

"I'm flying a twin-engine Cessna and I need some help getting this thing on the ground. Our pilot was injured. Are you there Love Field?"

"We see you. You're lined up perfect and cleared for landing. Remember at all times to keep her nose up just over the horizon and you'll do just fine. Do you read me?"

"Yes I uh…everything's just dandy. What do I do now?" Susan was determined to get this one right. With no backup she had no choice. Jim let out a groan.

"Oh Jim, I'm nervous enough as it is. Please don't make those sounds."

"I'm sorry…you're doing great sweetie…talk to the guy!"

"Uhh…tower, how am I doing?"

"Just fine…back off a little on the throttle…good." Susan was following his instructions perfectly. "A little left rudder…that's the control on the…"

"I know where it is!" Susan made the adjustment. "How's that?"

"Fine. KEEP THE NOSE UP!"

"You don't have to yell at me!" She raised the nose slightly. "Now what?"

"You're good, now kill the throttle." Just as Susan did, the Cessna banged down on the runway with the left wing scraping.

It quickly righted itself and she used enough flap to bring the Cessna to a halt next to a fire truck and an ambulance.

"Wow! It's over…my first touchdown!" She threw her arms around Jim who was still in shock and just happy to be alive.

"I'm proud of you sweetheart. Congratulations, that was one hell of a landing!"

"Do I detect a little sarcasm Mr. Flannery?"

"Absolutely not! That was one for the record books. You were great!" Jim held her face in his hands and kissed her warmly. "You know Miss McNeil, I think I'm falling in…" Jim stopped and kissed her again.

"What's the matter silly, can't you say it?"

"I just didn't want to be first. You know, I guess it's a guy thing."

"Hey Mr. Flannery?"

"Yeah?"

"I love you." Susan then kissed him deeply.

"I…Susan I've only known you a few days and I think I…I…"

She whispered in his ear – "You what silly?"

"I love you!"

"There, that wasn't so hard was it?"

"Well…no…but…"

"Did those three words put a dent in your masculine armor, Jim Flannery?"

"No…but…"

"This is better than a drive-in movie!" Came a voice from the back.

Jim and Susan turned around to find a conscious Arly Ferguson. "You heard everything Mr. Ferguson?"

"Yup."

"It was like pulling teeth trying to get those three words out of him."

"Yup. Ya know my head hurts, what happened? Where are we?"

Susan volunteered – "First, you were shot, in the head, doesn't appear too serious. Second, I flew the plane and landed it. Third, we're at Love Field in Dallas and fourth, there are a lot of people waiting out there with a lot of questions. So, we'd better not keep them waiting and besides, I'd like to get to a hotel. It's been a long night."

"You said I was shot?"

"That's right." Jim showed him the bullet hole in the cabin.

"But who?"

"We don't know that Mr. Ferguson. Do you have any enemies?" Jim and Susan had decided during the flight that to bring Bannister's name into this, would only draw attention from the Dallas police and not knowing the depth of the Dallas police involvement in the conspiracy, could only spell trouble.

"No one that would shoot me…I don't think…my head…"

"Come on Susan, Mr. Ferguson's in need of some medical attention."

As they exited the plane, a police car with siren blasting pulled up and stopped alongside the firetruck. The medical team helped a very shaky Arly Ferguson onto a stretcher and into the ambulance. Jim and Susan wished him well as the car sped off to Parkland Hospital.

The head of airport security Frank Donaldson approached Jim and Susan. "Can you two shed a little light here?"

Jim explained everything as it had happened, with the exception of their knowledge of Bannister. Donaldson then asked them to return with him to his office for further questioning. Susan protested: "Look Mr. Donaldson, we're both very tired…we've had a difficult night and we'd like to get some rest. Can this wait until morning?"

"Afraid not mam. A man has been shot and I'm not quite satisfied with the story I'm hearing. So, before I turn this over to the Dallas police here," Donaldson motioned toward Sergeant Hargis, "I have a few questions I'd like to ask. Now, if you'll just follow me." Susan rolled her eyes. "We've told you everything! What is it Mr. Donaldson that you want to hear?" Susan was tired and had very little patience for Donaldson's approach. Jim apologized for Susan – "I'm very sorry Mr. Donaldson, but we've had a very harrowing experience. The bullet hitting Mr. Ferguson and with my fiancee' having to fly the plane with so little experience…and saving all our lives…well, you understand don't you sir?"

Donaldson looked Jim up and down. "What do you do for a living Mr. Flannery?"

"I write a political column for the *Washington Post*, keeps me very busy these days. I'm here to do a story on the President's goodwill visit."

"I'll tell you what Mr. Flannery, you two show up at police headquarters in the morning, 10:00am sharp. I'll be there to lead the questioning…and uh Mr. Flannery?"

"Yes sir?" Jim wanted nothing more than to appease Donaldson

"Tell the lady to bring a different attitude with her."

"Right. Where can we get a cab?"

"You'll have to use the payphone. Over there." Donaldson pointed toward the main building, then turned and sneered at Susan as he walked away.

"The creep could have offered his phone!"

"Forget it Susan, let's get a cab and get out of here. I don't think we'll be seeing Mr. Donaldson again."

"Oh! Why?"

"Not now, later." Jim motioned to Susan and they walked to the payphone while Sergeant Hargis dug his thumbs into his belt and watched them out of the corner of his eye.

"Okay Ace, see that river down there?"

"Yeah, sure do."

"Drop down about a hundred feet and follow it. We're just about at the end of our ride."

No more than five minutes later – "That's it. Now swing past it and come in from the north for your landing." Bannister knew it well. He flew here himself, at least a half dozen times to visit with

Chief Curry when the plan was in its infancy stage.

"That's it Ace, good. Just take your baby right in."

The old single engine touched down and slowly came to a stop outside a dilapidated hangar.

"Here we are Mr. Flannery...safe an' sound...now about those C-notes?"

"Oh, yeah! How could I forget." Bannister drew the .44 and placed it against Emmitt Owen's temple. "Okay my old friend open that door."

Owen did as he was told. "But I thought we had a deal...you wouldn't...?"

Bannister squeezed the trigger. The explosive force of the .44 magnum sent Emmitt Owen out of the cabin, through the air, coming to a rest on the weed filled tarmac. His body writhed convulsively like an eel out of water. Bannister threw his big body across the empty seat, aimed and fired a second shot into the man's neck. The writhing stopped.

He thought – "Four down two to go." He then wriggled his large torso into the empty seat and fired up the engine, steering the old craft to the pot holed runway. He lifted off for the ten minute flight to Love Field.

When he arrived at Love Field, Bannister quickly guided the old single to a hangar in the south end of the airport. He walked to the main building where he saw a friendly face. Sergeant Billy Hargis was at a table with a cup of coffee. He saw Bannister approaching and quickly got up to greet him.

"Mr. Bannister, how are you?" The two men shook hands. "We had a situation here a short while ago that just might interest you. Geneveve! Coffee for Mr. Bannister."

"I'm fine thank you, a little tired from the days activities." Geneveve placed a fresh cup of coffee in front of Bannister. "Now Sergeant, that situation, let me guess: Could it involve a man, a woman and a plane?"

"Why...yes!"

"I'm all ears Sergeant...shoot."

XXIV

"We've been waiting for half an hour! Maybe we should call back?"

"Here he comes now."

A yellow and white Ford Galaxy marked – Dallas Taxi Service in large black letters, pulled up.

Jim followed Susan into the back seat.

"No luggage sir?"

"No, airline miscue. They're delivering it in the morning."

"Where to?" The driver was a young, well built man with no trace of the local accent. He dragged on a Lucky Strike while he flipped up the lever on the meter.

Jim had written down two hotels and their addresses from the phone book.

"Let's try the Piedmont."

"Good choice…center of town…nice place! Where you two from?"

"Washington D.C., we'll be visiting friends in the morning, then we're off to Los Angeles for Thanksgiving with my wife's family."

"Yeah, it's nice to get together with the family for the holidays. I'm gonna try to get back to Connecticut…my family's there."

"What brought you to Dallas? Couldn't be to drive a cab!"

"I came down here in July…I'm a football player. Tried out for the new team…well they've been around for a couple of years…the Cowboys. I made it to the final cut in late August and then they kinda pulled the rug out. I've been here since. Have to make a living so I drive this thing." He took another drag on his Lucky. "Took up these things after I got cut." He tossed the butt out the window.

"May I trouble you for one of those?"

"Sure lady." He handed her the pack and his Zippo.

"Mind if I take one?" Jim asked.

"Help yourself."

As Jim and Susan lit up, they both laughed. Jim whispered in her ear – "I like one once in awhile." "Me too." Susan replied.

"So what uh…position do you play?" Jim inhaled his first cigarette in six months, a little strong but it tasted good.

"I'm a linebacker…played for Boston University. The Cowboys cut me on account of speed. The coach down here, Tom Landry, he wants speed. I don't know…I may go back north. My father has an accounting firm in Hartford…I studied that at BU. It's something to fall back on, but I get bored with all of it…Hartford…accounting. I'd like to give football another try."

"Hey, I went to BU also. Journalism, class of '54" Jim leaned forward and extended his right hand. "Jim Flannery and this is my wife Susan."

"Pleased to meet you two. Dave Edwards, class of '62!" The two men shook hands.

"Well here we are, The Piedmont." Dave Edwards pulled down the lever, the meter read $5.50. Jim handed him a twenty and did not wait for change.

"Good luck with football Mr. Edwards!" Jim and Susan got

out of the cab.

"Thank you folks and enjoy your stay in Dallas!" As the cab drove off, Jim noticed a Dallas police car pull up slowly and park. He grabbed Susan's arm, directing her to the main entrance of the Piedmont.

"Susan, they followed us, don't turn around."

"Who?"

"The police. They just pulled up in front of the hotel."

They walked through the empty lobby to a door marked – EXIT. The clerk at the desk noticed as they walked by, but he was busy doing paperwork. He figured they were hotel guests.

The door led them to a sidestreet where they slowly walked along the side of the building in the opposite direction from the waiting police car.

"In the cab we passed a hotel…the uh…Richmond. Come on we'll cut through these side streets." Susan clutched Jim's hand as he picked up the pace.

After traversing a maze of streets – "There it is!" They entered the Richmond, checked in and quickly got on the elevator. Jim pressed the button for the fifth floor.

"It's a little after 2:00am. I'll try Hilsman when we get to the room."

"Isn't it a little late for that?"

"Susan, I'm running short on cash…I'll see if he can wire us something and I'll pay him back later."

"Hey silly, did you forget?"

"Forget what?"

"The President of the United States put us on his payroll!"

"Right, I did forget about that."

When they entered the room, Jim went right to the phone and dialed.

"Hello, John Scali here."

"John, Jim Flannery."

"Jim, where are you…is everything okay?"

"We're in Dallas and things are getting a little sticky. Is Hilsman available? I know it's late but I need to speak to him."

"He's sound asleep on the couch. The man's been at it all day and night. I don't think I should..."

"I'm awake. Who is it?" Hilsman had so much on his mind that it prevented him from getting the rest he desperately needed.

"Flannery, he's in Dallas...says he needs to speak with you."

"I'll take it." Hilsman slowly walked to the phone.

"Yes Jim?"

"Mr. Hilsman, I'm awfully sorry to wake you sir, but we have a slight problem here."

"Yes, go on."

Flannery told him of their journey from Lake Charles to Dallas, of Bannister, of the airport, the Dallas police and their shortage of cash.

"I'd say this is more than a slight problem. This man Bannister is turning into a real headache. He'll probably show up in Dallas, if he isn't already there. I can't do much about him, at the moment, but I can alleviate the problem with cash. Call Chief Deputy Paul Malinsky, he's staying at The Piedmont. He has an envelope for you. I thought you'd be running a little short at this point. Here, take down Malinsky's number." Hilsman read off the number.

"But Mr. Hilsman, that's the hotel where the police were watching us. I'm sure they think we're staying there."

"Hmmm, I wonder if they're on to Malinsky too? Look, don't move until you speak to him...he'll arrange a meeting place. Oh, by the way Jim, we're a little short on manpower, so I've told Chief Malinsky to call on you for a special assignment. I'll call you at your hotel in the morning. What's the number?"

Flannery read off the number and they both hung up.

"Well?" Susan was eager to hear.

"I'm going on a special assignment!"

"Where?"

"I'll find out right now." Jim dialed The Piedmont.

XXV

"I put a tail on their cab. So what do ya say we get in my car, radio ahead and find out just where the lovebirds are staying?"

"Good, good work Sergeant, Chief Curry told me about you, you're going places!" Bannister was confident now that the couple would soon be out of the picture.

They left the airport diner and walked to the back of the main building where Hargis had parked the patrol car. After getting in, the Sergeant made the call.

"Patrol four, Jesse do you read me? Over."

"Patrol four here. Yes Sergeant? Over."

"What have you got Jesse? Over."

"I'm parked in front of The Piedmont Hotel. The couple checked in about thirty minutes ago. Over"

"Good, I'm on my way. Over." Hargis placed the radio back in its holder. "It's only a short distance, we'll be there in no time."

Bannister felt for his gun, drew it and checked the chamber. Four spent cartridges, he thought – "I'll get more when the shops open." He then checked his ankle for the blood stained dagger. Feeling secure with his weapons, he settled back in his seat for the ride to The Piedmont.

They pulled up behind Patrol Four.

"Jesse, you can join Collins over in Oak Cliff, we'll take it from here."

"Right Sergeant."

"Now Mr. Bannister, let's see about that troublesome couple."

They entered the hotel and went straight to the desk.

"Good evening…uhh…Mr. and Mrs. Flannery…their room number please?"

"I'm sorry sir," the desk clerk saw the nametag, "Sergeant Hargis there's no one staying here by that name."

"Are you sure? Check again!"

"Like I said Sergeant, I don't have anyone…"

"Look, they checked in less than an hour ago…tall thin man, good looking woman in a black skirt…late twenties, early thirties…they may have used a different name?" Sergeant Hargis was becoming irritated, it usually didn't take much. Bannister stood there in silence, just waiting for the room number.

"Yes Sergeant, a couple matching that description came in a short while ago. But they quickly left by that door." The desk clerk pointed to the side entrance.

The two men stared at the exit. Bannister mumbled out loud – "Christ, they must have spotted the car. They're smart Sergeant, very smart."

"Look Mr. Bannister, don't you worry sir, we'll have every hotel in the city checked!"

"That won't be necessary…just those within walking distance. How many in say…a six or seven block radius?"

"Let me see…there's The Sheraton, The Long Horn Inn…The Richmond and a couple of seedy little places."

"We'll take them in that order. Come on!"

Bannister stormed out the door with Hargis following. They

jumped in the patrol car and went directly to The Sheraton.

"So Mr. Flannery, I'll expect to see you at 9:00am."
"Oh, and Chief, it's room 502."
"See you then Mr. Flannery." Click.
Jim stuck his head out the window and watched Susan. She was sitting on the fire escape staring out over the Dallas skyline.
"Chief Malinsky will be here at 9:00am for a room service breakfast. He says he'll discuss plans with us then."
"Good." She answered. She then climbed back inside and steered Jim to the bed. He then sat on the edge of the bed while she placed her hands on his shoulders. He looked up at her.
"After all this excitement, I'm not the least bit tired…how about you?"
Jim didn't answer. He lifted her blouse to just below her bra and gently kissed her smooth skin.
"Oh Jim…" Susan purred.
He then unbuttoned her skirt and slowly pulled it down, kissing the soft skin below her naval. He pulled her down onto the bed and continued.
Susan moaned.
When the couple fulfilled their desires, they drifted off into a deep sleep, entangled in each other's arms. From the open window a cool breeze gently blew over their naked bodies.

"That's two strikes Sergeant… what the fuck will be the third?" Bannister was very angry now. The couple's elusiveness was frustrating him and to compound matters, he hadn't had a drink in what seemed an eternity.
"The Richmond, that's the last of the better spots. I don't know about the seedy joints."
"The Richmond huh…let's go!"

XXVI

When they pulled up in front of The Richmond it was 3:40am.

They were given the same answer by this desk clerk – "Sorry gentlemen, there's no one here by that name."

Bannister slapped his hand on the desk – "Look, they…" He went on to describe the couple.

The clerk was beginning to feel a little intimidated by Bannister. "I'm sorry sir but I came on duty at 3:00am…I'm covering for Mr. Robertson who took ill and no one has checked in since."

Hargis interrupted – "Check the register and check it now!"

"Yes sir! Let's see…the last entry was a couple by the name of Mr. and Mrs. Dawson, we don't record the time we…"

"That' them!" Bannister's adrenalin was pumping.

"Mr. Bannister, how do you know that?" Hargis replied.

"Flannery used that name in my shop…the room number? Quick you little shit! The room number!" Bannister was wild.

"That's highly irregular…I'm sorry I can't…"

"Yes you can you little prick, this is official police business.

Now! The room number or do I have to come around there and get it myself?" The Sergeant's voice bellowed through the lobby.

"It's uh..uh..502!"

Bannister and Hargis quickly got into the elevator and pressed the button for the fifth floor.

As the door closed, the desk clerk who was shaking with fear, felt something was wrong and that the two men were lying. "Official police business...I don't think so. Probably another one of their greedy shakedowns...the Dallas police are famous for that." He then went to the switchboard and rang 502.

Jim opened his eyes and Susan mumbled – "Who could that be?"

"Could only be Hilsman or the Chief...I'll get it." Jim looked at the clock on the night table – 3:50am as he picked up the phone.

"Yes?"

"Mr. Dawson, I'm very sorry to wake you sir but this is the desk clerk and there are two men on their way to your room. Men that you may not be expecting...a police sergeant and I believe the other one... Bannister I believe his name was...he was very nasty and.." The line went dead. "Mr. Dawson...Mr. Dawson!"

"Susan wake up! WAKE UP!"

"What, what... just when I was falling..."

Jim pulled her to her feet. "Look, get dressed quick. Bannister is on his way up here with that cop...come on!"

The name Bannister got her attention real quick.

They dressed in record time. "Come on, we'll use the fire escape!" They both climbed out and Jim closed the window. He thought that it might give them valuable seconds. They made their way down five floors to the street.

"Don't knock, let's surprise them!" Bannister threw his burly torso, shoulder first into the door. It flew open and the two men entered with guns drawn.

"Now where the fuck are they?" Bannister was livid.

Hargis ran to the window, grabbed the two handles on the lower part of the window frame and pulled it open. He stepped out onto the fire escape.

Jim and Susan were running down the street and just as they ran under a street light, Hargis spotted them. "There…there they are!" He pointed in the direction as Bannister stuck his head out to get a look.

"Son of a bitch! Come on…the elevator will be faster!"

Running from the elevator past the front desk, Bannister pointed at the desk clerk – "I'll deal with you later you little prick!"

The two men jumped in the patrol car and swung around the corner in the direction where they saw the couple running.

"Nothing…shit!"

Hargis picked up his radio – "Patrol four, Jesse, do you read? Over"

"Loud and clear Sergeant. Over"

"Jesse, get back over here. I need you to comb the streets around The Richmond Hotel for that couple. No sirens. Over."

"They got away Sergeant? Over."

"Look Jesse, no questions. Just get your country ass over here and look for that couple! Over."

"Right away Sergeant! Over."

They searched for the next half hour and came up with nothing. Ditto for Jesse.

"All night diners, parks…parks! That's it Sergeant…It's the only place they can hide now, they know we're checking the hotels!"

"Right! Sam Houston Park is this way." Hargis picked up his radio – "Jesse, get your ass to the entrance of Sam Houston Park. Over."

"Right Sergeant. Over." Jesse was sick of being pushed around by his bully Sergeant. He considered quitting on more than one occasion, but he always thought about his lady and the four kids. "Gotta feed them," he thought, as he jammed the accelerator to the floor. He didn't want to keep the Sergeant waiting.

XXVIII

As he peered out from the side of the building, Jim saw that the police car was gone. Again, they entered the main entrance of The Piedmont.

"Mr. Paul Malinsky…would you ring him please?"

"At this hour sir?"

"Yes, this is an emergency." Jim and Susan were both breathing heavily.

"Who shall I say is asking?"

"Jim Flannery."

The clerk went to the switchboard and rang 712.

"Mr. Malinsky, there's a Mr. Flannery and a woman here to see you sir…I know the hour sir but the gentleman insists that this is an emergency." After a short pause, "Yes, right away sir." He turned to the couple, "You may go right up, room 712."

"Thank you." Jim grabbed Susan's arm and practically dragged her to the elevator. She was exhausted. Jim was too. They were working on their third or fourth wind, they didn't know. They lost track.

Exiting the elevator on the seventh floor, Jim and Susan found a man waiting for them in the hallway. "This way you two...I'm Chief Malinsky." Jim, then Susan shook the Chief's hand.

As they entered his suite, Susan made a beeline for the couch. She curled up in the fetal position as the two men just stared.

"Uh...Miss McNeil, there's no need for that...there's a second bedroom right through that door." The Chief pointed and Susan silently made her way to the bedroom. "What's with her?"

"Well Chief Malinsky, she's pretty tired and we uh...lost our sleeping quarters."

"Oh? And please...Chief is enough."

"Yeah, and uh...Bannister and the Dallas police officer...Hargis, they found us. I have no idea how they did it...I thought we lost them. We had to use the fire escape at the hotel to get away. We were lucky again, but our luck can't hold out much longer with this guy. He just keeps coming and coming, he's relentless in his pursuit. I know we lost them again but he'll find a way. He may be very coarse around the edges and everywhere else, but he is smart."

"No need to worry, you're safe here." Malinsky poured a glass of water and handed it to Jim. "I'm sorry I have nothing stronger."

"This is fine. Thank you."

"One of my men called earlier to report that a patrol car was parked in front of the hotel, then a couple entered and quickly exited, just as you told me in our earlier conversation."

"Yes, that's right. Your man saw us?"

"Yes, and he also reported that a police officer and a large man were here shortly after you and the girl left through the side exit. They sent the first patrol car off, but they were here for only a few minutes That had to be Bannister and this Hargis fellow. So they hunted you two down and you were able to give them the brush."

"Pure luck...believe me." Jim could think of nothing but sleep.

"Look Jim, get some rest. I'll call down for a large Texas style breakfast in the morning."

"That sounds great, thanks Chief. I guess everything else can wait until then."

"Goodnight Jim."

Dragging his feet to the bedroom, Jim collapsed on the bed, fully clothed. He was spent. Susan was already sound asleep making strange snoring noises. Jim never heard them.

"Yes, my name is Hewlett Clemons from The Piedmont Hotel. I was wondering, would it be at all possible to have Sergeant Hargis call me at the main desk? I have a bit of information that I believe he will find very useful. My number is 421-6377."

"Right. I'll get the message to him."

"Thank you so much."

"Yes sir, your welcome." Officer Tippet hung up. Desk duty didn't sit well with him. He didn't care much for the message taking and the oddball calls. He thought about the call for Hargis – "Probably more secret bullshit in that God awful plan they were working on. Covering up the murder of the President so that the Texan, Lyndon Johnson could take control and pump the big bucks into the pockets of a chosen few from the Dallas Police Department was downright satanic. When they approached me and said that I was a natural for their scheme, my reply cemented my doom. I've been up to my ears in paper work and desk duty since. When I gave my word to keep my mouth shut, I knew it was the wrong way for me and that I would never be able to live with it if they found success." Tippet picked up the phone and dialed The Piedmont. He found a soiled napkin and placed it over the mouthpiece in an attempt to disguise his voice.

"Piedmont Hotel, how may I help you?"

"Sergeant Hargis here, you have something for…"

"Yes Sergeant, that couple you were looking for…well they returned just twenty minutes ago…they went to a Mr. Malinsky's room. Room 712."

"Who?"

"Chief Deputy Paul Malinsky...from Washington D.C."

"I see and thank you." Tippet hung up. "Now what's Hargis up to...Chief Deputy from D.C....and a couple?"

"Sergeant, we need twenty men to effectively search this park. With only three of us they'll continue to stay one step ahead. I told you they were smart...smart little bastards!" Bannister was more than beside himself, he was tired and he could taste the Jack Daniels.

"I could really use a drink!"

"Well Mr. Bannister, what do ya say we call it a night. My shift was over at 4:00...that was twenty minutes ago. I know this wild all night place...The Cellar. It's run by our buddy Ruby...Jack Ruby."

"Sounds good and how is Mr. Rubenstein?"

"I think we should find out!"

"You lead the way Sergeant!"

Hargis picked up his radio – "Jesse, this place is a deadend. Book off. Over."

"Night Sergeant. Over"

Hargis didn't answer. He mashed the accelerator to the floor and turned on the siren.

"What the hell are you doing? There isn't a car on the road! Turn that fucking thing off!"

"Mr. Bannister, this is how we get around here in the early morning hours...kinda wakes the dead...ya know."

"Yeah, I know." Bannister put his hands over his ears as the Sergeant let out a howl. He was a real cowboy and loving it.

"Will you turn that fucking thing off? I can't think!"

"Okay, Okay!" Hargis obliged.

"Thank you." Now that he could think, Bannister's thoughts shifted to the couple – "Those two are either very smart or very lucky. They probably had some fairy fucking Godperson watching over them." He had no idea where to look next. For the moment he didn't care, he just wanted a drink. "Sergeant, stop at

The Richmond on the way. I wanna give that little prick behind the desk the beating of his life!"

"Oh Mr. Bannister, there's plenty of time for that. Give it a rest...hell, if you want I'll get you laid tonight...or this morning!"

"Yeah, this place The Cellar...what's it like?"

"It's got a lot of everything...all kinds of people to satisfy any desire you might have...you'll see."

"No faggots I hope?"

"Oh yeah, them too. Like I was saying, it's got it all."

"I hate fucking faggots..there's nothing worse than a faggot...NOTHING!"

"If you say so Mr. Bannister."

XXIX

Chief Malinsky knocked on the bedroom door. No answer. He turned the handle and entered.

"Wake up you two, it's 8:45am and our breakfast is here!"

Jim pulled himself out of bed as Malinsky closed the door giving them their privacy.

"Susan my dear, it's time to get up!"

"Oh Jim, not now. I need about twelve more hours, call me later."

"Not today. Come on, we'll take a quick shower…Malinsky has breakfast out there."

Susan struggled to her feet – "Okay, okay."

They showered together and got dressed.

"We need clothes. These are…they're filthy!" Susan made a face when she saw herself in the mirror.

Jim went out first leaving Susan in the bathroom.

"Good morning Chief….now that looks good!" Jim looked over the spread.

"Morning Jim. Have a seat."

The room service cart had all it's flaps up to accommodate the morning feast. It was covered with trays containing eggs, bacon, sausage, home fries, a bowl of fresh fruit, stacks of pancakes and toast, orange juice, two pots of coffee and all the accoutrements.

"Did they forget anything?"

"I don't think so. Dig in!"

Susan appeared from the bedroom with her hair pinned up. Jim never saw her that way. She greeted them.

"I like what you did with your hair…very nice…I haven't seen that before."

"I haven't either. You know a woman needs all her stuff. Make-up, rollers, clean clothes…"

Malinsky was taking it all in. "Oh, yes, this is for you!" Malinsky handed Jim an envelope.

Jim opened it and counted out twenty crisp one hundred dollar bills.

"What's all this for? We only need a little for expenses."

"Well Jim, Mr. Hilsman felt that an emergency may pop up and that you and the lady might need this. From the look of the two of you…your clothing…I'd say you need it."

"Well that's very generous." Jim fondled the money.

"After breakfast you take the lady shopping and pick up some things for yourself too...enough to get you both through tomorrow. A little after noon, take a cab to the Trade-Mart, I'll be watching for you. We'll spend some time there going over your roles. We'll be very busy…that I promise."

"Oh! That reminds me, Mr. Hilsman was going to call me at The Richmond!"

"Not to worry. I spoke to Roger before I woke you two. He knows you're here."

"You certainly have everything covered Mr. Malinsky."

"It's what I do Susan and please, everyone calls me Chief."

"And just what is it that you do Chief…if I'm not prying?"

"You're not prying Susan, remember I am a public servant…and what I do is chase criminals, a lot of fugitives…usually federal offenders and arrest them. We'll be doing a lot of that right here and in D.C…in the next 24 to 48 hours."

"We?"

"Yes Jim. Tell me…have you ever fired a gun"

"Well I've… before I went off to college, I did a little a little quail hunting with my father in New Hampshire."

Susan choked on her scrambled eggs. She hid her face as she spit up in her dish. Malinsky smiled and she returned the gesture.

"I'm sorry, something must have gotten caught in my throat."

Annoyed, knowing that Susan was laughing at him, Jim turned to Malinsky - "That's just about my experience with guns."

"Excuse me." Malinsky got up and went to his room, quickly returning with a duffle bag. He pulled out a government issue .45 caliber pistol. Removing the clip and checking the chamber, he handed it to Jim. Just as he did the phone rang.

"Have you ever seen one of these?" Asked the Chief as he walked to the phone.

Jim took the pistol and answered – "Yes, I believe I have. In the movie *Sgt. York*, I think he carried something like this…is that right?"

Malinsky was talking on the phone now while Susan was again choking. This time she could not help laughing.

"I'm sorry Jim!" Susan was sincere, but Jim wasn't buying it. Malinsky returned to the table.

"Well Jim, it's yours." He then put two loaded clips on the table next to Jim, "Here, you might find these handy."

"Handy! But I don't even know how to use this thing?"

"All you do is put the clip in there," he pointed to the bottom of the handle, "pull the slide back," again pointing, "and it's chambered, ready to fire."

"But Chief, do I really need this?"

"Look, just carry it for insurance. We're dealing with an assassination attempt on our President and if you're going to be a part of suppressing their plan, then just…"

"Yeah, I get your message…okay." Jim placed the .45 on the table and stared at it.

They spent the next ten minutes eating in silence, clearing a good portion of the food from the table.

"What kind of gun do you use Chief?"

"I like a Beretta or a Walther .380 Jim. Carried those exclusively when I was with the Agency."

"What agency?" Asked Susan.

"Central Intelligence."

"You mean as in the CIA?"

"Yes, for six years. Then I took the position as Chief Deputy. Funny thing, I worked side by side with the Director Allen Dulles and now I'm working to put him away."

"Why? What has he done?" Jim had a puzzled look on his face.

"He's the mastermind of this plot…along with a small group of Generals." Malinsky answered matter of factly.

"You've got to be kidding? Mr. Hilsman never told me any of this."

"There's a lot Mr. Hilsman hasn't told you."

"Yeah…I guess so…" Jim looked at Susan who was also staring in disbelief.

"And there's a great deal of information that you've supplied that the President is deeply indebted to. Without your input, we'd be somewhere up that creek without a paddle."

"We're both glad that we could help… and continue to do what we can. But tell me Chief, if the Generals are involved, who will arrest them?"

"Hilsman has that covered in D.C. Look, you two go on your shopping excursion now and don't forget the Trade-Mart around noon."

The trio got up and Malinsky led the way to the door. Jim left the .45 on the table .

"I forgot the….the gun." Jim stared at the table.

"I'll give it to you later. Now go get some clothes…you'll find all the stores in this general area. You won't have far to go."

"But what if Bannister and that cop are..."

The Chief cut in quickly – "There's a man in the lobby waiting for you...he's one of my men. He'll be with you...that call I received...it was him. Don't worry, the way is clear...you'll be safe."

"Whatever you say Chief." Jim and Susan left the room and got on the elevator.

"Susan, this is big...bigger than we thought...Generals...this reminds me of a book. Did you read *Seven Days In May*?"

"Yes, it is big and no I haven't read that...never heard of it."

"Well, let me tell you about it...this group of Generals attempt a coup d'etat against an American President who refuses to adhere to their desires for war......sound familiar?"

"Yeah, that's frightening!"

"Only difference here is that in real life they don't succeed."

"I hope you're right Jim!"

"Listen Susan, we have to do everything we can...everything that Chief Malinsky asks of us...to help President Kennedy."

"Yes Jim, but some of it scares me."

"Yeah I know Susan, but other than helping the President, there is a plus for you and I."

"And what might that be?"

"We're both journalists and this will be the story of the century!"

XXX

The breakfast was wrapping up and the President and First Lady shook hands with all the local politicos. From a hallway just outside the dining room, Colonel Prouty watched everything. His disguise was perfect, he fit right in. Even though, the President had recognized him from the description the Colonel had given. It provided a measure of security for the President knowing that the Colonel was there.

At 9:35am the Presidential party was driven to San Antonio airport for the flight to Houston. Aboard Air Force One, the President appeared to be much more relaxed.

"Jack, it was so nice to see you in such good spirits this morning."

"I feel good Jackie…revitalized…had a good conversation with Roger last night. He's got all the bases covered and Chief Malinsky is in Dallas right now with his team."

"I don't think I know this Chief Malinsky…Who is he?"

"The United States Chief Deputy Sheriff…he spent some time

in the CIA under Dulles. Roger is very pleased with the Chief's planning but I think there may be some sort of vendetta that Malinsky has for Dulles."

"Why?"

"Well Jackie, do you remember the takeover in Guatemala...I believe it was in 1954?"

"Yes, but...vaguely?"

"President Eisenhower had Dulles put together an operation to overthrow the Arbenz regime, who had become...let's say very unkind to American business. The operation succeeded with the installation of Castillo Armas...our friend...and of course American business thrived."

"What has that got to do with Chief Malinsky?"

"A lot Jackie. Mr. Malinsky at the time was considered the CIA's top operative. It was he who was the mastermind of the entire operation in Guatemala. However, Allen Dulles never duly cited him for his efforts and then took all the credit for himself. After, Eisenhower granted the Agency *carte blanche*, elevating Mr. Dulles to a kind of...espionage stardom."

"And Chief Malinsky?"

"Well it seems that Dulles felt threatened by the Chief's talents and as a result...reduced him to a desk job. I believe he stayed on for another year or so...became disenchanted and then moved to the Sheriff's office in Washington and I'm glad he did. He brings some very special talents to our counterplans."

The President and First Lady sat silently for the next few minutes. Both were focused on the plans ahead.

The President then broke the silence – "Jackie, I've made some decisions that you should know about."

"Yes?"

"I've decided to put Roger in the Attorney General's office."

"With Bobby?"

"No dear, in place of Bobby."

"But..he's your brother!"

"I know Jackie, I've decided to elevate my devoted brother."

"To…as?"

"The Vice-President. It's the right move…I've given this a great deal of thought. With Lyndon out, I want a man in there with strength and vision to help get our country through the aftermath of this mess. Bobby's the logical choice."

"I think that's wonderful Jack, does he know?"

"I haven't told him yet. When I do, I'm sure he'll be very happy. Roger knows and he's already accepted. I also plan to insert Colonel Prouty in Roger's position at the State Department."

"You have so much on your mind and in the works…it makes one wonder why some feel that the President's job is an easy one …that the country runs itself and the Chief Executive is merely a figurehead. Little do they know. You know Jack, I also think that promoting Bobby is the right move, but when I think of Lyndon and his involvement I feel very sad. I watched him in his dealings with you at the breakfast…and it just makes me sad."

"Me too Jackie…me too."

Air Force One then touched down in Houston.

XXXI

"I like the skirt!"

"You don't think it's too short?"

"No it's just perfect....hmmm."

"Oh Jim, cut it out. You just love my legs!"

"Yes I do."

"I know you do. I catch you staring at them all the time!"

"So? Come on let's cross."

They finished their shopping excursion and were now walking in the direction of the Trade-Mart.

"It's 11:45, let's skip the cab and walk. I think it's only about three or four blocks from here."

"Fine with me, but what about our protector back there?" Susan motioned behind them.

"He'll keep up."

Within minutes they had the Trade-Mart in sight and Deputy Powers had caught up.

"Okay you two, holdup...follow me."

They were led into an abandon garage. There, they found Chief Malinsky filling in Deputy Spencer on the government radio frequency they were using, which the Dallas Police could not tap into.

The Chief looked up as they entered – "I'll be with you two in a minute." He then turned to Powers – "Call Hardman over at Dealey on your radio and see if they've come up with anything."

"Right Chief. Hardman, this is Powers do you read me. Over" A moment later, "JP, Hardman here. We have a possible make at the Dal-Tex and the Depository. Two suspects went into the Depository about fifteen minutes ago, both carrying rifle size cases and just before your call, ditto at the Dal-Tex but with only one suspect. Nothing going on at the rail yards. Over."

"Let me speak to him." Powers handed the radio to the Chief.

"Hardman, this is the Chief. Good work, now send a man to each location and get the floor and exact rooms where they're setting up. You stick with the rail yards. Sounds like the two buildings are close to being ours. Let me know what you come up with. Over."

"Right Chief. Over."

"Powers, why don't you join the others in Building Three across from the Trade-Mart. Keep in touch before moving to Building Four."

"Right."

The Chief was a model of precision. Each location was thoroughly scrutinized. He wanted very much to outfox the old man at his own game.

"Well you two, that certainly is an improvement." Susan smiled and curtsied while Jim modeled his new blazer.

"Okay, fashion show's over, put your bags over there. Let's get down to business……Susan, wherever Jim goes, you follow." He handed her a thick black notebook, a small tape recorder and two pens. "Take notes or use the tape, but record everything as you see it…everything."

"Yes…everything."

He then handed Jim a 35mm Nikon F. "I know you can handle one of these, I've seen that you occasionly do your own photo journalism for the *Washington Post*."

"Yes, that's right." Jim looked over the Nikon.

"Now pay close attention. Tomorrow when the President arrives at Love Field, we'll be in Dealey to secure the three positions in sequence. In other words we'll start with the Dal-Tex, then move to the Depository, then to the picket fence at the railyards. At each position, we'll make the arrests and you'll photograph everything as it happens. Susan, you'll be recording all the details."

"Right."

"But Chief, why not cover them all at the same time?"

"Good point Jim. However, our problem is that we are limited with manpower. We had to break up the force we have between here and D.C., and we haven't assigned anyone to New Orleans, but with Bannister here in Dallas, he saved us a trip. So, you see our problem is manpower. On Friday, we'll have four men at Love Field, six in Dealey and eleven at the Trade-Mart which is the most difficult to secure…too many buildings for the number of men."

"Why are you paying so much attention to the Trade-Mart and Love Field, when we know that the crossfire is planned for Dealey Plaza?" Jim thought he made another good point, but he knew nothing of the alternate plan.

"Rain."

"Rain! What do you mean?"

"Well Susan, Hilsman found out that there's an alternate plan should it happen to rain, which will bring out the bulletproof hardtops for the motorcade. The problem is that we don't know the rain positions, we only know that there is an alternate plan. On one hand we like the idea of rain because the President has better protection in the hardtop…but on the other hand we're limited in our knowledge of where they'll try to make the hit. A similar problem presents itself at Dealey. If the skies are clear, we like the idea of shutting them down at the three positions that you two were able to uncover. However, should any of their positions change or new positions added, that we are unaware of, we don't like the idea of the President making the trip from Love to Dealey in a convertible. So, whether the sun is shining or the rain is falling, unknowns exist."

"Yeah, so if it rains you've chosen the only places where the President is out in the open - the start and finish – Love Field and the Trade-Mart…concentrating more on the Trade-Mart for the reasons you've stated."

"Precisely. You catch on quickly Jim. Susan, is he always this fast?"

"Sometimes he's too fast!" Susan smiled, the Chief turned to hide his laughter and Jim frowned.

"Well Susan, I haven't heard any complaints from you!"

"Oh I know Jim, I'm only fooling." She placed her hand in his, "All this stuff starts to get to me…a little humor doesn't hurt…I'm sorry."

Jim squeezed her hand and smiled.

"Okay you two lovebirds…over here." They went to the map where the Chief was using a pointer. "The President is expected at noon. When Air Force One hits the tarmac, we'll get a call. We'll have two men at the Dal-Tex and the three of us will be with them. We make the arrests, you do the pictures and you know your role Susan." Susan nodded. "When the three of us go to meet the other's at the Depository, my men at the Dal-Tex take their suspects out the back door of the building, then to an unmarked State Department plane waiting at Love Field. We'll repeat the procedure at the Depository and the rail yards, all before the motorcade arrives in Dealey. Now, with rain we'll still check Dealey, then join the eleven men posted at the Trade-Mart. You, Susan and myself, along with the six men orginally stationed in Dealey, that gives us a lot more eyes to find the snipers outside the Trade-Mart."

"After capturing them, why are you taking the snipers directly to the airport." Susan had the same thought.

"We can't rely on the Dallas police...we have no idea what we'd be up against. So we quickly move them to Love Field and fly them to D.C. for arraignment...this being a federal offense."

"Boy Chief, you certainly have this whole thing figured. You didn't forget anything!"

"As a matter of fact Susan there is something else and it's stuck in the back of my mind. The Dallas police Chief...Curry and the other one...Sergeant Hargis and of course Bannister. I want them on that plane with the others but I haven't figured out how I'm going to get them there...quietly, without anyone knowing."

"Couldn't you just issue warrants after this thing settles down and come back for them?"

"I could, but I don't believe that they'd hang around after all the brass are placed behind bars. Mark my words, they'd run, their kind always does. I'll figure something."

"You forgot something else Chief."

"What's that Jim?"

"My gun!"

"Is the old west getting to you?"

"No, but there's always the possibility that things may heat up a bit and I just want to be ready."

The Chief picked up his duffle bag off the floor and placed it on the table. He pulled out the .45 and handed it to Jim and then threw a shoulder holster on the table.

"Do I have to wear that?"

"I recommend it. You'll find it more comfortable than jamming this thing in your belt."

"But I really don't like it...it seems so bulky."

"Susan, is he always like this?"

"Unfortunately yes. You should have seen him on the plane!"

"Okay, okay, I get the message. Chief, you can count on me in any situation that comes up!" Jim took off his blazer and put on the shoulder holster. "I like this, it feels pretty good. Okay Chief, what's next?"

Susan rolled her eyes.

"Let's have some lunch first. There's a little diner around the corner. It's hidden on this side of the rail yards, come on." The Chief then hollered over to his deputy, "Spencer, we're going for a bite to eat, you hold down the fort. Do you want anything?"

"No, no thanks Chief. I'm not hungry now, I'll go out later."

The trio walked down the street in the opposite direction from the Trade-Mart. Jim was patting the bulge under his left arm. With the Nikon on one shoulder and the .45 under the other, Jim felt a little uncomfortable.

"Susan, you can see it, huh…you can tell that I have a gun, can't you?"

"No silly, I can't tell!"

"Don't worry Jim, you'll get used to it. I've worn one for years."

Jim stared down at the bulge.

"Yeah, but doesn't it stick out?"

Again, Susan rolled her eyes.

After lunch, the Chief took Jim and Susan by car to Love Field.

"Why are we here Chief? Is this a hint…you want us gone?"

"Oh no Jim…" The Chief smiled. "We're here for sort of a dry run."

Susan chimed in from the back seat – "Allow me gentlemen…we're about to make a timed run from here to Dealey Plaza then to the Trade-Mart…all at let's say…fifteen to twenty miles per hour…and if it were…Chief, how far are we from Dealey?"

"Ten miles."

"Okay then, you two are college boys…remember your physics class…time equals distance divided by rate or speed."

Jim and the Chief looked at each other with blank expressions. They were both absent from school that day.

"And simple math tells us that…if we travel at a constant twenty miles per hour for ten miles, the trip will take thirty minutes and at fifteen miles per hour...approximately forty minutes. Of course those figures do not take into account that stops will be made, traffic,etc....none of which can be figured into this equation because the President will be traveling non-stop. Very simple. Well guys?"

"Sounds a little complicated to me Miss McNeil. Here Jim, take this and keep time. Do you know how to work one of these?" The Chief handed Jim a stopwatch.

"Yeah, I know how to use this...are you ready Chief?"

"Yup!"

"GO!"

They left the lot at Love Field and began the ten mile trip.

"We'll do it at twenty miles per hour. Every time we stop I'll yell STOP and when I get back to speed I'll yell GO. Alright Jim?"

"Right Chief!"

Susan chuckled in the back seat watching the two men going through their laborious ordeal, after she had done all the figuring for them.

Following what seemed like an eternity of stop and go yelling, they reached the top of Dealey Plaza.

"Okay, what do you have?"

"Well Chief, are you ready?"

"Yeah, give it to me!" The Chief was on the edge of his seat.

"Twenty-nine minutes and fifty-six seconds."

Susan gloated, while Jim and the Chief let out very long sighs.

"Well boys?"

"Okay Susan, I owe you one......hey Jim, you too!"

"Me too what Chief?"

"Well you owe Susan too!"

"I'm sorry Chief, but this whole thing was your idea! Not mine."

"Yeah...." They all looked at each other and laughed. "I'll tell you what you two, dinner's on me...Chez Pierre...7:30!"

"That sounds pretty fancy to me...so in that case I may have to do just a little more shopping."

"Well, it's now 3:15 and I think I'll give you two the remainder of the afternoon off, I've got a few things to see to. Now let's make that run to the Trade-Mart for the final figure."

"Save yourself a trip Chief. How far is it?"

"About two miles."

"Just add about six minutes to my previous calculations."

The two men again had blank expressions.

"Well Jim, are you going to take me shopping?"

"What did I tell you…you owe her! Where shall I drop you two?"

"It's a beautiful day…let's walk Jim."

As Jim and Susan got out of the car the Chief leaned across the seat – "I'll see you at the hotel, 7:00pm." The Chief then drove off talking to himself. Let's see STOP and he clicked the timer…GO….until he got to the Trade-Mart...he couldn't believe his eyes…six minutes flat. He mumbled to himself – "How did she do that?

XXXII

Texas Governor John Connally joined the Presidential party for the luncheon at the Houston Hyatt. Colonel Prouty was there too. His small single engine charter all arranged beforehand by Hilsman.

Governor Connally and his wife were now a part of the Presidential entourage for the remainder of the trip. After the luncheon they continued their journey to Fort Worth. During the flight, the President and the Governor discussed Texas politics. They focused on the infighting between the Governor and Senator Yarborough. With the Vice-President also present and for other reasons, the President chose to keep the Governor in the dark concerning the conspiracy. He never for a moment suspected any involvement on the Governor's part, but he thought – "There's always the chance that he is."

It was 4:10pm CST when Air Force One arrived in Fort Worth, with Colonel Prouty's charter hot on their heels. The President's party was then driven to the Texas Hotel for the testimonial dinner in honor of a local representative.

As the party entered the Hotel, a crowd of well-wishers greeted them by the door. The President noticed a familiar face in the crowd. Cappetta nodded his head and the President returned the gesture. The Colonel was also there but the President did not see him.

"Good," the President thought, "Mr. Cappetta is here and he's probably got all the appropriate tables under surveillance." He admired Hilsman's efficiency.

The President and the First Lady were then led to the Presidential suite. The President's driver, Secret Service agent Greer took a turn at the watch outside the suite. Agent Kellerman would later relieve him.

"It was good to see a friendly face today, someone that I know for sure is on our side."

"Who are you speaking of dear?"

"Mr. Cappetta."

"The surveillance man, you saw him?"

"Yes, in the crowd by the door. He's here to get some tape at the dinner tonight…good backup for our case. I really have to say Jackie, that Roger Hilsman is one proficient man. He works diligently at leaving nothing to chance…and when I make a suggestion, he works it through, sort of cleaning up whatever rough edges I present, with the ultimate goal being perfection."

"You're a lucky man to have him."

"Yes I am. That's why I've chosen to promote him…he's earned it. By the way, what time are we expected for dinner?"

"I believe cocktails are at 7:00. Have you got your speech ready?"

"Tonight my dear I think I'll wing it…but right now I have a call to make…Hilsman…checking in you know."

"Well, you check in and I think I'll take a hot bath."

"A hot bath…huh? Maybe I'll join you…this shouldn't take long."

"I'll be waiting…Mr. President."

It was 1:55pm and Bannister slept through the day. His head felt like a bucket of cement. He had trouble lifting it.

"Must have been the booze," he thought, "I took that full bottle off the bar and drank all of it…and then it was empty." He then remembered smashing the bottle over a man's head, "he touched me between the legs…the faggot..he got what he deserved!"

He then looked around and didn't recognize anything. He got up from the couch and slowly walked through a hallway, finding a bedroom with a man and a woman sleeping. "Hargis." He mumbled. "And her, now I remember, boy she was good!" He then found the kitchen and helped himself to a plate of leftover fried chicken.

As the big man stuffed himself, he thought about Jim and Susan. With all his failures and time getting short, the anxiety crept into his body. "Hargis…Hargis!" Spitting bits of chicken breast on the table as he yelled, "Get your ass up!"

Less than two minutes later, Hargis shuffled into the kitchen fully dressed in civilian clothes.

"What's all the noise…?"

"Eat something and get rid of the bimbo..we've got to find those two!"

"Bimbo huh?" Hargis smiled, raised his eyebrows and poured a glass of warm beer from a half filled bottle on the counter. "You had a pretty good time with her…you told her that you loved her!"

"Bullshit!"

"Whatever you say Mr. Bannister." Hargis knew where to draw the line with the big man.

"Come on, eat something and let's go."

"Keep your shirt on, I'm thinking about where to start. Ya know that chicken's been around for about a week!"

"I don't care, it's good. Maybe we should get a few of your men to help?"

"I don't think that'll be necessary. Look, I got a report that some unidentified characters have been milling around

Dealey…and now I'm thinkin' that they just might be government people…ya know investigating the information that the couple found out at your shop." Hargis threw a cold hard look at Bannister. "I dunno, it's not so farfetched. I think the damage has already been done by those two. Killing them at this point will only draw more attention, and for you…it's to satisfy your revenge." Hargis wanted to say – "Your stupidity!" – but he thought better of it. "So the way I see it is killing them won't help the overall plan…let's face it, they've already spilled the beans and Washington is putting their own counterplans in motion."

"You might be right Sergeant…there is evidence that Kennedy knows what were up to."

"Yeah, how's that?"

"Remember I told you I chased those two through New Orleans?"

"Yeah, so?"

"At their hotel, I found two phone numbers they left behind…and no one knows this…but both of them were Washington numbers…I called both and one was…."

"Was what?"

"The Oval Office."

"Shit! My whole theory was just a guess…but it's…"

"Good guess Sergeant. I'd still like to get those two...they've been pissing me off…" Bannister continued gorging himself on the week old chicken.

"I've got an idea."

"Yeah?"

"We'll take my car, no police cruiser today…and we'll check out all of our positions…rain or shine…the three at Dealey and the Trade-Mart. We'll snoop around and maybe get lucky…and we'll pull them in on some trumped up bullshit charge and…tomorrow we drop the charges and release them after the fireworks in Dealey. Come on, we'll be fucking heroes and if your lucky, you'll be back in the good graces of Mr. Marcello."

"Not bad Sergeant, I like the way you think. But what about

the guy and the girl?"

"Will you FORGET THEM! We'll deal with those two when the time is right…this is more important."

"Yeah okay, we'll do it your way." Bannister had no such intention.

"Thank you Mr. Bannister. Now let's get cleaned up and then we'll hit the road!"

"I'm fine the way I am. Let's go!"

"Whatever you say Mr. Bannister."

Hargis shook his head as the two men headed for the car, leaving the 'bimbo' sound asleep in his bed.

"Wasn't it nice of Chief Malinsky to invite us to dinner?"

"It sure was Susan, the Chief is a great guy. We'll have to do something for him when this thing is over."

"Yeah we should, but right now let's walk over to that fancy little shop where we were this morning. I saw a short black dress that I know you, Mr. Flannery, are going to love."

"Yeah…." Jim was preoccupied with the sight of a red Plymouth Fury and it's occupants.

"Jim, what's the matter? Did you hear anything I said?"

"Oh…yes…I thought I saw…no it's nothing."

"Saw what Jim?"

"It was nothing Susan…come on, let's get that dress!"

Susan smiled while she held Jim's hand tightly, but in the red Plymouth Fury, Bannister was gritting his teeth.

"Let's not do anything crazy Mr. Bannister. We'll follow them to their hotel and leave it at that for now…and deal with them later…okay?"

"Yeah…right…later."

When they finished their shopping excursion, Susan was happy. She got her dress and black velvet heels to match. Jim, a new pair of loafers and a tie. It wasn't easy finding the loafers in a city that catered to the cowboy look.

"I think that about does it. Let's go to the hotel and relax a little before dinner, we haven't done much of that."

"You know Susan, I forgot to make that call to the Sunset Inn…our bags…your car!"

"We'll do that when we get back…come on, there's the hotel…I'll race you!"

"I can't race with this cannon under my arm…and this camera!"

Susan sped off alone while Jim walked the half block. He then noticed the red Plymouth Fury slowly pull up, stopping for a red light. There were two men in the front seat. His earlier suspicions were correct. He recognized the man riding shot-gun. He pretended not to see them.

Susan was standing in front of the hotel when Jim took her by the hand and led her past the hotel, down a sidestreet.

"Jim! What are you doing?"

"Just follow me…it's him!"

"Who?" She knew, but was afraid to say.

"Bannister! Come on, in here." They slid into an alley between two buildings and hid behind a row of trash cans. The red Fury slowly passed by. It continued up the street and disappeared from their sight.

"Good…they're gone, let's go."

Again Jim grabbed Susan's free hand pulling her back up the street to the side entrance of The Piedmont.

In the elevator Susan clutched Jim's arm.

"Don't worry sweetheart, we lost them."

"Don't worry Mr. Bannister, we found them."

"Yeah…The Piedmont."

The dual exhaust of the Fury rumbled down the street.

XXXIII

In the dining room of the Texas Hotel, all the dignitaries gathered to honor not only one of their own, but also the President of the United States. He was there to bring them together in the shared quest of unifying the democratic party of Texas.

In addition to the President and Vice-President, Governor Connally, the Mayor of Dallas Earl Cabell, and anyone else of importance in the state of Texas were all drinking, eating, and generally having a good time at this affair.

At one table, Mayor Cabell spoke with the Vice-President about securing funds for a major highway connecting Dallas with Houston. Cabell also recommended that the present federal courthouse be replaced with a modern version. The Mayor was turning the screw on Lyndon and the Vice-President knew it. Lyndon went along, he just wanted to be President. "Just make sure that all the loose ends are tied up…and the patsy takes the fall. You'll get everything you need Earl, and more. That's all I'm gonna say."

"Oh he'll be held accountable for the whole blasted thing…as a dead man. Ruby will see to that at the Texas Theater….and Chief Curry got Ruby to bring in this Cuban fella to silence Tippet. That's a real headache out of the way. Later, when things cool down a bit, we'll take care of the Cuban… and Ruby too." As he spoke, the Mayor puffed on a very fat, short and smelly cigar. The Vice-President couldn't stand the man and he wondered how he ever got elected.

"Well, it all sounds good Earl, but I should be returning to my…" Lyndon Johnson made a gesture in the direction of his table. He excused himself and quickly found his seat, two down from Jackie at the head table.

In his room, Cappetta watched the tape roll on all three tiny machines. He set a bug at the Mayor's table, and two at the head table: one under the Vice-President and the other under Governor Connally. The latter due to Hilman's recommendations, who was unsure about the Governor.

Cappetta didn't listen, it would be much too confusing to follow three conversations, he just watched, waiting to replace tapes when necessary.

With the Vice-President's wife Lady-Bird socializing with the locals, her seat was left vacant. The President quickly seized the opportunity. He sat in her seat and presented his latest plan to the Vice-President. It was the President's final test…he had to know for sure.

"You know Lyndon, I've got an idea about our ride through downtown Dallas tomorrow."

"Oh? Is that right Mr. President?" Lyndon's eyes lit up.

"I'm going to have Jackie ride in your car along with the uh…the Governor's wife."

"That's a terrific idea Mr. President, I'm glad you saw my point…you and the Governor should be the only ones in the lead car."

"Yes, I agree with you Lyndon, but with one exception."

"And what is that Mr. President?"

"You should join us."

"Me..."

"Yes, we'll change protocol I realize...however, having the nations top two leaders along with the Chief Executive of Texas in the lead car...well, it appeals to me. I like the idea, the three of us together. It's a display of party strength...after all, that IS what we're here for...isn't it?" The President smiled. He could hardly wait for Lyndon's response.

The Vice-President's jaw dropped as he searched for the right words, which never came. He could only produce a very lame response - "But Mr. President, I don't believe that what you're requesting is the proper way to handle this thing."

The President cut him off before he made a fool of himself: "Oh Lyndon, don't worry about a thing. Besides, this isn't a request, consider it an order." The President smiled again and patted Lyndon on his shoulder. The touch brought on an unexpected but recognizable feeling in the pit of the President's stomach – it sickened him.

"Yes...Mr. President...I see." Lyndon's voice dropped off. He had no idea how to change the Chief Executive's mind. The thoughts were swirling through the Vice-President's mind – "Those damned sharpshooters had better be just that...or else I'm..."

The President turned in his seat and addressed the First Lady: "Well, that's all set. Tomorrow, Lyndon and the Governor will be riding with me in the motorcade and you and uh...the Governor's wife will ride with Lady-Bird. It's uh...let me say...it's kind of a show of strength for the lead car. Don't you agree Jackie?"

"Oh yes, it's a marvelous idea. The people of Texas should see their successful home grown boy up front...don't you agree Lyndon......Lyndon?"

The Vice-President was deep in thought. He knew he was now deeply entrenched in the quagmire of his own evil doings, with no way out. After a long pause, he finally answered – "Yes

Jackie, it's uh…it's a fine idea."

The President determined that Lyndon Johnson failed the test miserably, so he got up from Lady-Bird's seat and returned to his own. As he sat, he reached out and took the First Lady's hand in his, then whispered in her ear – "Jackie, I love you."

She then turned, placed a finger on his lips and spoke softly – "I love you too dear…more than you'll ever know."

The President smiled, placed his napkin on his lap just as Lady-Bird returned to her seat, and he then announced – "Shall we eat?"

They all dug into the big Texas style offering of black angus steak with all the trimmings. Everyone that is, with the exception of the Vice-President. He lost his appetite.

XXXIV

"Dinner was wonderful…thank you Chief."

"You're very welcome Susan."

"Yes Chief, thank you, it was a pleasure!"

"You're welcome Jim, it was fun. Kind of got our minds off of things."

"And Chief?"

"Yes Jim?"

"When we get back to D.C., the next one will be our treat. You and your wife."

"That's very kind of you Jim…Susan…I'll put it at the top of my calender. Now you two get some rest…there'll be a guard at the door to my suite…so rest easy and I'll be back shortly. I've got to see to a few last minute details."

Jim and Susan got out of the Chief's car at the side entrance to The Piedmont. They were taking every precaution.

It was a little after 10:00pm when Jim and Susan passed Deputy Thompson at the door and entered the suite.

"Jim, the Chief is always seeing to some sort of detail…does he ever rest?"

"That's why he was chosen for this job. From the look of his plans, I'd say he's probably the best."

"And Mr. Flannery, what was that remark about US taking him to dinner in WASHINGTON, D.C.? Was that an indirect invitation for me to…?"

"Well Susan, I thought that you might…uh…"

"Might what, Mr. Flannery?"

"That uh…you would…"

"That I would accompany you to D.C. when this thing is over?"

"Yeah…something like that."

"With the intention of what my dear?"

"Well maybe we could try out…you know…an engagement or something?"

"Is that a proposal Mr. Flannery?"

"Well, yeah. I guess."

"You guess! Boy, I never thought that when it finally happened to me…that it would present itself in this manner."

"Well, what do you think?"

"About what Mr. Flannery?" Susan was now playing his game.

"You know…about us…what's your answer?"

"Do you want it now, or shall we toss this hot potato around for a while longer?"

"Come on Susan…will you…"

"Of course silly, what did you think?'

"Well, I didn't know what you'd say!"

The game was over when Susan seductively whispered in his ear – "Yes Mr. Flannery, I'd love to be your wife."

"But Susan! We'll uh…start with an engagement…sort of a trial run. Like the one this afternoon from Love to Dealey!"

"Yeah silly, I like that…Love to the big Deal." She placed her arms around his shoulders as he slid his hands along her delicate waist.

"Did I tell you how wonderful you look in that dress, my love?"

"Yes you did, about a thousand times."

"You must be getting tired of hearing it?"

"A woman never tires of compliments...you can tell me again."

"I'd rather show you." He then lovingly pulled her to him and kissed her deeply. They were locked in an embrace when the phone rang.

"I'd better get it...it seems every phone call these days is important."

"While you're doing that," Susan pointed to the ringing phone, "I'll be waiting in the bedroom and I'll slip out of this."

"Why don't you just go into the bedroom...I like you in that outfit...I'd like to..."

"To what silly?" Susan's seductiveness had Jim panting with desire as the phone continued ringing in the background.

"You'll see."

As Susan drifted into the bedroom, Jim answered the phone.

"Yes?"

"Hello, I'm looking for a Mr. Flannery. Might that be you sir?"

"Yes, I'm Jim Flannery. Who's calling?"

"This is Detective LaFleur of the Lake Charles Police Department."

Jim immediately thought that something happened to Susan's car. "Yes detective, how can I help you?"

"Does the Sunset Inn ring a bell sir?"

"Yes of course, we stayed there. I was going to call the Inn about our things, but it slipped my mind!"

"Slipped your mind sir?"

"Yes and our car is there too...I was going to..."

"To what Mr. Flannery? Let me get right to the point. Your bags were found in room nine along with the dead body of an unidentified man. Also, let'see...a 1962 dark blue Chevrolet Impala, parked in the front of your room, registered to a Susan McNeil of New Orleans...and the dead bodies of the motel owner and his wife."

"What?"

"We tracked you to Dallas through the roster sheet at the Charles Airport...and after a number of calls to various hotels, the desk clerk there at The Piedmont tells me that you and a lady...I gather that's Miss McNeil...are staying with a United States Deputy Sheriff. What's this all about Mr. Flannery?"

"Well, I...I was...dead bodies?" Just then Chief Malinsky entered the suite.

"Uh...detective...please hold for a moment."

Jim placed the phone on his shoulder and told the Chief about the events in Lake Charles.

"I'll take it Jim. Yes, this is Chief Deputy Malinsky, can I be of assistance?"

The Chief spent the next several minutes talking with Detective LaFleur while Jim sat staring in disbelief. "Had to be Bannister," he thought.

"Okay, thank you Detective, I'll be in touch." As he hung up the phone, he stared at Jim.

"You don't think that we had anything to do this?"

"Of course not Jim, this Bannister character is brutal. I'll be happy when we slap the cuffs on him."

"You better make sure they're big...the cuffs...he's got arms like tree stumps!"

"Yeah, the sad thing here is those unfortunate people in Lake Charles and their families...but we can't concentrate on that, now. We've got to stay focused on our plans here. Okay?...Jim?"

"Uh..yes, of course. I think I'll get some rest." Jim thought about the friendly face of the desk clerk and his wife, it seemed like eons ago. But the dead man in room nine, he had no idea.

On his way to the bedroom, he decided to tell Susan about Lake Charles in the morning. There was no reason to alarm her with it now, after all, the Chief had it all under control.

When he entered, he found the room dimly lit by the light on the night-table. Susan was lying across the bed, her dress pulled up to her thighs, revealing the tops of her nylons and the clasp of her garter belt. Jim looked over her shapely legs and the sensual curves created by her position on the bed. He thought – "Yeah, I'll tell her in the morning," as he pulled off his shirt and took her in his arms.

He marked each tape and then placed all six in a small container. He then placed the container, along with the tape machines in a briefcase. When he finished there was a knock at the door.

Cappetta opened it to find a man dressed in a cowboy shirt, string tie, tight jeans, and a cowboy hat and boots. The man smiled through a bushy goatee.

"Yes, can I help you?"

"Well, I'm a lookin' for a Mr. Cappetta?"

Cappetta thought the man spoke with a forced Texan accent. He also thought – "No one but the President and Hilsman know I'm here…who is this guy?"

"Yes, I'm Cappetta and who are you?"

The man removed his hat and pulled off the goatee.

"Colonel! Colonel Prouty! Please come in." Cappetta threw out his hand, grabbing the Colonel's and pulling him into the room. He continued shaking his hand while the Colonel cringed in pain from the vise. Cappetta knew nothing of his own strength.

"Mr. Cappetta! My hand!"

"OH!…I'm sorry Colonel." Cappetta closed the door and led the Colonel to a pair of seats by the window. As the two men sat, the Colonel continued shaking out his hand.

"You have some grip there my friend!"

"Please forgive me Colonel, sometimes I don't realize my own strength…Mr. Hilsman never told me to expect a visit…your disguise…I would have never guessed!"

"Yeah, it is a good one…remember, I'm supposed to be dead. I'm here watching everyone and everything that gets close to the President. So far no problems. Hilsman told me about your assignment, how did you make out?"

"I've got some very good tape on the Vice-President and Mayor

Cabell. From the sound of it, it seems as if the Mayor is the number one man in Dallas, with Chief Curry of the Dallas police a close second."

"Do the conversations implicate the Vice-President?"

"Like you wouldn't believe. I would have to say that he's dead and buried. Do you want to hear them?"

"There'll be plenty of time for that later. You know it's too bad...who would have thought that Johnson...well, good work...those tapes will be useful. Oh, by the way, you'll be joining me on my charter to Dallas in the morning."

"Oh?"

"Yes, we need all the hands we can get. We'll be leaving at 9:30am, about two hours before Air Force One and uh...do you mind if I take these two chairs for a little sleep?"

"No of course not...and take this." Cappetta pulled the blanket from the bed and gave it to the Colonel. "You'll need it...I've got to keep those two windows wide open, otherwise I can't sleep."

"Thanks." The Colonel put his feet up on the second chair and pulled the blanket over his body. "Geez!" he thought, "it's gotta be forty degrees in here!" Under the blanket he stretched out his hand trying to bring back the circulation, while on the bed, Cappetta was sound asleep the moment his head hit the pillow.

While Cappetta snored through the night, from his make-shift bed, the Colonel stared out the window and thought about the courage displayed by the President. "Courage," he thought, "the man operates at an extraordinary level...we can't let him down." The Colonel then slowly drifted off as the crisp November air filled the room.

XXXV

At 7:25am, Chief Malinsky, Jim and Susan finished their room service breakfast and went over last minute details. The Chief loved details.

"If you stick with a well thought out plan and work out every detail…your chances for success are increased. Now, from your perspective, can either of you think of anything that I may have overlooked?"

"Yes Chief, there's still the question of Bannister. Do you have something arranged for him?"

"Well Jim, when we pick up Chief Curry and the cop…Hargis, hopefully we'll get Bannister too."

"Yeah, hopefully!"

"Don't worry, even if we don't get him today, everyone else will be in our custody and he'll be without any support…we'll find him." Chief Malinsky turned on the television "Let's get the weather forecast."

When the local news wrapped up, the weatherman gave his

report –"Showers and some heavy downpours today for the Dallas-Fort Worth area." The Chief turned it off and slowly walked to the window. "Cloudy…maybe it'll hold off until later this afternoon...and maybe it won't. We'll just have to trust our plans either way."

The Chief then made a couple of final calls while Jim got into his shoulder holster. He put on his blazer and threw the motorized Nikon over his other shoulder.

"Well Susan, do I look like a tourist?"

"Yes Jim…Jim, I'm a little…"

"I know Susan, please stay by my side…we'll be okay." He had no idea if they'd be okay, he only knew what the Chief told them. "We'll just stick with the Chief and we'll be okay!"

The Chief finished his calls – "Don't leave anything of importance in the room…we won't be back."

Jim and Susan looked around, "Got everything."

"Okay you two…let's get this show on the road!"

Sergeant Hargis entered police headquarters at 7:45am, with his new sidekick Guy Bannister, bringing up the rear.

"Simmons, where's the roster sheet?"

"Yes sir, here it is Sergeant." Simmons was a small man, a six year veteran who always said yes, no matter what was asked of him. He figured it would help him move up in the department, little did he know that Hargis and his buddies liked having Simmons do their bidding. He was moving nowhere. Hargis never acknowledged the man as he and Bannister walked to Chief Curry's office reading the roster.

"Morning Chief."

"Sergeant, I'm glad you're here, there's something…." As he was about to finish, Bannister walked in. "Well Guy Bannister! I never expected to see you here on D-Day!"

Bannister extended his hand, "Extenuating circumstances, nothing serious. Besides, I thought I'd take in the noon time fireworks show while I'm in town."

Before Chief Curry could respond, Hargis cut in – "I see our boy Tippet is double shifted today…on patrol. I knew about his noon tour, but did you add the 4:00am shift?"

"Yup. Got'm walkin' the downtown beat from 4:00am to noon, then he takes the cruiser for the noon shift. By that time he'll be draggin' his ass. When Kennedy flies into the viper's nest, Tippet will be in Oak Cliff all by his lonesome. The Cuban will take care of him at the corner of E.10th. and Patton…oh I'll say 'bout forty-five minutes after Kennedy sucks his last breath."

"What about Oswald?"

"Ole Lee Harvey has been told to leave the Depository or Trade-Mart after and go directly to the safety of his rooming house in Oak Cliff an' wait for a signal to leave. He thinks we're clearing the way for his escape…but little does he know. Shall I continue boys?"

"You got the stage Chief!" Bannister replied, even though he heard Chief Curry go over this very plan at least ten times. Both he and the Sergeant knew that Curry loved to hear himself talk.

"Like I was sayin' boys, when Oswald leaves his rooming house, Tippet gets it from the Cuban. We got three witnesses lined up to swear to the fact that Ole Lee Harvey gunned down the cop. But I am getting a little ahead myself, ain't I now?" Bannister and Hargis said nothing.

"Well…let's see…where was I……oh yeah, while Tippet is lying in a pool a blood, Ole Lee Harvey heads to the Texas Theater thinkin' that his ticket outta Dallas awaits him there…ya know…to Cuba or some shit. He'll get a real fuckin' surprise when our boy Ruby blows his brains all over the screen…kinda spoilin' the matinee for the good payin' customers." Curry chuckled. He really did like the sound of his own monologue. "An' to wrap up my little tale, the dead Mr. Lee Harvey takes the rap for both the Kennedy an' Tippet murders, an' we close the fuckin' book."

"I have one question Dick Tracy?"

"Yes Mr. Bannister, shoot." Chief Curry loved when Bannister referred to him as the great comic strip character.

"What about Ruby and the Cuban?"

"I got a couple of outside boys to handle that…they're dead meat."

"Sounds good to me but we do have a small problem to see to."

"And what might that be Mr. Bannister?"

Bannister then told him about Jim and Susan.

"Holy shit!"

"That's what I said when he told me Chief!"

"Look, if they told those fuckers up in D.C. I'm sure they'd have done somethin' by now. Everythins' been real quiet…except for a few transients over in Dealey…Shit, I ain't worried." Chief Curry was now tapping his fingers on his desk and then running his fingers through what little hair he had. "Naw, I ain't worried…shit."

"Just for safety's sake Chief, let's you, me and Mr. Bannister go down to the Trade-Mart and have a look around. We'll stop along the way in Dealey, although it doesn't look like Dealeys an option with the forecast calling for rain."

"Yeah, that might be a good idea Sergeant…let's get down there. We can't have anything go wrong…Earl an' Lyndon will have my balls…and yours." He pointed toward Hargis. "What do ya say we have a little breakfast at the diner across the street an' then run right over there? Are you with us Mr. Bannister?"

"I wouldn't miss it for the world."

At 8:15am, a small twin engine aircraft landed at Love Field and parked in a deserted hangar at the south end of the airport.

A man of medium height and slight build stepped down. He wore dark glasses, a full beard that appeared to be manicured daily, a black Stetson, black suit with all the embroidered gold swirls on the front and shoulders, white satin shirt with long pointed collar, bolo tie with the head of a diamondback rattler drawing the strings to his neck and black cowboy boots made of the finest alligator skin.

He quickly got into the waiting black Chrysler Imperial and spoke – "Driver, to the airport entrance and park."

The driver did as he was told. When they arrived at a parking space near the entrance, raindrops hit the windshield. The man in the backseat took notice.

"Rain." He thought. "Driver, pay attention to what I'm about to say. When I say the word 'now' go directly to the Trade-Mart and pull around back. Let me out at the door marked deliveries and leave. Do you understand?"

"Yes sir." Once again the driver obeyed without question.

The man in the backseat did not speak again. He sat in silence, waiting.

XXXVI

Agent Greer knocked, then let himself in.

"Mr. President, it's 8:30 sir, your breakfast is here!"

The President appeared from the bedroom of his suite at the Texas Hotel, adjusting his tie.

"Thank you Mr. Greer, I'll take it from here." The President pushed the small cart over to the window and pulled up two chairs. Greer returned to his post by the door.

On the cart was a copy of *The Dallas Morning News*. The headline read – **JFK HERE TO UNITE PARTY**. The President sat, unfolded the paper and poured a cup of coffee.

The First Lady emerged from the bedroom dressed in a pink suit.

"Good morning dear."

"Good morning Jackie." The President rose to his feet and kissed his wife.

She sat, poured her coffee and then her juice. "Would you like some juice dear?"

"Uh..." The President was engrossed in the paper, "yes Jackie...uh...listen to this. There's a full page ad here taken out by H.L.Hunt and his right wing group. The ad is directed at me!"

"Well Jack, what does it say?"

"It says...**WHY DID YOU HOST, SALUTE AND ENTERTAIN TITO – MOSCOW'S TROJAN HORSE?** They just don't get it! That visit by Tito was an important link in our efforts with the Soviets. What do these men want – to annihilate the Soviet Union? Sometimes I just don't get it......we're really heading into nut country today."

"Oh Jack, please don't let it bother you. Mr. Hunt is a very frustrated man who despises anything un-American. He has no idea how to spend his fortune so he uses the press to unleash those frustrations. I wouldn't give it a second thought."

"Yeah, I suppose you're right dear, but..."

"No buts Mr. President. You've been in such great spirits...please don't let this get to you."

"Yes Jackie, you're right. You know it's nice having a quiet meal here with my wife...with no one else around. I don't think I could have made it through another meal with Lyndon!...Let's see, we had the luncheon at the Aerospace Medical Center in San Antonio, the testimonial dinner that evening, then the breakfast, then uh...the luncheon in Houston and last night's testimonial here. We've had a very busy schedule and now we're finally eating alone...like most Americans do."

"Yes my dear, so let's enjoy it."

The President reached across the table and held the First Lady's hand.

"You know Jackie, you've been a pillar of strength for me these last couple of days...thank you dear." The President pulled her hand to his lips and warmly kissed it.

"You're welcome dear, but there is reason for my motivation."

"Yes...and what could that be?"

"That I love you."

"I know dear...and you have all my love...all of it." They both smiled.

The President then sat back in his chair and again opened the paper. He looked out the window and back to the paper.

"Have you noticed something Jackie?"

"What dear?"

"It's very cloudy out there." The President motioned to the window. "And the forecast for Dallas is…showers and occasional downpours."

"Thank God!!"

"Yeah, I have mixed feelings about that."

"But Jack, the hardtops are much safer!"

"I know Jackie…I know."

No matter how hard he tried to block it out, the President quickly became immersed in his own thoughts – "If it does rain, where will they make their attempt?…the Trade-Mart…but how…when I exit the car?…When I'm speaking at the luncheon?…Or if the rain holds off and we're in the open top car…will they change or add positions?…Set up more sniper's nests that we're unaware of?…And if it does rain, will Chief Malinsky be able to secure the Trade-Mart area?…It's a lot to ask with the problems he faces with manpower……and Hunt…could he and his right wing group of millionaires be a part of this?…they certainly have the capital to arrange just about anything…What motivates men like this?…Greed…greed at the expense of the American people and for that matter, the people of the world…their actions affect everyone. These men want war!…And peace…peace is the answer…I have to survive to do my part to help bring about that peace. God be with us…be with all of us…be with those who have taken up this sordid affair...help them to see their mistakes…."

"Jack! JACK!"

"Oh……yes Jackie?"

"You were so far away."

"I was just thinking. You know, everything is going to be fine…I just know it dear."

Jackie smiled. She knew he was searching for the strength and she also knew that he'd find it.

When the President and the First Lady finished their breakfast, they had a little time to spare before preparing for their departure. The First Lady decided to occupy her mind with the crossword puzzle while the President made a call to the Oval Office.

Meanwhile in Dallas, a private plane flew over the motorcade route at a very low altitude and dropped thousands of handbills, littering the streets. On the handbill were two photographs, one full face and one profile. They were photos of the President of the United States of America. In bold letters, the text below the photos read:

WANTED FOR TREASON

"This man is wanted for treasonous activities against the United States"

The President was right, they were flying into nut country.

XXXVII

"Well Chief, at this point it doesn't look like it's going to let up."

"Yeah , if it keeps up we'll have no reason to cover Dealey."

The light intermittent showers had now developed into a steady rain. No downpours, just steady.

It was 9:45am and the trio of Jim, Susan and the Chief were joined by Deputy Powers in the Chief's car. They had a good view of the Trade-Mart from where they were parked.

Deputy Powers was running a team of men in the area and had received his final instructions from the Chief. He was about to exit the car when the Chief noticed a red car pass by.

"Wait Powers!...Close the door."

Powers pulled the door shut. "What's up Chief?"

"Jim, didn't you say something about a red Plymouth Fury?"

"Yes I did...Why?...Where?"

"It just passed. Heading in the direction of...they're parking."

"Oh God Jim, is he talking about Bannister?"

"The one and only Susan…Chief, how many were in the car?"

"I saw three heads and they've just pulled into a sidestreet and parked alongside the Trade-Mart…let's get a closer look."

Deputy Powers felt for his gun. Jim did the same.

As they slowly approached the Trade-Mart, Chief Malinsky pulled over and parked.

"They're getting out of the car…the one in the blue jacket with the umbrella is Chief Curry…I know him from our pictures. Jim, Susan, which one is Bannister?"

"He's the big guy with the rumpled up pants." Jim answered.

"So I take it that the other one is the Sergeant…Hargis?"

Jim answered again, "Yeah that's him."

"Shall we take them now Chief and get them out of the way?" Powers was anxious to get things underway.

"Powers, let's see what they're up to and then…" Chief Malinsky stopped just as Hargis and Bannister got back in the car and Curry entered the front door of the Trade-Mart.

"Powers, you stay here and keep an eye out for Curry. We'll follow the Fury."

"Right Chief." Powers quickly got out and took up watch from a doorway that offered shelter from the rain.

"We'll just see where these two are headed."

Staying two cars back they had a good view of the red Fury. They were heading in the direction of the airport.

"I wonder where they're going Chief…maybe police headquarters?"

"I don't think so Jim, my guess is Love Field."

"Love Field! That's over a half hour from here and…that'll be an hour round trip! Do we have that kind of time?"

"Boys, do I have to do the math again?" Susan cut in from the backseat and the boys didn't answer. "Yes, about thirty-five minutes if we're traveling at twenty miles per hour, but as I can see from the speedometer, we haven't been below forty miles per hour…which if my figures are correct…this trip to Love Field should take approximately…fifteen minutes."

The Chief turned and looked at Jim. They both had déjà vu, all over again.

"So guys, we're talking thirty minutes round trip."

Shortly after Susan finished her latest lesson, the red Fury turned into the main entrance of Love Field. The Chief pulled up and parked across the road. The rain was coming down harder now.

"They're parking…what are they doing?"

"I don't know Jim, but the car they parked next to…the black Chrysler Imperial…the rear window just came down."

Within moments the window went back up and the red Fury exited the lot.

The Chief picked up his radio from the seat. "Thompson, do you read? Over."

"Yes Chief, I'm in hangar three. Over."

"Thompson, there's a black Chrysler Imperial in the lot by the main entrance to the airport. Take the car and follow them wherever they go and let me know. Over."

"Right Chief, I'm on it. Over."

The Chief took up his place behind the red Fury, two cars back.

"Must have been important for them to make the trip all the way up here…whoever it is in that Chrysler…they're a part of this."

"We'll find out soon enough Jim. Thompson will keep a close eye on them."

The Fury continued along the return trip through Dealey to the Trade-Mart, with it's pursuers two cars back.

The Chief picked up the radio. "Powers, anything on Curry? Over."

"Yeah Chief, he left the Trade-Mart about five minutes ago, walked about a half block south toward me and he's been standing there under an umbrella. Over."

"Okay Powers, the Fury should pull up in about…Susan, how long?"

"Just about three minutes."

"Powers, you have three minutes until the Fury shows. Take

out Curry…cuff him. You have the warrants. Over."

"He's all mine Chief. Over." Deputy Powers put the radio in his pocket and pulled out his .38 special, then kept it concealed in the pocket of his raincoat. He crossed the street and walked toward Chief Curry. He pulled his gun and from his hip pointed directly at the stunned cop. The rain was falling harder now.

"Chief Curry, United States Deputy Sheriff Powers. I have a warrant for your arrest!"

"What? What the fuck kinda joke are ya pullin' buddy?"

"I'm not your buddy and this is no joke. You're charged with conspiracy against the Government of the United States of America. To be more specific sir, you are charged with conspiracy to murder the President of the United States!"

"Goddam, you must be crazy boy! Hey!…What are ya doin'?" Powers slapped one cuff on Curry's right wrist while attaching the other to his own left wrist. He held the .38 in his right hand while Curry continued to hold the umbrella in his left.

"Now we'll just wait for your buddies, nice and cozy under your umbrella."

"You'll never make it boy!"

"We'll see."

The red Fury pulled up and parked.

"Tell them to get out of the car. Make up something about going back inside the Trade-Mart." Powers whispered to Curry and motioned back toward the Trade-Mart.

The window came down on the passenger side. Bannister yelled out to Curry – "Come on, get in!"

Again Powers whispered to Curry, "Go on, get them out of the car or I'll blow your brains out right here."

"Uh guys, we got a little problem inside and I need your help." Curry gestured toward the Trade-Mart.

The window went up in the Fury. Both doors opened as Bannister and Hargis stepped out. When they closed the doors, they were immediately set upon by Chief Malinsky who had waited for the opportune moment. With gun drawn, the Chief grabbed Hargis and cuffed him, while Jim fired away with the Nikon through the pouring rain.

"Sergeant Hargis, you're charged with conspiracy to murder the President of the United States." The Chief took his gun and shoved him into the backseat of the Fury. He then instucted Powers to do the same with Curry.

During the twenty seconds it took to deal with Hargis, Bannister made off on foot and disappeared in an alley with Jim Flannery in pursuit.

Susan was now in the middle of the street yelling - "Jim…come back…let him go!" Jim had also disappeared in the alley.

"Powers, get Spencer over here from home base and you guys take these two to the airport…and get back here as soon as possible."

"Right Chief."

"And Powers?"

"Yeah?"

"When you get to the airport, use the side entrance. Stay away from the main entrance! Got it?"

"Right Chief."

Powers made the call and within two minutes Spencer arrived and rode shotgun while Powers drove.

"Now where the hell are Jim and Bannister?"

"They went through that alley Chief!" Susan pointed across the street.

Remarkably, not one spectator was drawn to the area, due to the quick work of the Chief and Deputy Powers.

As Chief Malinsky crossed the street, Jim emerged from the alley with the .45 in his right hand.

"I lost him…I just lost him…the big lug got away!"

"The tables have turned Jim, now he's running from you. Don't worry, we'll track him down."

They walked to the car and the Chief grabbed his radio from the seat.

"Hardman, do you read? Over."

"Yes Chief. Over."

"Take Rothman and Martino and comb the area on the south side and behind the Trade-Mart for a man on foot" He then described Bannister. "Find him and don't let him get away. Over."

"Right away Chief. Over."

"I don't see much hope in that, but it's worth a shot."

"Well Chief, if he gets away there's always the possibility that he'll alert the others and then we've really got a problem."

"That's what I'm afraid of Jim. Maybe Hardman and the guys will come up with something and we'll get lucky." No sooner had the Chief spoke, when Hardman cut in.

"Chief, Hardman here. Over."

"Yes Hardman, what do you have? Over."

"We spotted our boy Chief, he doubled back to the rear of the Trade-Mart. Right now he's hiding behind a delivery truck. He's going nowhere sir, we've got him surrounded. Over"

"Excellent work Hardman! Maintain your positions and I'll get back to you. Over."

"Right Chief. Over."

The Chief then noticed a black Ford sedan park in front of the abandoned garage. He turned the car around and approached the Ford to get a better look at its occupants.

"I don't recognize those two. Do you Jim, Susan?" They both answered in the negative.

The Chief then parked, checked his watch, 10:30am and got out of the car. As he did, the driver of the Ford also stepped out. The rain let up as they drew nearer.

The man wore a cowboy hat, jeans and cowboy boots.

"Chief Malinsky, how do you sir?" Came a voice through a bushy goatee. The man then removed his hat.

"I don't believe we've…Colonel Prouty!" The men shook hands and the Chief motioned for all toward the garage. The Colonel gestured to his passenger to follow.

Inside the garage, all introductions were made.

"I've heard a lot about you Cappetta, your surveillance work is first class. The President is very pleased."

"Thank you Chief Malinsky."

"Please, call me Chief…excuse me for one moment." The Chief pulled out his radio, "Hardman, do you read? Over."

"Yes Chief. Over."

"What's going on with Bannister? Over"

"No movement Chief, should we take him? Over."

"Not now, he's armed and very dangerous. Just keep an eye on him. I need Martino and Rothman at their posts, so send them and you hang onto Bannister. Any problems, use your radio. Over"

"Right. Over."

"Excuse me Chief, but did you say Bannister…the guy from New Orleans that gave these two such a hard time?" Cappetta gestured toward Jim and Susan.

"Yes, that's right. Why?"

"Well Chief, this guy is one tough cookie and I'd like to help your Deputy if I can?"

"Are you armed Mr. Cappetta?"

"No Chief, never touch the stuff." With his muscular arms by his side, Cappetta made two fists. The Chief and everyone else took notice.

"Take the alley on the south side of the Trade-Mart. That'll take you to the parking lot in the rear. When you and Hardman take him, have Hardman radio me and I'll send a car around to pick him up…don't bring him out into the street, we don't want anyone watching our movements. Okay?"

"I'm with you Chief. Now show me on this map just where we are in relation to the Trade-Mart?"

Cappetta watched as the Chief pointed out the best route to take. "When you leave, I'll alert Hardman that your coming and to meet you at the end of the alley."

"Wish me luck everyone…and keep an eye on this!" Cappetta left his briefcase on the table, then exited the garage.

The rain picked up again, "Damn!" Cappetta thought, "and no umbrella!"

He found his way to the alley on the south side of the Trade-Mart. It was roughly thirty yards to the end. As he approached the end, there was no sign of Hardman. Cappetta looked around the lot and saw only one delivery truck, "That's got to be where he's hiding," he mumbled to himself. There were at least a dozen cars parked in this area along with a row of brand new trash cans.

Stealthfully, Cappetta zig-zagged around the parked cars until he drew to within a car length of the delivery truck. As he prepared his next move, he felt a heavy blow delivered to his left shoulder, sending him to the ground. The pain was intense, but he still retained his state of mind and quickly rolled on his back, so as to get a better look at his attacker.

"Well well, you must be the infamous Guy Bannister?"

"I don't believe we've met." Bannister stood over Cappetta with a two foot section of lead pipe in his right hand.

"Where's Deputy Hardman?"

"Is that what he was...a deputy? He had another appointment...his last."

From his low vantage point, Cappetta scanned the lot, focusing on a body lying next to a drab colored station wagon. It was Hardman.

With his eyes on Hardman's body, Cappetta threw his legs in a scissors action around Bannister's lower legs and twisted until the burley man fell backwards to the ground. Cappetta climbed to his feet and leapt at the fallen Bannister, who had dropped the lead pipe when he hit the ground. The two men wrestled and struggled against each other's heft and strength. Bannister reached for his dagger. Cappetta sensed that he was groping for a gun strapped to his ankle, so he grabbed for Bannister's hand getting only his thumb. The vise twisted and pulled with his last ounce of strength until there was the sound of a ripping pop. Bannister let out a roar similar to that of a large wild mammal in pain. With Cappetta severely handicapped from the blow to his shoulder, he did all he could to hold the big Bannister to the ground.

The struggle between the two powerful men continued until a

hand found the lead pipe, lifting and swinging it violently.

The rain pelted down on the stuggling duo when the pipe struck Cappetta on the side of his neck, just above the shoulder. His body went limp. With his right hand, Bannister pushed Cappetta's body off and let out a long grunt. As the adrenaline found its way back to a normal level, the pain in his left hand increased. He got to his feet and looked down on his injured hand. His thumb was missing. He began shaking violently as blood gushed from the hole that once housed his left thumb. He mumbled, grumbled and swore incessantly. Shock and panic had set in as he began running around the lot in circles as if to make it reappear through some kind of raindance. He then stopped, looked at his thumbless left hand and lost his breath. He began breathing harder and harder and then fell to his knees. It was then that he refocused on Cappetta's prone body.

Again, he got to his feet holding his left hand tightly to his chest. He stared down at Cappetta and thought "Another time." Turning and running to the far end of the lot, the big man disappeared in the driving rain.

The rain continued to pour down on Cappetta's motionless body. With his head in a pool of water, he opened his eyes and tried to focus on the tire of a parked car. What he saw was a kaleidoscope of circles. He closed and opened his eyes over and over until the tire came into focus. He then felt a weight on his left shoulder. It was only a hand.

"Mr. Cappetta! Mr. Cappetta...are you okay?" Chief Malinsky noticed no blood or wounds as he turned Cappetta over on his back.

The rain poured down on Cappetta's face, aiding in his return to consciousness.

"Yeah...I'm okay." He got up with the Chiefs help. He wobbled on his feet.

"Are you sure?"

"Yeah, I'll be fine. A little sore." Cappetta felt his neck and shoulder with his left hand.

"We've got Hardman, he has a pulse. The boys took him. I think he's going to be okay."

"Good. He's alive…I thought he was dead."

"Where's Bannister? What happened back here?"

"Well Chief, all I remember is struggling with the big grizzly. He's a very strong man!"

"Well, there's nothing we can do about him now…wherever he went."

"Yeah, right. But he forgot something."

"What's that?"

Cappetta opened his hand revealing a souvenir of the battle. It was Bannister's left thumb. "He forgot this." Cappetta smiled.

Chief Malinsky squinted through the pouring rain at the sight in Cappetta's right hand. He appeared to be on the verge of letting go of what was left of his breakfast.

"What's the matter Chief, a little squeamish?" As Cappetta spoke, he favored his neck and left shoulder.

"A little I suppose…I've never seen anything quite like it." The Chief looked at his watch, 11:15am. "We're not doing too good on time but we could still get back on schedule. Let's get to home base."

"What's home base?"

"The garage."

"Oh."

As the two men walked in the rain, Cappetta lifted the lid of a trash can and deposited his souvenir of the battle with the big man. "I guess we won't be needing that!"

"No. I want what it was once attached to."

"Me too Chief. If it's the last thing I do, believe me, I'll find him."

With the rain pouring down, Cappetta placed the lid back on the can and looked at the Chief.

"Trust me, I'll find him."

XXXVIII

The man looked at his watch.

"Now."

The black Chrysler Imperial left the main lot at Love Field followed by Deputy Thompson.

When the Chrysler passed through Dealey Plaza, Thompson radioed ahead.

"Chief, Thompson here. Over."

"Go ahead Thompson. Over."

"I've got the Chrysler…we're just passing through Dealey. Over."

"Something tells me their destination is the Trade-Mart, stay with him Thompson. Over."

"Right Chief. Over."

When Cappetta returned from changing into some spare clothes kept at the garage, the Chief addressed the group.

"If I'm right, it looks like we've got a major player entering the scene."

The Colonel was the first to speak – "Who's that Chief?"

"Well, he should be arriving at the Trade-Mart in ...Susan?"

"Less than two minutes."

"Thank you Susan."

"You're welcome."

"Now Colonel, to answer your question, earlier at Love Field we spotted the Sergeant and the Bannister character meeting with an unidentified man or men in a black Chrysler Imperial. I put a tail on them and it seems as if they're headed in the direction of the Trade-Mart."

"Chief, Thompson here. Do you read? Over."

"Excuse me Colonel... Yes Thompson? Over."

"The Chrysler is pulling into the north end driveway of the Trade-Mart. Can't get a plate number...the rain is blinding now. Over."

"Thompson, there's another entrance about a half block south of where you are. Take it and you'll come out right next to the lot they went into. Over."

"Right Chief. I'm making the turn now...yeah...I can see them. The Chrysler is parked in front of a garage door that's marked in big letters – deliveries. The garage door is raising now and the back door of the Chrysler just opened. The man getting out is dressed in real fancy cowboy attire. Black suit, white shirt with tie, black hat and boots and some kind of swirls on the front and shoulders of the jacket. He's carrying a small black briefcase and an umbrella. He's going in the garage door...now it's closing. The Chrysler is backing out and he's leaving. Should I follow Chief? Over."

"No Thompson, that won't be necessary. Return to Love Field...you'll be needed there. Over."

"I'm on my way sir. Over."

The new man added to the mix had the Chief worried. This was one detail he had no answer for. But then he knew that something like this was bound to pop up. With time closing in, he had an idea. He went for the radio.

"Burke, do you read? Over."

"Yes Chief. Over."

"Burke, have you got the first delivery? Over."

"Yes Chief. Sergeant Hargis and Chief Curry are secured on the plane nice and comfy. Over."

"Listen closely, I need you to get whatever you can out of those two about sniper's nests…buildings, floors…whatever you can get…promise them the world…you know how to handle it. Over."

"It'll be my pleasure Chief. I'll get back to you. Over."

The Chief thought for a moment, then spoke into the radio – "Powers, Spencer, do you read?"

"Yes Chief, Spencer here. Powers is with me. Over"

"Good. You two guys park the Fury in the Trade-Mart area…on a sidestreet…leave the car and stay in that area until I call. It's a slight change in plan, I know, but you two will be using that car for a special assignment. You'll be ushering the Mayor to the airport. Wait for my call. Over."

The Chief thought that if they could fool the Dallas police into thinking that the Mayor was riding with Sergeant Hargis, then his men would encounter less resistance.

He then thought of Hilsman's men in Dealey. It was 11:40am. Back to the radio.

"Buchanan, do you read? Over."

"Yes Chief. Over."

"Anything in Dealey? Over."

"Nothing but pouring rain sir. Not a soul around and very little traffic. We've checked the three positions every quarter hour…all deserted. Over."

"Okay Buchanan, give them all one more going over and if nothing changes, you and your men go to your posts at the Trade-Mart. Over."

"Yes sir. Over."

Hilsman's men led by Buchanan, did one more check at the Depository, the Dal-Tex and the rail yards and found no takers.

They walked the half block in the pouring rain to their car and sped off to the Trade-Mart.

"Chief Malinsky?...Chief?...it's Martino, do you read? Over."

"Yes Martino? Over."

"I'm at Building Five with Rothman. We've arrested a man carrying a high powered rifle...in a case...found him in the stairwell on the fifth floor. Over."

"Make sure he's cuffed, then bring him out to the back, you know the plan. Hilsman's man Jefferson is waiting in the car behind Building Six. Tell Jefferson to wait, then you two go to Building Seven and assist Hilsman's men there. Over."

"Got it Chief. Over."

"Oh! Martino? Over."

"Yes Chief? Over."

"Good job, very well done. Over."

"Thank you Chief. Over."

Things were beginning to fall in place he thought. "We've got one sniper in custody and if their plan was to use three in Dealey, then we still had to find those other two." He then turned his attention to his favorite reporters.

"Okay Jim, Susan, you two stay with me. Jim, I want that entire motorcade procession on film...as they park and exit their vehicles...Susan you know your role." They both nodded. "Colonel, we could use a man to mill around in the crowd...and I see it's gathering...but stay close to the President's car."

"I've got it covered Chief."

"And Mr. Cappetta. How's that neck and shoulder?"

"A little sore, but if I can, I'd like to be as close as possible to the President's car...for a little extra security."

"Good idea Mr. Cappetta. Stay with the Colonel and you two work out your places."

"Right." Cappetta then opened his briefcase and removed the tapes, putting them in his pockets. He left the recorders.

"Okay, so we all know our roles?"

Everyone answered yes as Burke cut in on the Chief's radio.

"Chief? Burke here. Over."

"Yes Burke? Over."

"Air Force One is touching down sir! Over."

"Thanks Burke. Over." The Chief checked his watch and addressed the group.

"It's 12:03pm. That gives us fifteen to twenty minutes to arrival." He smiled at Susan as they all left home base.

On the way out the door, Cappetta crossed himself and offered to the group – "May God be with us."

In unison, they all answered – "Amen."

XXXIX

It was 12:05pm and Officer Tippet picked up his cruiser. He drove in the direction of the Trade-Mart.

"Officer Tippet, do you read me? Over."

"Yes Simmons. What is it? Over."

"Well Officer, I saw you leaving the station in a different direction than the one you're supposed to be on. Oak Cliff is the other way. Over."

"I know Simmons, I'm heading in that direction now. I'll radio in when I arrive in the Oak Cliff area. Over."

"Very good Officer. Over."

"Yeah, right Simmons. Over." Tippet slammed the radio against the dash, "and out, I'm out of this joke of a police force…once and for all!" He then pulled into a sidestreet behind the south end of the Trade-Mart and parked. He reached for a small duffle bag that contained civilian clothes. He changed in the car, then exited the vehicle and walked the two blocks in the pouring rain.

A sea of umbrellas had gathered at the Trade-Mart awaiting

the arrival of the President. Tippet found his way into the middle of the crowd and waited.

"Chief? Burke here. Over."

"Yes Burke? Over."

"We did a little squeeze on Curry and came up with Building One-second floor, Building Two-sixth floor and Building Five-fifth floor. All genuine sniper's nests! Over."

"Excellent work, Burke! We've got Building Five secured already…I hope you didn't promise too much because you know he gets nothing. Again, good work. Over."

"Thanks, my only promise was to cut his heart out. Over."

The Chief smiled. Time was getting close. He looked at his watch – 12:14pm. He turned to Jim and Susan – "We've got some good information here…excuse me…Buchanan, do you read? Over."

"Yes Chief. Over."

"You and Everet go to the second floor of Building One and send Rogers and Samuelson to the sixth floor of Building Two. Both sniper's nests…info straight from the horse's mouth. Work quickly, time's running. Good luck! Over."

"We're on it Chief! Over."

The Chief, with Jim and Susan stood across the street from the main entrance to the Trade-Mart waiting for a return call from the men in Buildings One and Two. The Chief thought – "If we can secure the last two sniper's nests, then we can deal with the crowd." He then turned to Jim.

"Jim, where's the Colonel and Cappetta?"

"I can see them in the crowd Chief." Jim pointed to the sea of umbrellas as the rain continued to pour down.

"Good…we'll just…" Before the Chief could finish his thought, the radio interrupted – "Chief, do you read? Buchanan here. Over."

"Go ahead Buchanan. Over."

"Buildings One and Two are secure sir. Both snipers cuffed and we're bringing them around back to Jefferson's car. Over."

"Well done Buchanan, now gather the team – everyone - and take the cars behind Building Seven and go directly to the airport. There's a phone in hangar three, have Burke call your boss at the Oval Office, he's got the number, tell him to get things underway in D.C., and make sure Air Force One is ready for a quick takeoff. I'm keeping Powers and Spencer with me. We'll meet you guys at the plane. Over."

"Right. And Chief? Over."

"Yes Buchanan? Over."

"Do you need any help down there sir? Over."

"If we do I'll call…thanks Buchanan. Over."

"Right Chief. Over."

The Chief was now feeling more confident that the plan would ultimately succeed with the exception of the unknown entity – the man in the black Chrysler Imperial. This is where he thought – "I made a major mistake in sending Thompson back to the airport…he was the only one who got a look at the man…there's no time to get him back here…I'll have to go on Thompson's description…the Colonel and Cappetta have it. He's got to be in that crowd." Just as he stepped off the curb to cross to the sea of umbrellas, the motorcade slowly rounded the corner with a long block to travel to its final destination. The street was now not only flooded with rain, but also with the Dallas police.

Officer Tippet began pushing through the crowd in search of the man. He knew the man was partial to disguises from the conversations he overheard at headquarters. He had no idea what to look for, he only knew that he was supplied by some big Mafia boss in New Orleans.

It was difficult to see through the heavy rain and the deluge of umbrellas didn't help, but he continued to look. Suddenly he saw him. He knew it was the man. It had to be. The outfit, the gold swirls on the jacket, he mumbled – "That's him! I know it!" He was about twenty feet from the man, but the crowd had thickened, regardless of the rain.

As the Chief looked over the crowd, he thought about his next problem and addressed Jim and Susan.

"Jim, in addition to the entire motorcade, pay close attention to the President's car and the fourth car, that's the Mayor's. Got it?"

"Yes Chief." Jim had the motorized Nikon F ready to record history and he could feel the adrenaline building. Susan stuck to Jim's hip. She didn't say a word.

The Chief then went to the radio as the motorcade approached.

"Powers, Spencer, do you read? Over."

"Yes Chief? Powers here. Over."

"You two jump in the Fury and park it by the fourth limo in the lineup. That's the Mayor's car. If you have to use the sidewalk to get it there - do it! NOW! Over."

"Right Chief. Over."

As the motorcade came to a halt at the main entrance, the Fury quickly found it's way to the fourth limo. Powers and Spencer were aided by the Dallas police who knew the car well and waved them through. Also, the driving rain prevented them from identifying the occupants. They took it for granted that it was Sergeant Hargis, exactly what Chief Malinsky was counting on.

Agent Greer stepped out of the driver's seat of the President's limousine. As he opened a large black umbrella, he checked the scene and was quickly joined by Agent Kellerman with a second umbrella. Kellerman pulled open the rear door. Governor Connally emerged first followed by the President and finally the Vice-President. As the trio stood under the umbrellas waving to the crowd in the driving rain, Colonel Prouty caught the sight of a long barrel of a handgun pointed in the direction of the President's car. Cappetta saw it at the same time. The President was standing directly in front of the Vice-President. He was suddenly hit with a jarring tackle just as the unmistakable sound of an exploding bullet filled the square. With the President on the ground under Cappetta's body, Vice President Johnson fell less than a foot away. There was a bullet hole in his forehead. He was dead before he hit the ground.

In the commotion that followed, a second shot rang out grazing the President's right shoulder as he attempted to get to his feet. Again, Cappetta smothered the President's body. Jim got it all on film.

While the Dallas police rushed to the President's car with guns drawn, the Chief was busy pulling Mayor Cabell from his car. He then stuffed him into the backseat of the Fury which immediately sped off for the airport with Powers driving and Spencer sitting in the back, cuffing the Mayor.

In the crowd, the Colonel and Officer Tippet had wrestled the slickly dressed hitman to the ground. More shots rang out. Tippet fell backwards into the crowd with two bullet holes in his chest. The Dallas police then focused on the Colonel. During all the confusion, Cappetta had assisted the President back into the limo and the Chief was screaming to the Dallas police waving his badge in the air:

"United States Deputy Sheriff Malinsky and that man is my prisoner!" Jim continued firing the Nikon with Susan at his side.

Every member of the Dallas police froze. They were stunned. While they all stood with blank expressions on their faces, Cappetta had found the First Lady's car and escorted her and the Governor's wife to the President's limo.

The Chief approached the President's car with Colonel Prouty holding the hitman in a headlock by his side. The Colonel flashed his credentials at the Dallas police – "Colonel L. Fletcher Prouty, United States Army, Personal Security Advisor for the President of the United States." Again, the Dallas police looked dumbfounded.

The Chief then turned to Agent Greer and Kellerman:

"You can secure this area boys, we're taking the limo." The Chief then instructed Jim and Susan to get in as he got behind the wheel and the Colonel wrestled the hitman into the middle of the front seat.

In the large backseat area were the President, the Governor, their wives, Jim and Susan, and Cappetta. The Chief started the engine and mashed the accelerator to the floor.

As the 1963 Lincoln Continental sped off to Love Field, the Trade-Mart square, which now held hundreds of onlookers was surprisingly silent. The only sounds to be heard were that of the driving rain.

XL

Halfway to Love Field, the Chief checked his watch, 12:53pm CST. His plan was to get everyone safely out of Dallas before 1:00pm. Everyone was safe, the prisoners were in custody, the timing was good but as far as the Chief was concerned, there was one glaring deficiency. The way he handled the man in the black Chrysler Imperial. He blamed himself for the President's wound. It was small, just a grazing shot and far from life threatening, but still it could have been avoided had he had the state of mind to keep Thompson at the scene.

Chief Malinsky was a perfectionist. That's the way he lived his life. This was a difficult assignment, the toughest he ever faced and yet he came so close to pulling it off without a hitch. He thought of the team of men he and Hilsman assembled. All first class. They did an exceptional job. He felt good about that but he didn't feel too good about the President's injury. He turned to the backseat.

"Mr. President sir, are you sure you're okay?" It was the third time he asked.

"Mr. Malinsky, I wish you'd relax. I'm fine and I'll be fine. You sir, along with Roger Hilsman and your men have pulled off something that most would have considered impossible. I am deeply indebted to you and your men...and I have a proposition that I will present to you later...at the Oval Office...and my hopes are that you will accept." When the President finished there was a short silence in the car that was interrupted by the sound of a distant siren.

The Chief checked his rearview mirror.

"Here they come!" The Chief wheeled the big limo around the corner to the main entrance of Love Field. He drove directly to Air Force One which was waiting with engines warmed up.

Again the Chief turned to the backseat.

"Okay Mr. President, we have to do this quickly. Jim, Susan and Mr. Cappetta, go with the President!" They all exited the limo with the exception of Colonel Prouty. He continued to hold the hitman in a headlock, despite the fact that he was handcuffed.

After making sure everyone was on board Air Force One, the Chief jumped back in the limo and drove to hangar three. Four Dallas police cruisers peeled onto the tarmac in pursuit of the limo. As they did, the President's plane quickly taxied and lifted off.

As the limo screeched to a halt alongside the waiting State Department plane, the Chief found a dozen of his men heavily armed and expecting a shootout with the pursuing Dallas police.

They jumped out and everyone got on board, leaving one large hatchway open with four men armed with shotguns loaded with 00 buckshot. As the four engine prop plane left the hangar, the Dallas police exited all four cars and stood with their hands on their guns not knowing what to do. When the old plane made it to the runway, one of the four engines sputtered and died. The pilot gave the remaining three engines maximum throttle, hustling the impaired craft down the runway and lifting off just as they reached the end of the tarmac. They were airborne. Everyone let out a sigh.

When the plane was safely in the air and on route, the Chief went immediately to State Department Agent Burke.

"Were you able to make that call to Mr. Hilsman?"

"Yes I did sir and Mr. Hilsman told me that the first stop was the Pentagon."

"Good and thank you Mr. Burke. You're a first class operative, I'd work with you on any project." The Chief extended his hand in a gesture of good will. Burke returned the favor.

"Thank you Chief. This was one I'll never forget and I'd consider it an honor sir, to work with you in the future."

"Me too Mr. Burke."

The Chief then looked over the lineup of conspirators and addressed them. "Sergeant Hargis and Chief Curry of the Dallas police, Dallas Mayor Earl Cabell, three ex-marksmen and Bat Masterson. Have any of you got anything worthy to say for yourselves?"

There was a long silence. The drone of the three engines produced the only sounds.

"That's what I thought."

The Chief then thought of the one missing person of importance, the Vice-President of the United States. He mumbled so that no one heard – "He's probably still lying in a pool of blood in the streets of Dallas Texas, USA."

XLI

Aboard Air Force One, the First Lady saw to the President's wound. Luckily, the bullet only grazed the skin of the right shoulder. She treated the area with supplies from a first aid kit and bandaged it.

"There, that will have to do for now. When we get back to the White House we'll have Dr. Manchester take a look at it."

"Thank you Jackie." The President then found a fresh white button down shirt in the closet of the Presidential quarters. As he buttoned it up, the First Lady approached him.

"Jack…it was so close…you could have been…"

The President put his arms around her waist and pulled her to him. She placed her head on his chest.

"I know Jackie, but I wasn't and we made it through…the first part." He kissed her on the top of her head.

"The first part! You mean there's more?"

"Well sweetheart, as we speak…Roger and Bobby are rounding up the brass at the Pentagon. By the time we land in Washington, everyone involved should be in custody."

"And then this whole thing will be over and we can spend a few days in Hyannisport for the holidays...like we planned?"

"Yeah, the kids are looking forward to going to the shore. Maybe we'll take John and Caroline sailing. I think it's time my son had a lesson in seamanship."

"But Jack, he's only three!"

"He's just the right age." The thought of their children brought a smile to their faces.

Until now they avoided the subject of the Vice-President. The President was about to broach the subject when his phone beeped and the small red light flashed. He stood and picked up the phone. He knew who it was.

"Yes Captain Cutler, how are you?"

"Oh I'm fine Mr. President. Are you and the First Lady comfortable sir?"

"Yes, thank you Captain we are."

"I just wanted to let you know sir that our ETA in Washington, D.C. is 5:45pm EST. And one other thing sir, turn your television on to CBS. Walter Cronkite is doing a report on the events in Dallas."

"Thank you Captain, I will."

The President placed the phone in its cradle and turned on the TV. With his sleeves rolled up, the famed CBS anchor stared into the camera with a grave look on his face.

"Once again I repeat, Vice-President Lyndon Johnson was killed by a sniper's bullet outside the Trade-Mart in Dallas, Texas, at 12:29pm CST. We're told that President Kennedy is safely aboard Air Force One enroute to Washington, D.C. Reports we're getting are a little sketchy at this time but...just a moment......we have Dan Rather at the scene...go ahead Dan?"

"Yes Walter, it's still a mass of confusion here, but we have a little better description of what actually transpired from eyewitnesses. It seems that the bullet that struck and killed the Vice-President was actually meant for President Kennedy! An unidentified man tackled the President just as the shot went off, moving the President out of the way and leaving the Vice-President in the path of the bullet. I'm sure there'll be an indepth investigation into just what happened and also Walter, the story we're getting from eyewitnesses is that, and get this, two men identifying themselves as Government people of some sort, made off in an unidentified plane with the gunman. That's all I have for now Walter...this is Dan Rather in Dallas."

"Thank you Dan."

The President turned off the TV and addressed the First Lady.

"I need to prepare a statement in honor of the Vice-President's life in politics...something to show how proud this administration is of his achievements...and then we'll plan a full military funeral, with burial in Arlington."

"You mean that your not going to..."

"No Jackie, I'm not. At this juncture there's no point in besmirching the man's name...unless of course if one of the conspirators implicates Lyndon through testimony, then that's an entirely different story. No, I think the best route for the administration to take is to deny any knowledge of his involvement. I'd like to do that out of respect. Did you see him......there in the street?"

"Yes I did. It was absolutely awful!"

"Yes and without Mr. Cappetta, it would have been me there in the..." The President's voice tailed off as he sat back in his chair. The First Lady drew her legs up on her chair, put her head back and closed her eyes. She was exhausted.

"Jackie, why don't you lie down on the bed...get a little rest and I'll call you before we land. I think I'll go out there and have a chat with Mr. Cappetta."

The First Lady found her way to the bed. The President bent down and kissed her on the lips, then turned off the light and quietly left the room.

"Mr. Cappetta, could I have a word with you?"

"Yes, of course sir."

The President led Cappetta to a small conference room aboard Air Force One.

As he closed the door, the President extended his right hand.

"Please, go easy Mr. Cappetta."

Cappetta smiled and shook the President's outstretched hand.

"Without you my friend, I would not be here right now. I am deeply indebted to you."

"It was my pleasure Mr. President and I'm just glad I could help!" Cappetta was not looking for accolades. As far as he was concerned, the President was injured and he didn't do enough to prevent it.

"Well, my hopes are that I can pull you away from your surveillance work and have you work with the administration…as my personal Secret Service man. Of course that would require you to go everywhere I go…and we'd work out a salary that I'm sure would be very attractive. Is this something that you might consider?"

"I'm honored sir that you would extend the offer, but sir, won't I have to go through some sort of training period with the Secret Service?"

"Mr. Cappetta, you've already passed all the tests…and besides…I am the President and through a special order, I will appoint you to your new position. After what you've done, I can't see anyone objecting. Can you?"

"No, of course not sir and yes I accept!" Cappetta stood and reached for the President's hand. The President winced.

"Mr. Cappetta!"

"Oh! I'm sorry sir, sometimes I just don't realize my own strength."

"I know and uh…congratulations."

"Thank you sir."

"Good, that's all set. Now if you'll excuse me, I'd like to spend a little time with those two reporters. They did some exceptional investigating and I'd like to…"

"You just sit and relax sir, I'll send them in."

"Thank you Mr. Cappetta."

"Your welcome sir and please call me Pete."

"Okay Pete, send them in."

While waiting for Jim and Susan, the President took the opportunity to reflect on the events in Dallas. He thought – "I'm a very lucky man…and the Vice-President wasn't."

XLII

In the east wing of the lower level of the Pentagon, the three Generals were meeting in Conference Room B. They never received the call from Dallas, but they did see the broadcast. Everything had gone wrong.

At the main entrance, seven visitors arrived and went directly to the receptionist.

"I'm here to see Generals LeMay, Lemnitzer and Smith."

"Why of course Mr. Kennedy. They're in conference, I'll just ring for them."

"That won't be necessary, if you'll just direct us to wherever they are?"

"I'll do better than that Mr. Kennedy, I'll take you there myself." The receptionist came out from behind her station and led the Attorney General and a group of six men dressed in business suits down a long corridor to a door marked Conference Room B.

The receptionist knocked and the Attorney General and his

men entered.

General Lemnitzer rose to his feet. "Why Mr. Kennedy, what brings you here sir?" LeMay and Smith remained seated.

The Attorney General placed his hand in the inside chest pocket of his jacket and pulled out three envelopes.

"Gentlemen…and I use the term loosely, in representing the Department of Justice of the United States of America, I have warrants for your arrests." He handed each man an envelope.

LeMay blurted out – "On what charge Mister…Kennedy?"

"Generals Lemnitzer, LeMay and Smith you are all charged with conspiring to murder the President of the United States of America." The Attorney General then stared at General LeMay – "My brother, Mister…LeMay!" He then turned to his team of men, "The cuffs boys."

As Hilsman's handpicked men put the cuffs on the Generals, everyone remained quiet with the exception of General LeMay.

"This is ridiculous Kennedy, what are you trying to pull here? You'll never make this stick!"

"Right General. Take them away boys."

As the Generals were led to an unmarked police paddy wagon, the Attorney General and two of Hilsman's men got into a black limousine and directed the driver to an office building in downtown D.C.

As the black limo pulled up and parked, the three men got out and entered the building. They checked the directory and took the elevator to the seventh floor. When they reached the office they found the door slightly open.

The Attorney General pushed it open the rest of the way. The only light in the room came from the windows through the venetian blinds. A chair was pushed in at what appeared to be the secretary's desk. The office was deserted. The Attorney General walked to the only door in the room. It was marked – Mr. Allen W. Dulles. He knocked. No answer. He then turned the knob and opened it half way to his right. On the wall to his left was a shadow. The shadow of a man hanging by a rope that reached to the ceiling. He pushed the door open all the way to his right. The light coming through the blinds backlit the hanging body of Allen Dulles. His head was cocked to the right and his tongue protruded from his mouth.

The Attorney General, Anderson and Scott all looked at the hanging body in disbelief.

"Do you want us to cut him down Mr. Kennedy?"

"No, I think we should leave him. I'll make a call." He didn't want to use the phone that sat on the desk a foot from the dead man's dangling feet. He went to the secretary's desk and called the D.C. police, giving them all the information and then hung up.

They left the building in silence and got into the limo.

"The police will take care of things for now…I'll deal with them later. Right now, let's see how Mr. Hilsman's doing with General Cabell."

The Attorney General then instructed the driver to return to the Oval Office.

When the limo arrived at the designated space near the West Lawn, the Attorney General, Anderson and Scott made the short walk to the glass doors. It was 4:25pm EST and the sun had begun its vanishing act on the horizon. They entered the Oval Office.

"Roger, has he arrived yet?"

"No Bobby, he called. Says he's going to be a little late. He said 4:45 at the latest."

When the President was making his run through Texas, the Attorney General and Roger Hilsman had developed a rapport and decided to drop the formalities. They were now simply Roger and Bobby.

"And everything I hope went okay at the Pentagon?"

"Oh yeah Roger, the Pentagon went very nicely with the exception of the usual belligerence from LeMay. It was Dulles that was a bit unsettling."

"And?"

"In his office…he hung himself."

"He was a tortured man. Well, we certainly don't want to see any human suffering…but he WAS instrumental in their plans to murder our President…your brother!"

"Yeah…he must have seen the broadcast. Speaking of the broadcast, it's really too bad about Lyndon. Either way, dead or alive…he suffers."

The conversation was then interrupted by the intercom.

"Mr. Hilsman sir, I'm awfully sorry to interrupt, but General Cabell is here to see you."

"Thank you Miss Lincoln, send him right in." Hilsman instructed Anderson and Scott to wait outside by the West Lawn, which they did and then turned to the Attorney General – "Here we go Bobby!"

To which the Attorney General replied, "It's your show Roger!"

The door to the Oval Office opened and General Cabell walked in.

"How do you do sir?" Hilsman greeted the General as did the Attorney General. Hilsman then led them to the seating area.

"Now Mr. Hilsman, you said in our phone conversation that reinstatement to my post with the CIA was under consideration. Is that correct?"

Hilsman wondered if the General had seen the television broadcast from Dallas.

"Yes, the President has been rethinking the entire situation and he feels that your case requires special attention." Hilsman then handed the General an envelope. "It's all laid out in there General…your future!"

Hilsman smiled as the General opened the envelope and read it in it's entirety.

"You've got to be kidding! Is this some kind of prank?"

"No it is not sir. It's a warrant."

"I can read!!"

"General Cabell, you're charged with conspiring to murder the

President of the United States."

"This is preposterous Hilsman...you're out of your mind! Who do you think you're dealing with?"

"With a murderer General." Hilsman then signaled to his two men outside the glass doors. Anderson and Scott entered. "Cuff him boys and get him out of my sight." Hilsman decided that he'd had enough of the General's tone, so he thought he'd rub it in a little. "Your brother will be joining you in approximately...Mr. Kennedy, when is that State Department plane due?"

"About 6:15 Mr. Hilsman."

"Good. Look at it as a kind of family reunion General." Hilsman flashed a smile while the Attorney General hid his. This was Hilsman's show.

"Very funny you son of a bitch! I promise you Hilsman, I'll have your job for this!"

Hilsman turned to Anderson and Scott, "Take him away boys."

As the General was being led out the glass doors to the waiting limousine by the West Lawn, he began yelling obscenities about Hilsman, the Kennedys and anyone else that came to mind in the present administration. Anderson removed his soiled handkerchief from his chest pocket and stuck it the General's mouth. "I have very sensitive ears General, PLEASE."

"Well Bobby, the last one is in custody and I have to say that it's been one hell of a week!"

"Yeah, one I'll never forget...and my brother...he's been through hell with this thing. You have to admire his strength and courage, not to mention the trust he placed in all of us. I don't believe I know another man that would have gone through with that trip. It takes a special kind of..." The Attorney General paused. "That's why he's the President."

"You're absolutely right Bobby."

"You know Roger I've been thinking. My brother is going to have the problem of selecting a new Vice-President."

"Yes he is."

"I'm going to highly recommend you for the position. You're an ideal candidate."

"Well thank you Bobby, but I believe the President will want someone that has more public appeal. Someone close to him in the administration." Hilsman wanted to tell him that he would soon be the ex-Attorney General but he thought better of it.

"I still think that you would be an excellent choice."

"Again, thank you Bobby, but I'd rather you said nothing about it to the President."

The two men then sat in silence waiting for Air Force One to touch down at Dulles Airport.

XLIII

The airport was swarming with reporters, police, security guards and a host of onlookers. The President's limo awaited his arrival surrounded by twelve Secret Service Agents.

It was Friday, November 22, 1963 at 5:40pm EST when Air Force One touched the tarmac at Dulles Airport.

As the President's big jet came to a stop, the portable stairway was quickly connected to the front door. When the door opened, the Governor and his wife appeared first and after a short pause of ten seconds, the First Lady and the President emerged from the cabin to a rousing welcome.

Descending the stairway, the First Lady turned and looked over her shoulder at the President. "It's so good to be back!"

"Yes it is Jackie." They both wore big smiles.

As the President was led to his car, an army of photographers were snapping away while reporters were clamoring for a story. The President stopped as he was about to enter the limo and addressed the group.

"I will attempt to answer all your questions at the White House press conference tonight, 8:15 sharp."

The President, the Governor and their wives were now seated in the limo for the short ride to the White House. The President noticed that Jim, Susan and Cappetta were missing. He put down his window and said something to a Secret Service Agent. Within moments, the trio got into the Presidential limo.

"I would like all of you to be with us at the White House tonight…unless of course you have other plans?"

The trio all answered yes we'd like to and no we don't.

"Good!" The President then signaled to the driver to get underway.

Susan then grabbed Jim's hand and whispered in his ear – "Jim, we're going to the White House!" Everyone in the car heard her and smiled.

Jim was also smiling as he thought – "I've been there a dozen times for press conferences." But he knew that this time would be different. This time they were not only guests of the President of the United States but also they had the story that no one else had.

The President's car pulled up to the main entrance. In front and behind the President's limo were cars holding the twelve Secret Service Agents. They surrounded the President and his party as they entered the White House.

"I think I'll show Mrs. Connally to her quarters dear, then I'll send Dr. Manchester to the Oval Office…that is where you'll be, isn't it?"

"Yes dear and thank you." The President kissed his wife then turned and directed the Governor, the two reporters and Cappetta to the Oval Office.

When they walked through the reception area, the President's secretary jumped to her feet and grabbed her bosses hands.

"Oh Mr. President, it's so good to see your handsome face sir, welcome back!" Miss Lincoln was more than elated to see her

President.

"Thank you Miss Lincoln and it's wonderful to see you!"

He shook her hands and continued through the doorway to his office.

When he entered, the Attorney General was standing at the window looking out over the West Lawn. When he turned he saw the President. They walked slowly with eyes locked until they were a foot apart. Everyone watched in silence as the brothers threw their arms around one another, patting each other on the back. The Attorney General had tears in his eyes when he spoke.

"Welcome home big brother."

The President's eyes were also swelling with tears as he responded.

"Thank you Bobby…and uh…what do you think about your new title?" The President paused. "Mr. Vice-President!"

"Well…I uh…don't…I don't quite know how to…however, Mr. President…let me say this about that!"

The President and the new Vice-President both laughed out loud. Everyone else in the room followed.

The President then introduced Jim and Susan to Roger Hilsman and the Attorney General, who then greeted the Governor and Mr. Cappetta.

The atmosphere in the Oval Office had now changed from the near hopelessness earlier in the week to a sense of glee and celebration. Some were standing, some sitting, all busily involved in conversations about the events of the last few days. The President then changed the mood as he asked the group for quiet.

"I know this is a joyous time for all of us gathered here, but we mustn't lose sight of the fact that a great politician gave up his life earlier today. That person deserves the respect given when one spends an entire lifetime in the midst of the struggle for democracy. As a tribute to Lyndon Johnson's years of service to our great country, I believe a full military funeral and burial at Arlington National Cemetary are in order."

Everyone was silent with the exception of Jim and Susan. They clapped lightly. They were unaware of the Vice-President's involvement. The Governor was told aboard Air Force One on the flight from Fort Worth to Dallas, when the President gave him the option of riding in another car. When he declined, he won the President's confidence.

Hilsman responded first – "But Mr. President you can't mean…"

The President quickly cut him off.

"No disrespect toward you my dear friend, but there's no point in dragging the Vice-President's name through the mud. If those behind bars choose that route, so be it. However, I would like this administration to take the stance I've just stated and I know this may be difficult for some, but I ask all of you to respect my wishes."

The Governor, Hilsman, the new Vice-President and Cappetta all agreed, while Susan had no idea what had just transpired. In his mind, Jim was putting together the pieces of the puzzle. He whispered to Susan.

"I think the Vice-President was involved."

"Involved in what Jim?"

"In the conspiracy Susan!"

"Oh my God, do you really think?"

"Yes."

"Jim, this story has mushroomed into something that we need to get to work on as quickly as possible. I've got to get to a phone and call Mark at the *Sun*."

"Remember Susan, you can't let on about the Vice-President, we have to keep that part of the story quiet…and I've been thinking." Jim paused.

"About what Jim?"

"I think we should write this entire story together…for the *Post*. We'll get all the facts from Mr. Hilsman and the Attorney General about how the operation was handled here in D.C., then combine that with our experiences and we'll have…"

"But Jim, I love the part that has us writing the story together, but my editor is expecting a story from me."

"Look, we'll take care of your boss. We'll give the *Post* the exclusive with the stipulation that your paper immediately follows with the same story, word for word…right? Now stay with me."

"Okay…and?"

"We give it to the *Sun* right after the *Post* hits the streets!"

"How about a few hours before it hits? I'd like to see the *Sun* come out of this with something."

"Okay, that sounds fine. Now let's see what we can find out from Mr. Hilsman and the Attorney General."

"That's the second time you said that."

"Said what?"

"The Attorney General!"

"So?"

"He's now the Vice-President Jim."

"Oh yeah, right!"

"I wonder who gets his old job? Geez, this is fun…musical chairs at the White House!"

"I think I can answer that for you." The President was standing a few feet from Jim and Susan. He overheard the last part of their conversation.

"May I have everyone's attention please, just for a moment…thank you. Now that you all know that my brother is the new Vice-President, well before the public announcement, some of you may be wondering who his replacement will be at the Justice Department. Well, the man I've chosen is here tonight…and he and I have already discussed the uh…musical chairs routine." The President smiled at Susan. She managed to return the gesture through her embarrassment. "And he has accepted. My dear friend Mr. Roger Hilsman, the Attorney General of the United States of America."

They all lined up to congratulate the new Attorney General. When it was his predecessor's turn to shake his hand, Hilsman offered a very good excuse before the Vice-President could speak.

"I couldn't tell you Bobby, that would have betrayed the President's trust. I felt that it would be a very special moment between the brothers."

"Yes it was special Roger and thank you. And uh...congratulations!"

"Thank you Mr. Vice-President."

"Now that title is going to be a little difficult getting used to."

Their conversation was interrupted by the buzzing intercom.

The President pushed the answer button.

"Miss Lincoln, I looked forward to hearing your lovely voice over this contraption during my entire stay in Texas. What is it that I can do for you dear?" The President was clearly glad to be back.

"Thank you Mr. President and Dr. Manchester is here to see you. Shall I send him in?"

"Yes, please, thank you Miss Lincoln."

"You're welcome sir."

The President then addressed the gathering.

"Now if you'll all excuse me, my doctor is about to perform some kind of surgery on my shoulder. I shouldn't be long."

Dr. Manchester was greeted at the door by the President, who led him through another door to a conference room for the 'surgery.'

Jim and Susan spent the next twenty minutes talking to the Attorney General and the Vice-President about how they received their information from Colonel Prouty and the Cappetta tapes. During the conversation, the Vice-President stressed to the two reporters that Lyndon Johnson's involvement was off limits. They agreed.

XLIV

It was 5:15pm CST when he crossed the Texas border into Louisiana. The left hand was taped tightly enough to stop the bleeding, but still, medical attention was required. The pain was intense. He took another slug from the bottle of Jack Daniels. It helped, but he knew he had to get to a doctor.

He pulled over the stolen '59 Ford wagon and went to the payphone. After placing a coin in the slot he dialed.

"Hello! Bannister's can I help you?"

"Rhoda, it's me. Listen…"

"Guy! Guy! Where are you? Is everything okay?"

"No Rhoda, it isn't. Don't ask anything else, just listen!"

"Yes Guy?"

"In my safe there's a little over $12,000 in cash." He gave her the combination. "Put all of it in an envelope and give it to Hank at the meeting tonight. Tell him to meet me at The Kingston Motel on route 19 in Baton Rouge tomorrow morning…no later than 9:00am. Have you got that?"

"Yes Guy. When will I see you?"

"I'll call you in a day or two, just be patient Rhoda. The entire operation collapsed in Dallas and I've gotta lay low for awhile. I'm sure that you'll be swamped with Feds within the next twenty-four hours, so remember, you know nothing…NOTHING!"

"Yes of course, I know…" and the line went dead.

The big man returned to the stolen wagon and continued the painful trip to Baton Rouge.

The President returned to the Oval Office from 'surgery' sporting a big smile.

"Dr. Manchester informed me of his prognosis…I'll live!"

The group applauded which now included the First Lady and the Governor's wife.

"Mr. President, I took the liberty of ordering a buffet for our guests. It'll be delivered here at 7:15, I thought you might like to wait for Chief Malinsky and the Colonel."

"That sounds wonderful Jackie." The President then sat in his favorite rocker and addressed Governor Connally who was sitting on the couch with the new Vice-President.

"I must say Governor, you exhibited a great deal of courage when you chose to exit the limo first. You placed yourself in a very dangerous position."

"Well Mr. President, looking at the situation objectively, you and I…and Lyndon knew that you were the only target. Considering that he chose to exit the limo last, leads me to believe, that he fully expected the hitman to accomplish his task well before he stepped out. When he found himself out in the open without any shots fired, he had no idea where to stand. So, foolishly he placed himself directly behind you, believing that was the safest place to be. Then of course Mr. Cappetta performed his flying tackle at the very instant the shot rang out, which left the Vice-President directly in the line of fire. And the rest is history."

The President was about to reply when Miss Lincoln called.

"Mr. President, there are two men out here who say they have an appointment with you sir, but they refuse to give their names and I have no idea who they are!" Miss Linclon knew exactly who they were.

As the President turned to Hilsman with a puzzled look, the door to the Oval Office opened and in walked the Colonel and Chief Malinsky, both looking a little tattered from their experience.

"Welcome home gentlemen!" The President announced.

As the three men hugged and shook hands, a lavish buffet fitting a King and his court, was wheeled into the Oval Office.

While all the White House guests were busy eating and socializing, at 8:15pm, the President was led to a jampacked Press Room. His guests would watch from the Oval Office television.

The President expertly fielded an array of questions until 9:00pm, never once letting on to his knowledge of the conspiracy. That would come later, in his national address on Saturday evening. There, the President would reveal the entire story, with the exception of the involvement of the man he once believed to be his friend.

XLV

Early Saturday morning the President was busy working at his desk in the Oval Office. He let Jackie sleep after the evening's activities where they entertained their guests until well after midnight. Considering the hour, the President insisted they all spend the night, which they did. They were now having breakfast in the White House dining room where the President excused himself to catch up on his work.

It was Miss Lincoln's day off but she insisted on coming in to help the President who was sorting through some paperwork when she entered with a telegram in her hand.

"I'm sorry to interrupt you sir, but the telegrams are piling up on my desk and this one," she held out a yellow envelope, "I believe will be of interest to you." She handed him the telegram. The place of origin stamped on the envelope in large letters – HAVANA, CUBA.

"Hmmm…I wonder if this could be…" The President opened the envelope and read the telegram in silence. He then placed it on his desk and looked up at Miss Lincoln.

"I believe Miss Lincoln, that arrangements for a trip to the Caribbean are in order."

"Do you mean you're going to Cuba sir?"

"Yes I am Miss Lincoln. This is just the opening we needed." The President then handed the telegram to his secretary.

"Go ahead Miss Lincoln, you can read it."

The telegram read:

From the Palace of the Presidente ~ Havana, Cuba

Dear Mr. President Kennedy,

When I received the news that an attempt had been made on your life and in addition to that Mr. Johnson had been murdered, I sir, felt a great sadness.

That an evil mind or minds would resort to such doings in your great country, makes one believe that no leader is safe, anywhere in this world.

And, after spending a considerable amount of time with the writer Jean Daniel here in Havana on Friday, where he informed me of your wishes, the following decisions were made by myself and my advisors:

1- To put an end to the hostilities between the United States and the Republic of Cuba.

2- To unite with your country in an effort toward world peace while Cuba maintains her role with the Soviet Union.

3- To invite you, the President of the United States to my Palace in Havana, to open friendly talks here and hopefully you will make a similar offering to have me and my staff to the great White House.

Please feel free to have your staff call my Palace at your earliest convenience, so that we may arrange for your visit.

If I'm not moving too quickly Mr. President, the week after

your Thanksgiving holiday would be ideal for me and my staff.
Do be in touch Mr. President.

Sincerely and best regards,
Fidel Castro

She put the telegram down on the President's desk.

"Yes Miss Lincoln, I'm going to Havana. Call the Palace and arrange for the Monday following Thanksgiving. If that's acceptable to Mr. Castro, then call Captain Cutler and have him sort out the details for Air Force One. Then a memo to Roger and Jim Flannery, the *Post* reporter. I'd like both of them to attend all the meetings in Havana." He paused.

"Anything else sir?"

"Yes, I'll dictate letters to Chairman Khrushchev and Prime Minister Macmillan...they should be kept up to date."

Miss Lincoln sat down as the President dictated the two letters. When he finished, she returned to her office.

The President then walked to the glass doors and stepped out onto the West Lawn. It was a glorious autumn morning. He walked and thought – "This was a dream…and now just maybe…a reality."

XLVI

It was 9:10am when Hank Ripperton walked into the diner at the Kingston Motel in Baton Rouge. He spotted Bannister and sat in the booth directly across from the big man.

"You're late Hank."

"I know, I had a little…"

Before Hank could finish his excuse, Bannister came right to the point.

"Did you bring the envelope?"

Hank slid the envelope filled with $100s and $50s across the table. Bannister opened it and counted out $12,350.

"I knew I could count on you Hank." Hank was always there for Guy Bannister. He knew if he wasn't, something dreadful would happen to him.

Bannister then peeled off two $100s and handed them to his friend.

"Thanks Guy. What's with your hand?"

"A little accident in Dallas."

"Boy, what a mess over there, huh?"

"Yeah, the entire fucking operation went up in smoke and it's all because of those two reporters."

"What reporters?"

Bannister then told Hank about Jim and Susan.

"Do you want me to see what I can do about those two?"

"Yeah, I want them taken care of. They're probably in D.C. right now. You see to it Hank, I've gotta hide out for awhile. I'm the only one they didn't get and they'll be coming...all because of those two fucking reporters!"

"What are you gonna do?"

"I want you to call Lester at the docks. Tell him I'm coming and I'll need a boat...maybe to Key West...I don't know...anywhere. I was thinking of hiding out in South America for awhile...change my identity and when the time is right...back to the states."

"I'll call Lester when I get back to New Orleans. Oh, by the way, we got your car back from the Lake Charles Airport. No problems."

"Good, I've got enough of those. Look, you take off, I'm going over to Baton Rouge General to get this thing stitched up." He looked down at his left hand. "And tell Lester I'll be there before dark."

"Right Guy."

Hank left the diner as Bannister drank his third half cup of coffee. The other half was Jack Daniels. He needed it for the pain.

After breakfast in the White House dining room, the President's guests were milling around saying their goodbyes.

Governor Connally and his wife were heading back to Texas where an investigation into Dallas Police activities would soon be underway.

Colonel Prouty would have a lot of explaining to do when he showed up at home. After all, he was murdered at Idlewild Airport.

Chief Malinsky was planning his own investigation in New Orleans concerning the activities of the missing Guy Bannister.

Jim and Susan were given a conference room off the Oval Office complete with two typewriters, one UNDERWOOD and one ROYAL. There they would start work on their story, undisturbed. The two reporters were also offered a room in the White House for the weekend when their bags arrived early Saturday morning from Lake Charles. Chief Malinsky had arranged for their shipment through the Lake Charles Police. However, they declined the offer because Jim wanted to show Susan his apartment.

And with the President busy working in his office for the weekend, Mr. Cappetta was given the time off.

Hilsman thought he'd stick around to help the President get back in the swing. He also had a difficult time leaving after spending the last few days and nights heading up the Oval Office command post. He had become very fond of the place.

He entered the Oval Office and found the President working at his desk. The President looked up.

"I understand Bobby's dealings with the Pentagon went smoothly."

"Yes sir, they did. However, the Dulles discovery was a bit unsettling for your brother."

"I know, it bothered him to speak about it. It's been all over the news this morning and the papers. Well Roger, a tortured mind will present drastic choices and more often than not...make rash decisions. Perhaps it was best for him this way, maybe he's found peace. And uh...my brother tells me that your strategy with General Cabell was a classic in deception. He said he'd rather you told me."

"Of course sir, I'd be glad to." The President smiled as Hilsman continued. "You remember the Cappetta tapes of Caball at the Hyatt where he alluded to you as a dead man?" The President nodded. "Well sir, I suppose I was seeking a way to give him a taste of his own medicine. So, I extended an invitation to the

General to meet with me under the premise that his post at the CIA was under reconsideration by you. When he arrived, we briefly discussed just that and then I handed him an envelope with the warrant for his arrest. Before he opened it I told him that his future was all spelled out in the contents of the envelope. Well," Hilsman chuckled as he continued his tale, "after he read it he was just beside himself, swearing and carrying on. As a matter of fact, he was shouting obsenities about all of us as my two men Anderson and Scott escorted him to the car parked right out here. Anderson later informed me that he got so tired of listening to the General's tirade, so he stuffed his well used handkerchief in the General's mouth!"

"He did that?"

"Yes sir, he did."

The two men had good laugh.

"That's a wonderful story Roger!"

"Thank you sir. It kind of ended the whole ordeal on an upnote."

"Yeah it did…and Roger?"

"Yes sir?"

"Good work."

"Thank you sir."

"Well, on that note I think I'll get to work on my speech for tonight. Hang around if you can, perhaps you can give me a little help with some of the details?"

"Certainly sir."

The President and the Attorney General spent the next three hours preparing the President's national address, where the American public would hear it all.

In the conference room, Jim and Susan were starting work on what would be the story of their lives.

"Jim, do you think Bannister's crazy enough to come up here after us? I certainly don't want to go back to New Orleans with him on the loose."

"Don't worry sweetheart, Mr. Hilsman told me that he got a

photo of Bannister through the New Orleans Police after our first contact with the Oval Office. On Friday, he put it out on the wire service. Seems Mr. Bannister has an extensive record."

"That comes as no surprise."

"Right. So don't worry, he'll be picked up eventually."

"I hope you're right."

"Let's forget about him and get started here."

"Okay Clark Kent and where do we start?"

"From the beginning, when the Colonel was given his assignment in New Zealand."

"Good, you take the White House angle and I'll begin with our meeting at the Bourbon Street Grille. You my dear, lifted the lid off this thing with your barroom confrontation with Bannister. So…let's see…" Susan quickly had the ROYAL at full speed while Jim labored away with two fingers on the UNDERWOOD.

XLVII

Doctor Audette neatly placed the twenty-fourth and final stitch in the man's hand.

"Just how did you do this Mr. Dawson?" Jim Flannery's fraternity brother's name was getting even more mileage. This time it was being used by Bannister.

"Ya know Doc, I was cutting down a tree in my yard and I guess I got a little careless with the chain saw."

"But this wound appears to be at least twenty-four hours old. Why did you wait so long to get medical attention?"

Bannister did not like being questioned, but he managed to stay on his best behavior.

"After it happened Doc, I went into the house and taped it up. It hurt like hell so I had a few drinks to ease the pain and I kinda passed out and slept through the night."

"You were probably in shock Mr. Dawson. Do you realize that?"

Bannister thought – "Of course I realize it you fucking little shit…I went through it didn't I? I'd like to put you in shock and see what you think…what the fuck do you know about being in shock…other than what you read in some half assed textbook. I'll show you fucking shock!"

"Yes, your probably right Doc, I must have been in shock. The whole thing was so careless of me."

"You need not worry Mr. Dawson, I believe we've got the bleeding under control now. But you'll have to take these three times a day for the infection." Dr. Audette handed him two bottles of pills.

"What's the other bottle for Doc?"

"Those are for the pain Mr. Dawson, which you'll continue to feel. No more than three a day and NO ALCOHOL."

Bannister thought – "He must be out of his fucking mind if he thinks I'm not gonna have a drink. Pain! What the fuck does he know about pain. He's never felt pain in his pampered fucking life. I'd like to show the little prick some real fucking pain!"

"Yes Doc, I got ya…absolutely no alcohol. I want this thing to get better."

"Good. That just about does it Mr. Dawson, so take care of yourself and come back in ten days and I'll remove the stitches…and please, be more careful when handling power equipment."

Bannister thought – "Yeah, I'll be more careful you little fucking runt. I'll come back in ten days to shove a chain saw right up your tight fucking ass."

"Right Doc and thanks!"

Bannister went to the checkout at Baton Rouge General and paid his bill.

Ten minutes after the big man left, the nurse who assisted on his procedure, sat at her station and picked up the Saturday edition of the Baton Rouge Gazette. There was a picture of a man named Guy Bannister on the front page. She thought he looked an awful lot like Mr. Dawson. She read the article beneath his picture which stated that Bannister was wanted in connection with the assassination of Vice-President Johnson. She picked up the phone and dialed the Baton Rouge Police.

After their visit to Baton Rouge General, the police put out an APB and also alerted the New Orleans Police. From the nurse's description of Bannister and his injury, they were now looking for a large man in a soiled short black trenchcoat, crumpled up khaki pants and a heavily wrapped left hand. They had no idea what kind of car to look for, but considering he escaped the scene in Dallas on foot, the odds were high that he was driving a stolen car with Texas plates.

Roadblocks were set up on all the major roads in Baton Rouge, but the '59 Ford wagon with Texas plates was now on the outskirts of New Orleans, where it pulled off the road next to a payphone. Bannister stepped out, went to the phone and called Hank.

"Yeah it's me Hank."

"Lester's got it all arranged. Take route 1 south all the way to the end. That's Grand Isle. Go to the docks, Lester will be waiting."

"Thanks Hank." Bannister hung up and jumped in the car and sped off to Grand Isle. He figured it was about a forty-five minute drive.

He was close. A little less than an hour later, he pulled up at the Grand Isle docks.

Lester LaValle was sitting on a bench smoking his pipe. The bench overlooked a marina filled with pleasure boats. When Bannister got out of the wagon he saw his contact and quickly walked in his direction.

"You're all set to sail Guy. Haley's Comet in slip number nine is your ticket, but you know this won't be cheap."

Bannister never liked Lester LaValle, but he knew at this point that the old man was his best way out.

"Okay Lester, hit me with it."

"Five thousand and that includes a Cuban and South American

passport."

"What the fuck do I need a Cuban passport for?"

"I've got it all planned for you Guy and it wasn't easy. You go directly to Key West...you're already checked in at the Southernmost Motel…it's at the south end of Duval St. Wait for a man named Walter to be in touch with you. He's arranging boat passage to Havana…a night trip. He'll set you up with a contact there. You're hotel is already taken care of…it's the El Floridita. The Tuesday after Thanksgiving your contact in Havana will put you aboard a steamer for Buenos Aires…and then you're on your own my friend."

"I'll pay Thirty-five hundred."

"No you won't. You'll pay five thousand or else the engines in Haley's Comet stay ice cold."

"You were always a tough bargain Lester." Bannister reached for his gun.

"If you use that Mr. Bannister, you'll be out in the cold with no contact in Key West. You see, the people down there are waiting for my call. Now what will it be?"

Bannister considered blowing the old man's brains out all over the docks, but instead he counted out five thousand in one hundred dollar bills and handed the wad to LaValle.

"That's what I thought Mr. Bannister. Now follow me." They walked down the dock and quickly arrived at the ninth slip, which held a black 34 foot twin engine inboard. Lester asked the big man about his left hand. Bannister ignored him as he stepped on board while Lester untied the speedy looking craft and gave the man at the helm a signal. The engines came to life with a roar.

Within moments, the sun dipped behind the horizon and Haley's Comet was at full song as she exited the harbor for the Gulf of Mexico.

XLVIII

The speech was ready. It was 6:10pm and the President had a little under two hours before air time. Another busy day in the life of the Commander in Chief.

In addition to the correspondence with Moscow, Great Britain, Cuba, and the sixteen page speech written with Hilsman's assistance, the President also received an important call from the Justice Department.

Assistant Chief Prosecutor Bill Dillon informed the President that all the conspirators from Dallas and D.C. had been officially arraigned and charged. Bail was denied due to the recommendations of Attorney General Kennedy.

The President then dined with the First Lady and Roger Hilsman in the White House dining room, while Jim and Susan left for the *Post.* There they would work on the final draft of their story in preparation for the Sunday edition.

From the Oval Office at 8:00pm, the lights were lit and the

cameras were focused on the President of the United States.

The President sat at his desk and looked straight ahead. He began.

"Good evening. With great sadness in my heart I come to you tonight. This past Friday, shortly after noon, our country lost a distinguished leader and friend to all," the President paused, "Vice-President Lyndon Johnson."

"Lost to the bullet of an assassin on the streets of Dallas Texas. Lost forever to his family and friends."

"I too…was to have met with that same assassin's bullet. Due to the heroics of a very courageous man, my life was spared. My thanks to that man and to the brilliant strategy of a small team of men whose perseverance and hard work brought this plot against our government to a halt."

"Yes my fellow Americans, a plot…a conspiracy. A conspiracy that began in the halls of the Pentagon."

The President then gave a detailed day to day account of the plans for and against.

In closing, he returned to the subject of the murdered Vice-President.

"And I declare Monday, November 25th, a national day of mourning for Vice-President Lyndon Johnson. The Vice-President's body will lie in state in the Capitol Rotunda on Sunday, followed on Monday by a full military funeral with burial at Arlington National Cemetary."

"I now call on all Americans to offer their good will and prayers to Vice-President Johnson's family. May God be with all of you. Goodnight."

From coast to coast, Americans remained glued to their televisions. The shocking revelations and the President's desire to share this information with the American public well before it hit the press, boosted the public's trust in the Commander in Chief. If he ran for re-election tomorrow, he'd win by a landslide.

At 9:15pm, the television crew packed up and left the White House, leaving the President with his brother and Roger Hilsman in the Oval Office. They all remarked that the address went smoothly and effectively. The President looked a bit worn. He was exhausted.

"I know it's been a long day sir, but there is another matter that requires your attention."

"Yes Roger, what might that be?"

"The uh…the flight from Honolulu arrived at Idlewild while you were giving your address sir…….they're on a commuter flight to D.C. now."

"Are they all coming here?"

"Yes sir. The Vice-President took the call from Idlewild and they would like to meet with you tonight."

The Vice-President offered, "I told Bundy that you would probably be unavailable after the broadcast, but he insisted on them seeing you tonight."

"Okay Bobby, Roger…when they arrive, tell them that I'm unable to meet with them until Tuesday morning…at 9:00am. They're all to be here at the Oval Office at that time…ALL OF THEM. They'll meet with the three of us…draw up warrants…for all of them with a charge of…" The President rubbed his chin, then ran his hand through his hair. "Treason."

XLIX

The lights were on and the door was locked at Bannister's Books. Rhoda did not like spending night after night alone at home, so she busied herself at the shop.

At 10:05pm she decided it was time to close up and go home. As she gathered her things there was a knock at the door.

Through the glass she saw a man standing at the door waving. She walked to the door and opened it. The man was short, of medium build, dark red hair and a moustache.

"I'm sorry sir but we're closed."

"Oh gee, my wife and I are going back east in the morning and I was told by a friend that your shop has the best selection of books on the B-17's role in World War II. Would it be possible? I'd only be few minutes."

"Yes of course, come in." She stepped aside to allow the man to enter. As he did, he pushed the door closed, drew the shade and turned off the lights with the switch by the door. They stood in near darkness. The only light came from the twelve foot tall streetlamps that lined Dauphine Street.

Holding a small European semi-automatic with silencer attached, he lifted it to her temple. She froze.

"Where is he?"

"Who?"

"You know who, your husband!"

"I haven't heard from him in days!"

"Look lady, your time is coming to an end and…I just might spare you if you come clean. NOW WHERE IS HE?"

"I'm telling you the truth…I don't know!"

"Last chance lady."

She closed her eyes as the man pulled back the hammer. He squeezed the trigger. The silenced small caliber bullet let out a noise similar to that of opening a soda bottle after being shaken.

The man placed the gun in his belt, pulled his jacket closed and exited the shop as the phone rang.

The shelf next to the front entrance held an array of books on the life of Adolph Hitler. They were all covered with blood.

The phone continued to ring.

After seven rings, Guy Bannister slammed the phone on the hook.

While Haley's Comet was being refueled at a dock in Clearwater Florida, Bannister called Rhoda to tell her that he wanted her with him on his odyssey through Central and South America. "That's strange," he thought, "she wasn't home and she's not at the shop." He'd call her again when he got to Key West.

The Dallas Police officer walked straight through the overcrowded club to a short hallway leading to a door marked PRIVATE. He knocked, then entered.

The man sitting at the desk was counting money. He had stacks of bills in front of him. With an unfiltered cigarette dangling from the left side of his mouth he looked up at the cop.

"Good evening officer. What can I do for you? A little action tonight? I've got this sweet thing out there, but she's only here for the night."

"The program...it went sour...and we need to make a few adjustments."

"And what do you have in mind?" He continued to count the mid-evening's receipts.

The officer drew his gun and walked around the desk behind the man.

"Wait...what? What are you doing?"

The cop held his gun to the man's head and handed him a pair of handcuffs.

"Put one on...your right hand!"

The man put one cuff on his right wrist while the cop pulled his left arm behind and shackled the man's hands to the chair.

"Officer, what's this all about?"

The Dallas policeman did not answer. He removed a nylon cord from his jacket pocket and quickly placed it around the man's neck. He pulled both ends tight. The man squirmed and violently wriggled in the chair while the cop pulled tighter. The body stopped moving.

When the cop released his grip on the cord, the man's body fell forward with his head hitting the desk.

The Dallas Policeman walked to the door, opened it, looked around and left The Cellar by the rear exit.

Jack Ruby's head sat on the neatly stacked rows of singles, fives, tens and twentys. He was dead.

L

At 10:15pm, Mark Lane's cab arrived at the main entrance of *The Washington Post*. He was late. After getting Susan's call early Saturday morning, he tried to get a direct flight but he was forced to take a commuter to Atlanta where he picked up his connection to Dulles Airport.

Jim and Susan had just put the final touches on their story and handed it to Jim's editor Joe Muldoon when Mark Lane entered the office. Susan greeted her boss and then introduced him to Jim and the Editor of the *Post.*

"I'm sorry I'm late…plane travel…you know. Someday they'll perfect it."

"Here Mark, take a look!" Susan handed her boss a copy of the story.

"While you people go over the story I'll get this down to typeset and we should have a complete copy of the Sunday edition by…" he looked at his watch, "a little after midnight." Joe Muldoon excused himself and left the office.

"Where are you staying Mark?"

Mark Lane was immersed in the story. "What was that Susan?"

"I said where are you staying?"

"I'm not. I've got a direct flight back which leaves at 11:15...I came myself because I didn't want this in anyone else's hands. We're shooting for the Sunday run...they're holding the presses until I get back. It won't hit until noon Sunday...six hours later than our usual Sunday release, but that's okay." He sat there reading in silence. When he finished he looked up at the two reporters.

"You two really had...?"

"Yes Mark. It all happened just as it's written."

"But Susan and......Mr. Flannery...this is one powerful story...and it's beautifully written." Jim and Susan smiled at one another. "I've got a ticket for you Susan, you are coming back with me tonight?"

"No Mark, I don't believe I'll be going back to New Orleans, except to visit my mother."

"What are you talking about, there'll be a promotion and...a raise after this!"

"I've been offered a position here Mark and......I've taken it." She then placed her hand in Jim's and smiled at her partner and lover.

"Oh...so that's it...you two...well, there's always a place for you at the *Sun* if you tire of the political hub."

"Thanks Mark, but Jim and I are going shopping for......for a ring."

"A RING! Boy, you two aren't wasting any time! Speaking of time I'd better get moving.....Well Miss McNeil, I guess this is goodbye." Mark hugged her and shook Jim's hand. "You're getting quite a woman here Mr. Flannery."

"Yes I know."

"Well, good luck to you both."

"Thank you Mark." Susan smiled at her ex-boss.

Mark Lane left the *Post* with the story in his briefcase. "Christ!" He thought. "Somebody will probably make a movie about those two!"

He hailed a cab and got in.

"Driver, Dulles Airport…there's an extra twenty in it if you can break the sound barrier."

"You got it mister."

Mark Lane settled back in his seat and thought about Susan. "I'll miss her, but the kid's on her way up. Talent like that doesn't come around every day."

It was Sunday 12:35am when the first run came off the press.

"Perfect. The boys downstairs did a hell of a job and we're right on schedule." Joe Muldoon then turned to Jim and Susan. "Nice job you two." He then gave each of them a hot copy of the Sunday edition. "Take off and get some rest. I'll want both of you to cover the funeral on Monday, then you're off for the holiday."

"Thanks Joe and goodnight."

"And welcome to the *Post* Miss McNeil!"

"Thanks Chief!" As she said it, the title brought back memories of the adventure in Dallas. Jim caught it also.

The two reporters picked up their luggage outside Joe Muldoon's office and exited the *Post*. They found a cab and took the short ride to Jim's apartment in Georgetown.

Jim inserted the key in the front door of the well kept brownstone. "I'm on the second floor, come on." At the top of the stairs he opened the door, turned on the light switch and stepped aside allowing Susan to enter first.

"Jim, this is beautiful." Susan put down her suitcase and walked around the large living room.

The room was tastefully decorated with a combination of Victorian antiques and modern furniture. French doors led to a small balcony overlooking a courtyard. Jim opened the doors.

"Let's get a little air in here."

He then led her to the dining room which had as the center piece, a large round tiger oak table with four upholstered chairs

"This is terrific Jim, I knew you had good taste. After all, you picked me!"

"Yeah, most of the antiques came from a great aunt who passed away two years ago. Nobody in the family wanted them, so I had them shipped down here from Newton."

He then took her hand and led her to his study. Positioned in front of a large window was a long solid looking ebony desk. On one end of it sat a telephone while on the opposite end a ROYAL typewriter.

"Someday I hope to spend some real time in here…you know, write the great American novel."

"You just lived it my dear. Now it's just a matter of getting it all down on paper…and I don't mean a newspaper story."

"Susan, we should collaborate on this…write our story…a book."

"That's a great idea sweetheart, but right now I have to find a place for myself…have my furniture and car shipped up here. I've got to start putting down some roots…I did take the job you know!"

"Why don't you uh…jusy stay…you know."

"Is this another invitation I'll have to ask myself…and give you the answer?"

"Well, kinda but…"

"But what silly?"

"But……but I love you Susan and I want you to stay here with me."

Susan beamed with happiness.

"I love you too Jim, but do you think we should live together…you know my mother is an old fashion girl and……what the heck, let's try it!"

They threw their arms around each other and consummated the arrangement with a kiss.

"That reminds me, I should call my mom." With her arms

around Jim's neck, she looked at her watch. "It's kinda late, but she is a night owl."

Jim led her to the phone on his desk.

"You're in charge of the phone bill."

"That's not a bad deal."

"And the groceries!"

"Let's shake on it Mr. Flannery."

Jim took her hand and placed it on his shoulder. He then wrapped his arms around her waist and lifted her onto the desk. He slowly unbuttoned her blouse.

"I guess that call to mom will have to wait until morning." Susan was now purring, very seductively.

Jim didn't answer as they both quickly became immersed in the passion of the moment.

LI

The engines of Haley's Comet slowed as she entered the marina at Key West. It was Sunday, 6:50am and the sun was just making its appearance.

The man at the helm found an empty slip and neatly backed in. He cut the engines and jumped out holding the black beauty by a line.

When Bannister stepped onto the dock, the helmsman named Ramon handed him a folded sheet of paper.

"The directions to the Southernmost Motel are there…it's a short walk…maybe ten minutes. Your room is number twenty-one. You'll find the key in the plant by the door. At 8:00pm tonight go to the bar at the Casa Marina…it's on Reynolds Street…order a Margarita…"

"I despise Margaritas!"

"Please Mr. Bannister, just order it and leave it on the bar in front of you. Walter will find you…good luck!" The man named Ramon got back onboard and brought the twin engines to life.

The exhaust note of Haley's Comet resonated through the morning air as the black boat slowly found its way out of Key West harbor.

Less than fifteen minutes later, Bannister found the key to room twenty-one. It was exactly where the man named Ramon said it would be.

By 10:00am, the District of Columbia was abuzz with activity after the Sunday edition of *The Washington Post* hit the streets.

Jim Flannery's and Susan McNeil's detailed accounting took the President's address to another level. As wire services got hold of the story, papers across the country were calling in their help to work overtime at getting an unheard of late Sunday edition in the hands of their readers.

At Jim's flat, Susan called her mother in New Orleans. A decision was made to fly her up to D.C. early Wednesday morning for the Thanksgiving holiday.

When Susan hung up, Jim called his family in Newton Massachusetts. They insisted that their son, his fiance and her mother join them for the holiday. Jim made the plans to leave D.C. by train on Wednesday at 4:00pm. Susan lost the debate that focused on plane versus train travel. She reasoned that the train, although at times could be romantic, in this instance with her mother along, was a highly inefficient way to go. She lost the debate. Jim hated flying.

It was 8:02pm when Bannister entered the bar at the Casa Marina. He ordered the Margarita and when it was delivered he sat and looked at it. He thought – "A real fucking faggot's drink."

"Bartender, bring me a double Jack Daniels...straight."

"Is there something wrong with the Margarita sir?"

"No there's nothing wrong with the Margarita sir. Just bring me the double...OKAY!"

"Yes sir, right away!"

When the bartender placed the double on the bar, a short stocky man dressed in a white linen suit sat on the stool next to Bannister.

"Mr. Bannister, I am Mr. Starno…Walter Starno."

"Okay bartender, you can flush the green slime now!"

The man behind the bar quickly disposed of the Margarita.

Bannister then turned to the man next to him.

"So you're Walter huh?"

"Yes my good man and I have your itinerary in order."

"My itinerary huh? How about my fucking boat ride to Cuba."

"If you insist my friend, but first there is still the small matter of money."

"Money! I've already paid LaValle!"

"That is correct sir. And now you will pay me."

"Pay you what?"

"Three thousand dollars…American, please."

"And what's this three thousand American supposed to get me that I haven't already paid for?"

"I do not know what Mr. LaValle told you my good man, but if you wish passage to Cuba along with the correct papers, you will pay now. Otherwise, I will leave and I am sure that the Federal officials here in the United States would like very much to know your whereabouts."

"Why you prick!"

"Yes. Now the money Mr. Bannister."

The big man was steaming. Out of character he kept his cool and counted out three thousand and handed it to the man in the white suit.

"Thank you Mr. Bannister. Now, on Wednesday evening at 10:00, you will meet me at the same dock where Ramon left you. There I will give you your Cuban passport and you will be taken by boat to Havana. A room at the El Floridita Hotel is reserved in the name on the passport. You will meet your contact in the lounge of your hotel the following Monday at 8:00pm. His name is Esteban Ortiz. Wait for him at the bar. He will have further instructions concerning your Tuesday departure for Buenos Aires."

"Do I have to order another fucking Margarita?"

"If you would like, that is entirely up to you. Until Wednesday at 10:00 my good man." Walter Starno bowed his head and quietly left the bar, disappearing through the foyer.

Bannister downed the double and asked for another. He thought about the money. Five thousand to LaValle and three to Starno. That left about four thousand and he hadn't even left the United States yet. "I still have a few big ones in the safe at the house.......I'll call Rhoda when I get back to the room." He downed his second drink and asked for another. He continued to ask for another and another, until he was asked to leave.

LII

The front page of *The New Orleans Sun* carried the word for word story that appeared in *The Washington Post* earlier in the day. The only exception being that Mark Lane inserted a file photo of Susan McNeil with the hopes of boosting her career. He figured it was the least he could do. Carlos Marcello had other ideas.

It was Sunday evening at 10:45 and the New Orleans mafia boss sat in his study staring at the front page. He picked up the phone.

"Canelli, it's Carlos."

"Yes Mr. Marcello, how are you?"

"Not too good. What's up with the book shop dummie?"

"Nowhere to be found. The wife knew nothing, I iced her anyways…just like you said. I'll keep looking for him if you want?"

"Put that aside for awhile, he'll surface. I need you to do another job…the front page of today's *Sun*...do you have it?"

"It's sitting right in front of me."

"Good. The article on the Kennedy mess...the girl's picture at the bottom."

"Yeah. Nice looking...she's the hit?"

"Right. And the other mick...her boyfriend...Flannery. They're in D.C., can you do it?"

"Of course. And Mr. Marcello?"

"Yeah?"

"This one's on the house, I feel I owe you one."

"Let me at least give you a few thousand for expenses. I'll send a man with an envelope."

"If you insist."

"And listen. There's no rush on this one. Enjoy the holiday with your family. After the weekend...Monday, Tuesday...whatever you can do, but please get those two."

"Consider them history."

"Good." Marcello hung up.

Bobby "Long Pockets" Canelli now had another assignment from the big boss. He was beginning to make a name for himself in the New Orleans underworld due to his precise hits. Until now, he was much more famous among his Mafia buddies as the guy with short arms and long pockets. Seems that whenever the boys went out for a few drinks, he never picked up the tab. The late Frankie "The Onion Head" Ingenito would comment: "Long pockets over there never goes for a fucking dime!"

On Monday, the President hosted dignitaries from around the world who had arrived in Washington D.C. to pay their respects to the slain Vice-President and his family.

Jim and Susan did an exceptional job of covering the ceremonies, complete with pictures for *The Washington Post*. Joe Muldoon was proud of his new addition to the staff.

Early Tuesday morning, the President along with his brother and Roger Hilsman studied the Honolulu Cappetta tapes.

"I'd like to handle this one and I'd say that Bundy and Lodge will be the only recipients of these." The President waved the envelopes containing the warrants.

The threesome sat in a conference room off the Oval Office, awaiting the arrival of the members of the Honolulu conference. In the center of the conference table sat a silver tape recorder, on loan from Mr. Cappetta.

At 9:00am they all filed into the conference room. After greetings were made, each expressed their grief and concern for Vice-President Johnson and his family. The President acknowledged all with the exception of Bundy and Lodge.

"Gentlemen, I've asked you all to come here today to listen to a rather revealing piece of tape." The President then placed his hand on the machine. They all watched in silence. "And there are some present that may become a bit uncomfortable with what they hear."

Beads of perspiration were now visible on the brow of McGeorge Bundy and the pen in Ambassador Lodge's hand was nervously tapping an irregular beat. Both got the attention of the Commander in Chief.

"However gentlemen, shall we listen?" The President asked the question, but did not wait for a response. He pressed PLAY.

The first voice heard was that of the United States Ambassador to Southeast Asia, Henry Cabot Lodge.

"Well Mac, the pullout plans of the pretty boy would have handed everything to the North on a silver platter."

"Yeah well, his days are numbered...he'll be gone and Johnson will meet with the Generals on Wednesday next week...they'll put the final touches on what I've drafted here...on NSAM 273." The President threw a cold hard stare at McGeorge Bundy.

Bundy's voice continued to fill the conference room: "Lyndon tells me that we're preparing for a long bitter war. He's looking for a way to get the American public behind him...he alluded to a plan in the Gulf of Tonkin with the Agency. If all goes well, he sends in the troops and then massive bombings in the North. This could go on for years."

"It's what the Generals and the complex want Mac...we'll all be there for the payoff."

The President then turned off the machine.

"After studying a series of these tapes, there is nothing incriminatory concerning those of you present who were not just heard. It was important that you hear this exchange so you will know what kind of criminal minds you were dealing with. You two remain in your seats," the President motioned toward Bundy and Lodge, "The rest may leave and do have a wonderful holiday gentlemen." As they slowly filed out, through their grave expressions they all returned the holiday gesture.

The President then handed both men an envelope. They each read the contents. The President then spoke:

"As the President of the United States of America, I charge you McGeorge Bundy and you Ambassador Lodge, with conspiring to commit treasonous activities against the office of the President and the Government of the United States. Do either of you have anything to say to the man who placed absolute trust in you after hand selecting you both for the posts you hold?"

There was nothing but silence in the Oval Office conference room.

"That's exactly what I thought." The President then nodded to Hilsman who pressed a call button on the table. Anderson and Scott entered.

"Mr. Anderson...Mr. Scott...would you mind cuffing these two...uh...gentlemen?"

"It'll be our pleasure Mr. President...ALL our pleasure sir."

The conspirators were then led out to a waiting car for transport to the D.C. police station. There, Assistant Chief Prosecutor Bill Dillon would set up the arraignment and formal charging. Once again, bail would be denied.

"I think that about does it for the first part of our agenda."

"What else do you have in mind Mr. President?"

"First Bobby, I'd like to do something for the man who was killed at Idlewild…you know…something for the family."

"We've checked into that and the man…Larry Merriam, had no family sir. What would you like to do?"

"Well, let's provide a burial of some kind. Bobby, would you have Miss Lincoln arrange for that?"

"Yes of course. Anything else sir?"

"The appointments…yours and Roger's…and Colonel Prouty to Roger's post at the State Department. Oh, and Chief Malinsky…he's the only one who has yet to give me an answer."

"We have his answer. I took the call and he declined. He said he's very happy serving in his present position. He also told me that you could call on him at anytime for anything."

"Well, if that's what the man wants…at least we still have him with us in some capacity. However, I've sent my recommendation to Congress to waive protocol on all appointments due to the nature of the events in Dallas and here in Washington. I more or less told them that I had already made the appointments and that I was leaving the formalities in their hands."

"Have you heard anything yet sir?"

"Yes Roger, as a matter of fact I have. Tip O'Neil informs me that there has been no opposition to my request…and that he and many others expected that I would move in this manner considering the circumstances. So, as the President I would say that it's a done deal. Welome aboard Mr. Attorney General and Mr. Vice-President!"

The three men shook hands as they left the conference room and entered the Oval Office.

"Hyannisport is sounding real good about now. We're getting an early start Wednesday and I think I'm going to take the kids sailing. You have a wonderful holiday Roger and my best to your family."

"Thank you sir and you too. A peaceful holiday to both of you and your families."

Roger Hilsman left the Oval Office feeling much more at ease.

He thought – "We've accomplished our mission and it's now time to spend a few quiet days with the family." He smiled as he left the White House. He never entertained a thought about Cuba.

On Wednesday, a little after 9:00am, the President and his two brothers along with their families, left the White House aboard two Presidential helicopters for the trip to the Hyannisport compound. The return to the salt of the sea always had a calming effect on the President. After the nightmare of Dallas, it couldn't have come at a better time.

LIII

At 4:00pm Wednesday afternoon, Jim along with Susan and her mother boarded the train for Newton, Massachusetts. Earlier they had lunch at Jim's apartment in Georgetown where Susan made sandwiches and her mother expressed her displeasure with their living arrangements. Susan tried to get one by her mom with a feeble explanation of her love for the second bedroom. Mrs. McNeil wasn't buying it.

After all the back and forth, Susan decided to herself that her mom would just have to get used to it and eventually she would. On the other hand Jim said nothing. He did all he could to make his future mother-in-law comfortable.

By the time they arrived in Newton, Susan's mom had taken a real liking to Jim. During the trip, he asked her to accompany them to a jewelry store in Boston to assist her daughter in selecting a ring. He also talked about a house in the suburbs, raising kids and all the necessary things that a mother wants for her daughter. With Jim's charm and love for Susan, the elder McNeil quickly accepted their living arrangements.

At 10:00pm Bannister strolled down the dock to the designated slip. Walter Starno was standing next to an old fishing boat talking to a tall curly haired man with a deep tan.

"Mr. Bannister, I would like you to meet Javier. For this leg of your journey my good man, he is your guide."

"Yeah, good to meet you…Javier."

"Senor Bannister, it is a pleasure. Please, get onboard sir."

The big man stepped on the fishing boat which smelled like the day's catch.

"Don't you ever clean this fucking thing…it stinks!"

"Mr. Bannister, you are embarking on a ninety mile trip that will take less than three hours. And during that time, I am quite sure that you will become accustomed to the smell. I am told that the stench of rotten fish performs wonders on the human sinus. Enjoy your journey Mr. Bannister."

Bannister did not answer. Instead, he pulled out his .44 and pointed it directly at Starno.

"That will not help Mr. Bannister. Once again, as Mr. LaValle had warned you before, your escape relies on you my good man, maintaining your composure and steering clear of rash decisions."

Bannister placed the big .44 back in his belt.

"Good. That is a wise choice. And I nearly forgot, here is your Cuban passport." Starno handed Bannister the passport which he opened immediately. "For your stay in Havana, you will go by the name of Jose Melendez. If it so happens that you become attached to your assumed name, arrangements can be made for you to keep it for the remainder of your pilgrimage to South America."

"One question."

"Yes Mr. Bannister?"

"Where and how did you get this picture of me?" Bannister held open the passport.

"We have our sources my good man."

At that moment Javier started the engines of the old fishing boat. The area quickly became immersed in a thick blue smoke.

When it cleared, Walter Starno had disappeared. The old boat then chugged through Key West harbor and began the ninety mile journey to Havana.

LIV

Thanksgiving as usual was a day of eating and family games. When Friday morning rolled around the President was eager to set sail. He scooped up John Jr. and took Caroline by the hand and headed for the dock. Their uncle Bobby, the new Vice-President also went along.

The air was crisp and the sea was a bit choppy but everyone onboard had a good time. The President adored the sea and there he gave his children their first real lesson in seamanship. The little ones each spent time at the helm and they were also introduced to the intricacies of the sport. The kids were catching on quick and the President felt that someday his son would be a fine sailor. It was a great way to spend the holiday.

From the shore, the usual number of Secret Service agents kept watch on the President. In addition there was a newcomer sitting on a rock overlooking Nantucket Sound. The newcomer was Peter Cappetta and he never once took his eyes off the President's boat.

When they returned from a very pleasurable holiday in New England, Jim and Susan put her mom in a cab for Dulles Airport. Susan promised to get down to New Orleans as soon as possible for a visit and her mom promised to arrange for the contents of Susan's apartment to be shipped to D.C., Susan would have to tend to her car through the Lake Charles police. That evening, Jim thought it was the right time to break the news to Susan.

"Susan, would you have a seat here please?....there's something I need to tell you."

Susan jumped on the couch. "Sure, what's on your mind?" She held out her left hand, "This is such a beautiful ring...thank you sweetheart."

"You're welcome...yes it is very nice...uh...Susan, I'll be away tomorrow on an assignment."

"Oh yeah, where to?"

"Havana."

"Havana! As in Havana, Cuba?"

"Yup. The President requested that I accompany him along with Mr. Hilsman...he wants me to report on the meeting with Castro. We leave tomorrow morning at 6:00am."

"Castro! That's wonderful...what an opportunity...I had no idea that the President was looking to close the wounds with Cuba. That is what the trip is about isn't it?"

"Yes it is... and you're not upset?"

"Why would I be upset? Your career is really taking off...this is wonderful...and so is mine."

"What do you mean?"

"Chief Muldoon gave me an assignment at the Senate for the next two days...I'm thrilled to death!"

"The Senate! But that's my beat!"

"I know. He gave it to me because you'll be away...I didn't tell you because I was afraid YOU would be upset. You'll be with the President and Castro...how exciting...this is history in the making...and you're worried about the Senate!"

Jim felt dumb. "Pretty silly huh?"

"Yeah silly, you really are. It's probably why I love you so much."

"Why?"

"Because you get goofy over the silliest things."

"I'm not goofy! Am I?"

"Of course silly, now come over here."

Jim quickly slid across to Susan's side of the couch, leaned over to the end table and turned out the light. The only light came from the rays of the full moon through the French doors.

"Ooooh, Mr. Flannery!"

"Yes Miss McNeil?"

"Lower."

"Gotcha."

LV

Captain Jayson Cutler had Air Force One ready for departure from Dulles Airport. It was 5:55am, Monday December 2, 1963.

The President's secretary had taken care of all the arrangements for the trip. Hilsman, Flannery and Cappetta, along with twelve Secret Service agents would accompany the President on the one day excursion to Havana Cuba.

At 6:05am, the President's limo pulled up alongside Air Force One escorted by the team of Secret Service agents.

When everyone was aboard, Captain Cutler taxied Air Force One to the runway, and as usual, he lifted the big jet off with the grace of the bird on the Presidential Seal.

In the Presidential quarters, the President sat at his desk going over the presentation of his plans concerning the lifting of the embargo with Roger Hilsman. The President picked up his buzzing and flashing phone.

"Good morning Captain!"

"Good morning Mr. President. Just want to let you know the schedule sir. Weather permitting, we should be touching down in Havana at 9:10am."

"Thank you Captain."

"Your welcome sir. If there's anything you need, just call."

"Yes, as a matter of fact there is. When we're within range, radio ahead to Havana and see if you can find out if the limos they're using are hardtops or convertibles."

"Yes sir, as soon as I get something I'll ring you."

"Thanks Captain." As the President hung up, Hilsman quickly got to his feet.

"I overlooked that sir! How could I…"

"Don't worry about a thing Roger…please…sit down. I really don't think it matters what we're riding in. In all likelihood, uh…Mr Castro will have our limos surrounded with his militia. He'll take every precaution to avoid an international incident…after Dallas. He's a smart man…and I'll bet he's looking for the world to view his beloved island in a new light. These talks will be very enlightening Roger…and I'm glad Flannery is with us to bring the story back."

"Yes…and what was your take on the hot-line conversation with the Kremlin sir?"

"Well, you know Roger…with the translators on the line and all, the conversation becomes…shall I say…for the lack of a better word, disjointed. However, overall I thought Khrushchev seemed very positive. He did suggest that if all went well in Havana…that a summit should be arranged involving our three countries."

"Did he have a venue in mind?"

"No. But in my phone conversation with Prime Minister Macmillan, he extended the invitation to host the talks in Great Britain, which I believe would be ideal. Having the Prime Minister involved…kind of equalizes the representation of our contrasting systems of government."

"I like this Mr. President. This is very encouraging."

"Yes Roger it is. I believe we're on a very good path here."

The phone on the President's desk buzzed and flashed.

"Excuse me Roger...... Yes Captain?"

"Mr. President, sunny and warm in Havana with open top limos sir!"

"Thank you Captain."

As the President hung up, he stared at Hilsman.

"Convertibles."

LVI

At 9:05am, Air Force One touched down on Cuban soil. It was the first time since early 1963, when the President sent U.S. Representative James Britt Donovan to meet with Fidel Castro. Donovan successfully negotiated the release of over 1,200 imprisoned Cuban exiles from the Bay of Pigs fiasco. In exchange, the United States paid out over $50 million in medicine and aid to bring back the freedom fighters. The deal ultimately added to the tensions between the United States and Cuba which led the American President to seek his present path toward an easing of those tensions and peace.

As the President exited Air Force One, he was greeted by hundreds of Cubans at the Havana Airport. In perfect unison they chanted – "PRES-SI-DENT KEN-NE-DY, PRES-SI-DENT KEN-NE-DY." As he waved to the crowd, they became even louder.

The cheering continued as the President got into the backseat of the open top limousine with Roger Hilsman on his left. Jim

Flannery and Pete Cappetta sat in the jumpseat behind the driver.

Limos for the twelve Secret Service agents sat in front and behind the Presidential car. However, six of the agents were instructed by Hilsman to ride on the doors and trunk of the President's car and to shield him as much as possible.

Again the President was right. When the mini-motorcade got underway, a total of eight troop transport trucks filled with uniformed members of Castro's militia, surrounded the limos and led them on the slow ride to the Palace of the Presidente.

As the motorcade entered the Palace square, throngs of Cubans continued the chant heard at the airport – "PRES-SI-DENT KEN-NE-DY."

The President waved to the crowd as the motorcade came to a halt at the Palacio del Gobierno. As he exited the limo, he noticed at the top of a long flight of stairs, the President of Cuba.

After making the fifty step climb surrounded by Secret Service agents and Cappetta glued to his side, the President was now face to face with Fidel Castro.

"Welcome to my country Mr. President Kennedy!" He extended his hand in peace.

"Thank you Mr. Presidente. Your people," The President looked out over the square, "I wasn't expecting such a warm welcome."

"My people have developed a great respect for you Mr. President. They know that your efforts toward peace and unification will be beneficial to their lives. Come, let me show you my Palace." As the two leaders disappeared through the main entrance to the Palace, the throngs continued their chant in support of the American President.

Fidel Castro then led the Presidential entourage on a personal tour of his stately residence.

The tour ended when they entered a large conference hall with domed ceiling and a long table in the center, capable of seating as many as fifty people. At the end of the large room were ornate glass doors, which were fully opened leading to a balcony overlooking the square.

Inside the glass doors were six stuffed chairs arranged around a large coffee table. One of the chairs was a rocker.

On the walls were large paintings in ornate gold frames of Jose Marti, Che Guevara and Fidel Castro.

Castro then led the President to the seating area next to the glass doors.

"This one is for you Mr. President." He motioned toward the rocker. "And when our talks are complete, it is my gift to you. My hopes are that you will find use for it in the great White House."

"That is very kind and generous of you Mr. Presidente. It will have it's place in my home."

The two leaders were easing their way into the formal discussions when Jim Flannery and Roger Hilsman joined them. When they did, Fidel's brother Raul took the seat next to President Kennedy.

Two Secret Service agents took up positions on the balcony, while outside the conference hall the other agents were given chairs. That left Cappetta. When asked by a Cuban official, he refused to leave the room. So he took a seat at the long conference table. He wasn't letting the President out of his sight for a moment.

The first topic of discussion focused on the embargo. An agreement was reached that allowed 90% of participating American businesses to function in every city on the island with the exception of Havana where the other 10% were allowed to operate. The reason for this was to employ as many as possible in the poorer outlying areas. In addition, from those businesses a 7% tax on everything exported would be payable to the Cuban government on a quarterly basis. The plan then called for the United States to purchase a small percentage of the yearly Cuban sugar production and a percentage figure to be named later concerning rum and cigar exports. Just as the subject of cigars was approached, a short heavy set man in what one would assume was the Cuban rendition of a butler's outfit entered the hall. He was carrying a large humidor filled with the finest Cuban cigars, which he opened and made his first offering to the President. Of course the President indulged as did Hilsman and Flannery. When offered to Cappetta he replied – "I never touch the stuff, thank you."

As the large room filled with smoke, the two leaders continued their talks. Up to this point they had little difficulty in reaching agreement concerning the lifting of the embargo. The rest of the talks would benefit from this. Every area discussed whether it be the Soviet Union, Southeast Asia, the Congo, or Central America, they were all dealt with the single goal in mind that would benefit all, peace.

Jim Flannery recorded everything. Periodically he directed a question toward the Cuban leader, but for the most part he took notes. On the other hand, Roger Hilsman's experience in the State Department kept him up to speed with foreign policy and he was instrumental in touching on areas of concern that the President may have overlooked. Time was flying by. It was 12:50pm so the talks were adjourned for lunch in the Palace dining room.

After dining on grilled prawns in a carmelized sauce and garden salad served with a fine white French Bordeaux, the leaders returned to the conference hall to continue their negotiations. The subject of Central America was now a hot topic with Hilsman and the President.

It was agreed upon that the Cuban leader would assist the Americans in moving U.S. businesses into as many areas as possible in Central America, in an effort to educate and employ those in need. This sphere of discussion continued until 5:00pm. There the talks were halted with the promise to continue by both sides at a later date in Washington D.C.

The President and his small staff were then shown to their quarters for rest and freshening up before the 7:00pm dinner in the Palace dining room.

Outside their rooms, the President convinced Cappetta to take the evening off and visit the nightspots in Havana. Cappetta reluctantly agreed.

"Air Force One is scheduled to leave at 10:00pm…so Mr. Cappetta, enjoy the nightlife in Havana while you have the chance."

"Thank you sir, but are you sure you won't be needing me? You know there are a few people here that I just don't trust sir."

"Don't worry Mr. Cappetta, I'll be fine…go on, have a good time and uh…you might want to try the El Floridita Hotel…if memory serves me correctly from a trip in '57…the lounge there was a pretty hot spot."

"The El Floridita…hmm…I'll try it sir!"

At 7:00pm, the President, Roger Hilsman and Jim Flannery attended the dinner in honor of the President in the Palace dining room. At 7:15pm, Pete Cappetta left the Palace and walked to the El Floridita Hotel.

LVII

The sandwich board on the sidewalk was plastered with photos that Cappetta knew well. He had difficulty reading the Spanish but he was well-acquainted with the woman's picture and her name.

He met Laura Collins when she sang at the Copacabana in New York in 1957. She was the star attraction and from the moment they were introduced, they carried on a torrid affair that was cut short when she left the city seven months later. When she disappeared without any warning, his life was never the same. He always felt that she left for another man, but the truth was that her ties with organized crime were responsible for her departure.

At that time the Mafia boss running the club and casino activities in Havana was Santos Trafficante. He also had a piece of the Copa in New York where he made frequent visits in search of new talent for export to the Cuban operations. When the Copa signed Miss Collins, little did she know that she had become the property of Mr.Trafficante. In Havana, she again became the number one draw until 1959 when Castro's revolution hit. The new Cuban leader then gave the Mafia their walking papers and by that time Miss Collins had taken a shine to life in Havana. When the turmoil of the revolution had settled down, she signed on with the El Floridita where she continued to pack the house.

He stared at the pictures and thought about the times he spent with the only woman he ever loved. Against his will, he turned and entered.

It was 7:55pm and the lounge was nearly filled to capacity in anticipation of the 8:00pm show. Cappetta found a small table in the back of the lounge. He wanted to be as far from the stage as possible. When the waiter took his order for a gin martini, the lights faded over the tables and a spotlight was focused on the lovely Miss Collins.

She opened with an old favorite that Cappetta remembered well:

"Set em up Joe!"

"Make it one for my baby,"

"And one more for the road."

He listened to the number that one time brought a smile to his face. This time his eyes swelled with tears. He picked up his drink and walked to the bar. It was farther from the stage but her voice still echoed through the memories.

As she finished her opening number she saw him sitting at the bar. It had been over five years but she knew it was him. She reminisced of their times together midway through her second song where she stumbled and missed a beat. Quickly regaining her composure, she went on to finish a third song. She then placed the mike in its stand and took her first break.

When she got to the bar, he stood and stared. Words were in short supply for both. She spoke first.

"I saw you from the……"

"Please……" He pulled the stool out for her to sit.

"It's been a long time Peter. You're looking well."

"Thanks. You look wonderful Laura…you haven't changed. I had my reservations about coming in here tonight…I guess curiosity got the best of me."

"I'm glad you did…it's so good to see you!"

"It is? Seems to me you didn't feel that way five years ago when you disappeared without even a phone call."

"Please Peter, don't go there. You don't know the circumstances…it was out of my control."

"Was it another man?"

"Of course not! I loved you!"

"Forgive me if I'm prying…then what was it? I think I'm entitled to that much."

As Laura Collins searched for the words to explain, Cappetta saw a man at the opposite end of the bar that looked very familiar. He could only see the side of the large man's face through the rising cigarette smoke and he was talking to a tall thin man. He knew it was him.

"I don't believe it, he's here…in Havana!"

"Who's here?"

"Uhhh…an old friend…he's at the other end of the bar." Cappetta couldn't take his eyes off the man.

"Buy him a drink and invite him over if you'd like!"

"He's not that kind of friend." He continued to stare.

"Peter, why are you here in Cuba? Are you in some kind of trouble?"

"Trouble! No. My new position in life is to prevent trouble. I work for the Government now." He continued to stare at the man.

"The Cuban Government?"

"No Laura, the American Government. Let's just say that I kinda work as the President's personal agent. Everywhere he goes, I go."

"He's here today…with Castro…that's why you're…"

"Yes and that man over there had a big part in the attempt on the President's life…in Dallas. I'm sure you read about it."

"Yes. He was very lucky to escape that horrible…that man was part of it? Were you there?"

"Yes he was part of it and yes I was there. It was something I'll never forget."

"Didn't a man push the President out of the way just as the shot was fired?"

"Yes he did."

"The papers down here never gave the man's name. Seems to me he was the hero and he receives no recognition!"

"He preferred it that way. Excuse me Laura." The big man was now alone. The tall thin man he was talking to had gone.

"Where are you going? Are you going to arrest him?"

"Something like that." Cappetta picked up his drink and walked to the far end of the bar.

When he reached his destination he placed his drink down. The bartender stood directly in front of him, blocking his reflection in the mirror. The big man's taped left hand was resting on the edge of the bar when Cappetta grabbed it and squeezed. The man's face contorted in pain.

"Fancy meeting you here Mr. Bannister!"

"I don't…ug…ahhh…believe we…..ahhh…we've met." The pain was intense as Cappetta continued to squeeze until blood seeped through the bandages.

"Yes we have. Does the parking lot behind the Trade-Mart ring a bell? It should, after all, I believe you left something of importance behind that connected to this!" And he squeezed harder.

"Why you…it was you!" He could hardly speak. His hand was on fire with pain.

A half bottle of Jack Daniels sat on the bar in front of Bannister. He slowly placed his right hand around the neck of the bottle and swung across his body to his left, striking Cappetta's forehead dead center. Cappetta released his grip and fell backward, landing on the floor. As he struggled to get to his feet, he fell to the floor again. Bannister pushed his way through the crowd, quickly exited the lounge and disappeared down a sidestreet.

When Laura got to Cappetta, he was still on the floor in a semi-conscious state. As he lifted his head, blood trickled in his eyes and down his left cheek from the wound to his forehead. She knelt by his side.

"Peter! Peter!"

"Yeah…yeah…I'm alright." He got to his feet and took a wad of napkins off the bar and wiped the blood from his cheeks and eyes. "Where did he go?"

"He just ran out…let him go…here." She handed him a clean bar towel. He threw it down on the floor and headed to the door.

When he reached the street, he looked both left and right. He saw nothing but two older women walking arm in arm. They appeared from the street that ran alongside the El Floridita. He rushed toward them.

"Americano…hombre…largo Americano…did you see him?" With his hands and arms he described a large man.

They understood and pointed in the direction from which they just came. "Por alla!"

As Cappetta ran down the sidestreet, Laura Collins exited the hotel and stood in front not knowing which way to go. She then heard his voice in the distance bellowing through the balmy night air.

"BANNISTER……BANNISTER……I'M HERE!"

She followed the voice.

Wild with anger from the latest incident with the big man, Cappetta ran blindly down the dark sidestreet. Suddenly, with no warning an arm appeared from an alley hitting Cappetta square in the face and knocking him on his back. Again, as in Dallas he was looking up at his attacker.

"I don't know who you are, but you've pissed me off one too many times!" Bannister pulled the .44 from his belt. As he cocked the trigger aiming the big gun at Cappetta, Laura Collins jumped on the back of the burly gunman. An errant shot rang out as the singer struggled desperately to hang onto Bannister's right arm.

Cappetta then flew to his feet with the agility of a cat and managed to get hold of the big man's right arm just as he tossed the singer off his back. As the two men struggled, a second shot rang out. This one found a target.

The sheer force of the .44 magnum lifted Laura Collins off her feet, driving her backwards and depositing her lithe frame in the middle of the cobblestone street.

The struggle continued as they wrestled in the dark until the gun dropped to the street. The two men followed with Cappetta landing on the big man's back. Grabbing Bannister's left arm and twisting it around his big torso, Cappetta called on his last ounce of strength until the big man's left arm cracked at the elbow. Bannister roared in pain and in one last effort to free himself, violently threw his bare right elbow around striking Cappetta's nose and rendering him unconscious. At that moment, sirens could be heard approaching the scene.

The big man got to his feet and with his right hand picked up the gun and tried to run. The pain in his left arm and hand was fierce. The left arm dangled at his side as his large silhouette could be seen lumbering through the darkness and finally fading into the night.

As the Cuban police car rounded the corner, Cappetta got to his feet. He saw the still body of Laura Collins lying face up in the street. He rushed to her side as the police car screeched to a halt. He placed his arms around her back and lifted, her head dangled backwards. He then placed his face in her neck as the tears flowed from his eyes.

"Laura! Laura! I'm so sorry…forgive me." She did not answer. He felt for a pulse…nothing.

"Senor…Senor…" The Cuban policeman then said something that Cappetta did not understand.

"Americano…largo…that way!" He pointed in the direction that Bannister ran off.

The cop then shoved his gun in Cappetta's back directing him toward the waiting patrol car. Cappetta resisted.

"No! You don't understand…the man who shot her got away…he went that way…we have to find him!" Again Cappetta pointed in the direction.

The policeman had no idea what the American was trying to say, he only knew that he was guilty.

When he pushed him into the backseat of the patrol car, two more police cars pulled up, both carrying two Cuban cops. They all exited their cars and one of them said something to the first cop. Cappetta watched from the backseat as the five policeman stood over the body of the woman he still loved.

LVIII

It was 10:10pm when the car entered the lot of the Havana Police station. On the way, Cappetta pleaded with the cop to search for Bannister but to no avail. The language barrier had him frustrated. He couldn't make the cop understand. Also, through his frustration he had completely forgotten about the President and Air Force One. All he could think of was her body lying in the street.

When they insisted on taking his watch before entering the cell, he looked at it for the first time since he entered the El Floridita lounge. It was 10:20pm and Air Force One was scheduled to leave at 10:00. Again he tried to reason with the cops but they were having none of it. After pushing him in the cell, the arresting officer made a comment that Cappetta understood completely. "Senorita Laura Collins…you Senor…kill!" He then paused, "You Senor…Queremos verte muerto!" He then made the motion of running his hand from one side of his neck to the other.

" Roger, something must have happened...he should have been here a half hour ago. Driver! The El Floridita Hotel...PRONTO!"

"Si, Senor Presidente!"

The President's limo sped off to the El Floridita, closely followed by the two limos carrying the team of Secret Service agents.

When they pulled up at the hotel, Roger Hilsman got out and instructed three agents to check the lounge for Cappetta.

Three minutes later they returned.

"Mr. Hilsman sir, the bartender spoke English...he told us that a man fitting the description I gave had a fight with a large man with a heavily bandaged left hand...he said the big man left followed by the man I described...and get this...he said our man called the big guy...are you ready sir...BANNISTER!"

"How could that be?"

"I don't know sir but he also said that moments after the two left...the singer," The agent pointed to the sandwich board on the sidewalk, "followed and then there were sirens heading in that direction." The agent then pointed to the sidestreet.

"Let's go!" Hilsman and the agents got back in their limos.

Hilsman called out to the driver – "Driver, that way!" He pointed to the street alongside the hotel.

"Mr. President sir, it seems that Cappetta is on the trail of ...of all people sir...Bannister!"

Jim Flannery responded before the President had a chance. "Bannister! What on earth is he..."

The three limos then came to a stop behind the two police cars and an ambulance, all with flashing lights.

"Mr. President, please stay in the car." Hilsman then looked at Flannery, "Jim, it's time to use that Spanish again."

"Right." As Hilsman and Flannery stepped out, Hilsman motioned to the men in the other limos to guard the President. The President's car was quickly surrounded by the twelve Secret Service agents.

After a brief conversation between Flannery and one of the Cuban police, they returned to the President's car.

"Mr. President, he's at the Havana Police station."

"Who is?"

"Mr. Cappetta sir."

"Why?"

"They're saying that he murdered a woman sir." Flannery pointed to a stretcher being placed in the ambulance.

"So what about Bannister?"

"I don't know. They say they found Cappetta and the dead woman at the scene…they took him to the station…they know nothing of Bannister…he must have gotten away again sir."

"Have the driver radio to the Palace…I'll speak to Mr. Castro…and let's get to the police station."

"Yes sir!"

As the President's cars were speeding to the Havana Police station, Bannister was slowly finding his way through the dockyard. He found an empty skidplate to rest on behind a row of crates containing refined Cuban sugar. The crates were to be loaded aboard the *Rio Escondido* at sunrise for export to South America. It was also Bannister's ride.

The big man removed a tarp from one of the crates and with his knife he fashioned a sling for his broken left arm. He slipped the sling over his head and tried to bend his left arm at the elbow. The bones were shattered at the elbow and the pain was excruciating. He then remembered the pills. Digging into his left pocket with his right hand he pulled out the small vial from Dr. Audette. He counted out four pills, threw them in his mouth, chewed and swallowed.

After waiting what seemed an eternity, fifteen minutes later the pills began to perform their magic. He then bent his arm at the elbow and placed it in the sling. His mind was numbed, cutting off the signal to his brain from the throbbing left arm.

As he lay on the skidplate the thoughts of money swirled through his mind. "I'm down to less than $3,000 and I haven't been able to contact Rhoda. It'll have to wait until I get to South America."

With the help of Dr. Audette's medication, the big man lazily drifted off to a deep sleep.

Jim Flannery spoke with the arresting officer in the man's native tongue. Once again he was having none of it. As far as he was concerned, Cappetta was guilty of murdering the very popular singer and he would pay the price. The cop alluded to the fact that the firing squad was in order.

"Mr. Hilsman sir, I'm getting nowhere with this man. He's already talking quick justice…the firing squad! Has anything come of the President's conversation with Mr. Castro?"

Just then the President entered the station surrounded by the twelve Secret Service agents.

"Roger, Jim uh…Mr. Castro is on his way here right now. We'll get this thing straightened out…we're not leaving this island without that man. Roger, send two of your men to the El Floridita and have them bring back the bartender. We need him to corroborate Mr. Cappetta's story. He's the only one who's seen Bannister that has so far come forward…and with no gun at the scene…they have no case."

"Right sir." Hilsman sent his two best agents on the job then continued. "Mr. Flannery is having a difficult time with the cop sir…they're talking firing squad!"

"What!"

"Yes sir…they uh…they do things a little differently down here."

"I know they do Roger…but they have nothing to…"

As the President was about to finish his statement, three machine gun toting guards entered the station followed by the Presidente of Cuba. Three more guards brought up the rear.

"Mr. President, I rushed here as soon as I got your call."

"Thank you for coming so quickly. There's a matter here that I believe requires your attention."

The President and Hilsman then filled him in on the events of the evening. The Cuban police did the same with their leader.

"You see Mr. President, the problem here is that your man was the only person at the scene of the crime and the murdered ex-patriot American singer became something of a national treasure for my country."

Hilsman cut in. "But Mr. Presidente, the evidence against Mr. Cappetta is purely circumstantial…the murder weapon has not been found…and when my men return with the bartender from the El Floridita, he will be able to support the premise that another man was involved…the man who shot the singer and escaped. We know who that man is...his name is Bannister."

"I see Mr. Hilsman." The Cuban leader now had an angry look on his face. "You have taken it upon yourself to have your American agents perform a…an apprehension of a Cuban citizen while you are here as my guest?"

"Forgive me for interrupting Mr. Presidente, but it was I who instructed Mr. Hilsman to send for the bartender. I knew that as soon as you arrived, you would have seen the necessity of his presence and you would I believe sir…have done the same. I was in no way overstepping your power and authority…I was merely expediting the matter."

"Your reasoning is very logical Mr. President and I appreciate your honesty…I believe that you were looking to save me the needless aggravation of waiting for the witness to arrive. I may have acted as you Americans would say…a bit rash. Please accept my apologies Mr. Hilsman."

"Of course Mr. Presidente."

No sooner had Hilsman finished, when the two agents and the bartender entered the station.

When questioned by the Cuban leader, the bartender gave his account of what he knew. Hilsman, Flannery and the President watched and listened as they spoke in Spanish. Flannery understood the entire conversation. However, the President and Hilsman heard only one word that came from the mouth of the bartender that they understood – 'Bannister.'

"Mr. President, I have made my decision…further investigations are required into this affair. We will put out an alert for this man Bannister...we will want to question him. My country as you know does not treat murderers lightly and I am not quite satisfied with the explanation that I am hearing. But," and he pointed his index finger straight up in the air, "I will release the prisoner in your custody...and if our investigation should point in the direction of his guilt...I fully expect that extradition will not present a problem. And Mr. President, I would hate to think that the progress made here today...between our two countries, could be jeopardized by such an ordeal."

"I fully agree and you have my word on that."

The Cuban leader then gave a signal to the arresting officer and within moments Cappetta appeared. The two leaders then shook hands as the Presidential entourage boarded the limos for the ride to the airport.

It was 11:35pm when Air Force One left the Havana Airport with Cappetta on board. At that very moment in Washington D.C., the doorbell rang at Jim Flannery's apartment in Georgetown. Susan used the intercom.

"Yes, who is it?"

"Police ma'am. D.C. Police!"

"Police! Just a moment I'll be right down."

When she reached the bottom of the stairs she quickly pulled open the outside door revealing a policeman with red hair and a moustache. He was short with a medium build and held his hat in his hand.

"Yes officer, how can I help you?"

"Well ma'am, we've been investigating the two murders that occurred in this area over the last week and do you mind answering a few questions?"

"Officer, isn't it an odd hour to be questioning residents? Don't you usually do that at a more reasonable time of day?"

"Your absolutely right ma'am...but sometimes we can't get a hold of everyone because of their work schedules. Now in your situation ma'am, I tried you three times earlier...at a more reasonable hour and no one was home."

Susan thought about what the man just said – "He's right, I was at the paper until a little before ten getting the Senate story out."

"Yes officer you're right, my job kept me very busy tonight. What is it that I can do to help you?"

"Like I said ma'am, just a few questions." The officer opened a small pad to take notes, he then looked up and around. "Geez, a little dark out here…I can't see my pad!"

"Officer, please come in…it'll be easier inside."

"Thank you ma'am, this will only take a few minutes." He stepped in and closed the door behind him.

"This way officer." Susan led the policeman who she thought had a touch of a Louisiana accent, up the stairs to the apartment.

"Nice place ya got here ma'am."

"Thank you, just make yourself comfortable officer."

Bobby "Long Pockets" Canelli found a chair and made himself very comfortable.

"Yeah, real nice ma'am."

LIX

Air Force One touched the tarmac at Dulles Airport at 2:25am. It was a long day for the President and his men. Most had slept through the entire flight.

The limo's first stop was the White House where the President gave further instructions to his driver.

"Mr. Garrett, please see these gentlemen to their homes. I'll see you all at our meeting tomorrow…excuse me…today at 3:00pm. Goodnight gentlemen, get some rest."

Mr. Garrett then stopped at Roger Hilsman's residence and continued on to Georgetown.

"Peter, why don't you stay with Susan and I tonight? I know the ride to your place from Georgetown is a little over an hour. You can take the spare bedroom."

Cappetta thought that being around people might be the best way to keep Laura Collins off his mind. "I think I'll take you up on that Jim…thank you. Are you sure it won't be too much of a bother?"

"After what you've been through, a good night's sleep and one of Susan's southern style breakfasts is just what the doctor ordered."

"Say no more."

Moments later, the limo dropped Flannery and Cappetta at the brownstone in Georgetown.

"You know Jim, it's such a nice night I think I'll take a short walk. I won't be long."

"I'll leave this door open, just come right up."

"Thanks."

Jim went up the stairs to his apartment and Cappetta strolled down the tree lined street. He needed the time alone to think. The memories of Laura Collins shattered in the streets of Havana began to haunt him. He wondered if he would have been better off had he gone directly home. Right now he wanted to be alone. He headed back to Jim's place with the intention of thanking him for the offer. He'd call a cab and go home.

As he approached the brownstone, he saw the silhouettes in the second floor window. He recognized the tall thin figure as Flannery, but he thought, "The short one couldn't be Susan…it's a man's body…and he has a gun!"

He ran to the front entrance and stopped. He turned and ran along the side of the house to a courtyard in the rear. The gate was locked. He quickly scaled the fence. Looking up he saw a small balcony and two glass doors. There was a trellis leading to the balcony. He climbed it. When he reached the top he looked through the glass doors. The end table light was the only light on in the room. In the corner of the room Susan was tied to a chair with a gag in her mouth. He slowly opened the glass door. When Susan saw him he placed his finger over his mouth. He slipped the gag from her mouth and motioned for her not to speak. He then heard voices and followed the sounds to the master bedroom.

"I'm just gonna finish tying you up and then you can watch the show…Mr. Reporter! Your little lady there is a sweet dish…I'll bet she'll be a lotta fun and just think…you'll have a front row seat!" After tying up Flannery, 'Long Pockets' picked up the small caliber silenced .380 and left the bedroom. "Here I come you sweet thing!"

He began whistling "Zipadee-doodah" on his way to the living room. Just as he turned the corner from the hallway, Cappetta's fist struck the short man's neck below the chin. 'Long Pockets' hit the floor sliding across the room. As he gasped for air, Cappetta landed on top of the man dressed like a cop. The little hitman was no match for the muscular Cappetta but he still hung onto his gun. A shot went off as Cappetta lifted the man to his feet and drove him like a cowboy tackling a steer to the front window and through the glass. Cappetta stood alone in the room. He then went to the bedroom and untied Jim.

"Susan needs you…go untie her." When Jim left the room, Cappetta tried to follow, but the bullet lodged in his abdomen caused his knees to buckle. Jim didn't see him in his haste to get to Susan.

When Jim had untied Susan, they stood in the living room wrapped in each other's arms. Jim turned to the hallway and called out for Cappetta.

"Peter…Peter." There was no answer. Jim and Susan looked at one another then turned and ran to the hallway outside the master bedroom.

Cappetta's body was stretched out on a throw rug which was now covered with blood. He held his stomach as he tried to speak.

"A doctor Jim…get me to…" Then nothing.

Jim felt for a pulse, it was faint. Susan ran to the phone in Jim's study and called the police. She instructed them to send an ambulance as quickly as possible and gave the address.

Jim held a towel to Cappetta's stomach and pressed in an effort to control the bleeding until the medical team arrived. They then heard the sound of sirens approaching.

"I'll go down and open the door." When Susan got to the

bottom of the stairs she found the door open. She then directed the medics up the stairs. After a quick preliminary exam, a breathing apparatus was placed over Cappetta's mouth. They put him on a stretcher and quickly transported him to the waiting ambulance which sped off as soon as the doors were closed.

In the street, Jim stood over the body of Bobby 'Long Pockets' Canelli. His head was crushed to half it's original size. Jim mumbled out loud as Susan held his arm, "He must have landed head first…who is this guy?"

"That's exactly what I'd like to know. Captain McDuffie, D.C. Police, maybe you two can shed a little light here."

Jim turned to see the policeman flashing his badge.

"Hey! Aren't you the two reporters who did the story on the President…and Dallas…and all that?"

"That's right, this is Susan McNeil and I'm Jim Flannery and I'll tell you what Captain…you take us where our friend in that ambulance is going and we'll tell you the whole story."

"Hop in!"

Captain McDuffie then instructed his men to take over the crime scene as he got behind the wheel of the D.C. patrol car and followed the ambulance.

"Now from the beginning Mr. Flannery."

Susan cut in. "Before my fiance begins Captain, would you mind calling your partners back there and ask them if the dead man in the fake police uniform has any ID?"

"Sure Miss McNeil……Whitaker do you read. Over."

"Yes Captain. Over."

"Check the stiff for an ID. Over. This will just take a minute. Have you any idea who he might be? After all, he did a beautiful dive out of YOUR front window."

"Neither one of us knows who he is Captain, but I have a pretty good idea where he's from."

"Oh yeah? Where might that be young lady?"

"New Orleans."

"Captain, he has no ID sir, but we did find a stub in his pocket that reads…let me see…Costume Bazaar, New Orleans. That's all I have sir. Over."

"Thanks Whitaker. Over. Now Miss McNeil, do you want to tell how you knew all that?"

"Have you got about a week Captain?"

"I've got all the time in the world."

The D.C. Police car then came to a halt as the stretcher carrying the critically wounded body of Peter Cappetta was wheeled into the Arlington Hospital emergency room.

LX

In a steady rain the big man wrapped the canvas tarp around his shoulders. He stood at the east end of the loading docks where the sugar crates once sat. They were all loaded aboard the *Rio Escondido* and all that remained was to wait for the tall thin man.

It was Tuesday 7:45am when Esteban Ortiz spotted the big man who appeared even larger in the canvas tarp.

"Good morning Senor Bannister, come with me." The two men walked to the gangplank of the cargo ship. "You've become a very popular man with the Havana Police."

"What are you talking about Ortiz?"

"After I left you last night…the murder of the nightclub singer…you are wanted for questioning. The police…they have turned the city upside down looking for you. I don't know how you've managed to avoid them, you know this is a very small city. I would suggest we get you onboard as quickly as possible Senor."

"She got in the way, too bad. Now how about my new passport?"

"Captain Machado has it. He will ask you for money, American money. Are you prepared to pay him Senor?"

"Another fucking chiseler! What's he gonna want?"

"I don't know Senor…that is him there…we will find out now."

Captain Machado was now walking down the rain slickened gangplank.

"Good morning Captain……Captain Machado…Senor Bannister."

"You are a very hot item at the moment Senor Bannister."

"So I hear Captain."

"And I am…a little reluctant to gamble my assets to benefit your escape. If I take you onboard and then later it is discovered by Cuban officials that I did so…then Senor, I could lose my investment in all this." Machado waved his arm toward his ship.

"Just what are you getting at Captain?"

"Well Senor Bannister, in order for me to immerse myself in such a dilemma, I will have to receive some sort of monetary compensation."

"How much?"

"Say……two thousand in United States currency?"

"Say……you can go fuck yourself!"

"Yes you can…and good day Senor." Machado turned and headed back up the gangplank.

"Captain! Captain! I will reason with Senor Bannister…please!" Machado turned and walked back slowly. Ortiz and the Captain had this whole routine down pat.

Ortiz turned to the big man.

"Senor, he is your only escape from the island. Believe me, if the Cuban officials should arrive here, you will not want to deal with them."

Bannister was too tired and in too much pain to put up much of a fight. But he still wanted to protect what little money he had left.

"Okay Captain…what do ya think about a thousand?"

"Not much Senor."

"But I already paid your buddies...LaValle and Starno!"

"Really Mr. Bannister. I know nothing of those men, they are not my...as you Americans say...buddies. Whatever you paid them was money well spent...after all, you've managed to get this far without interference from the authorities. So Senor, if you want to board my ship, my fee as I've previously stated is two thousand American dollars. It's your decision...my ship will depart in less than fifteen minutes and time is running Senor."

The big man counted out the money and handed it to Ortiz.

"Here...pay the creep."

Bannister then walked up the gangplank and when his back was turned, Ortiz pocketed half the wad and gave the rest to the Captain.

"You'll need this Senor...Melendez." He handed Bannister the South American passport. "Come...I'll show you to your quarters."

Ten minutes later, the *Rio Escondido* steered slowly through the thick fog which now enveloped Havana harbor. In three days time the old ship would reach it's destination and the big man disembarking would call himself Jose Melendez. Even though the villainous Guy Bannister escaped and disappeared from the North American continent, he would forever linger in the minds of those who courageously tried but failed to bring him to justice.

LXI

"Jim…Jim…wake up!"

"Yeah…I'm awake…what time is it?"

After an exhausting interview conducted by Captain McDuffie and the not too encouraging reports on the condition of Peter Cappetta, the two reporters camped out in the Arlington Hospital emergency room.

"It's 8:30 sweetheart and I just got off the phone with Chief Muldoon."

"Oh! Right! My story. I forgot with all the excitement last night."

"Well I told him all about our encounter with that…with the psycho cop and he gave us the day off…but he still wants your story on the meetings in Havana."

"I just have to deliver it…last night I finished it on the plane. And how's our friend Peter doing?"

"Surgery went fine. They got the bullet out and he's resting, but the doctor said that he's still critical. The bullet mushroomed and tore up his insides…he's going to have a long recovery."

"Well I'm glad he's alive…that man saved our lives last night…without him………can we see him?"

"The doctor prefers that he rest with no visitors. Maybe tomorrow."

"If there's no reason to stay then let's get a cab and go home. I've got to get over to the *Post* and then to a meeting at the Oval Office."

"We're certainly coming up in the world aren't we Mr. Flannery!"

"Oh it's no big deal Susan…it's just another meeting with the President."

"Do you hear yourself…just another meeting with the President! Most reporters would give their eyeteeth to have five minutes with President Kennedy!"

"I'm not most reporters…and neither are you."

"What do you mean?"

"Well, on the plane last night the President asked if you were available for today's meeting."

"And what did you tell him?"

"I told him you were busy…I don't know, you were planning to go grocery shopping or something."

"Jim Flannery! You didn't?"

"Of course not! He's expecting us at 3:00pm, something about the campaign."

"The Presidential campaign?"

"Yeah, he wants us to cover the entire campaign through the *Post*. He's already talked with Chief Muldoon about it."

"This sounds very exciting Jim. Boy, things have certainly changed in our lives since the Bourbon Street Grille."

"Yes they have…HEY TAXI!…come on Susan he's stopping."

Outside Arlington Hospital the two reporters climbed in their cab and headed for Georgetown, while in the Oval Office the President watched the morning news. The story that caught his attention was the incident in Georgetown.

The President pressed the call button on his intercom.

"Miss Lincoln, see if you can get a hold of Jim Flannery at the *Post* and uh…call Arlington Hospital and get an update on the condition of Mr. Cappetta."

"Right away sir."

The President sat back in his chair, deep in thought. "The man who saved my life in Dallas was now near death from a gunshot wound…" Just then the buzzing intercom broke the silence.

"Mr. President sir, the hospital reports that the patient came through surgery fine but he's still listed as critical and I found Mr. Flannery at his residence. He's on line two sir."

"Thank you Miss Lincoln." He then pressed line two.

"Hello Jim! I got the news about last night…are you and Susan okay?"

"Yes sir we are but Mr. Cappetta is in a bad way. He's still listed as critical."

"Have you got time to fill me in?"

"Yes sir. When we arrived at my place last night, I invited Peter to spend the night with us. I thought he could use the company after his ordeal in Havana."

"Yeah?"

"He decided to go for a walk and I went up to the apartment where I found Susan tied up in a chair. When I started untying her sir, a man dressed as a cop appeared out of nowhere and placed a gun to my head. He forced me into the bedroom and tied me up. He wanted to get Susan in the bed and have me watch…a real sicko. When he left the bedroom to get her that's when I heard the sound of two men fighting and then a shot went off. Then only moments later I heard glass breaking. Peter threw the man out of the front window and he landed head first in the gutter. Unfortunately, the shot got Peter in the stomach and I really thought we were going to lose him. Susan called the ambulance and that's it sir. Oh! The man had no ID but in his pocket the police found a stub from a costume shop in New Orleans."

"New Orleans!"

"Yes sir. He could be some kind of hitman sent by Bannister...I guess to try to even the score."

"Well this character Bannister...remains the only one at large and I have to think that he's already left Cuba for God knows where. I spoke with Chief Malinsky earlier and his investigation in New Orleans turned up nothing but Bannister's dead wife."

"Bannister's wife sir?"

"Yes. She was murdered in the book shop. The Chief seems to think that it was a professional hit...underworld style."

"So maybe those same people sent the hitman after Susan and me!"

"That's possible Jim...I think it's time to launch a full scale investigation into their activities down there...but you and Susan stay away from this one...no reporting on this and stay out of the limelight for now. We'll put some pressure on them so that they'll have to backoff from going after you two. When we meet this afternoon you can give Chief Malinsky all the details...it might help, but I really have the feeling that Mr. Bannister was not involved in this one and he could be running not only from us, but also from his underworld connections...and in all probabilities...we'll never see or hear from him again."

"I hope you're right sir and uh...at this afternoon's meeting I'll bring you a copy of my story...it's scheduled for tomorrow's edition."

"Good. I'll see you then." When the President hung up he called for his secretary.

"Miss Lincoln, could I pull you away from whatever you're doing? I have a couple of letters to dictate."

"Yes, of course sir."

The President's secretary entered the Oval Office and took her usual seat for dictation.

"Now Miss Lincoln...let's see...a letter to Chairman Khrushchev, Mr. Castro, Prime Minister Macmillan and uh...copies to Roger, my brother, Mr. Rusk and Mr. Flannery. Also Miss Lincoln, flowers to Arlington Hospital for Mr. Cappetta...the card should read…From all your friends at the Oval Office."

"Very good sir. Which letter would you like to start with?"

"Mr. Castro."

"Oh! That reminds me…excuse me for one moment sir."

Miss Lincoln left the Oval Office and moments later returned with a yellow envelope. She handed it to the President.

"This came a few minutes ago sir."

"Thank you." He opened it and unfolded the telegram. It read:

Dear Mr. President Kennedy,

I hope your return flight to Washington was a pleasant one.

The news that I have to report to you is good. My investigators have uncovered two witnesses who claim to have seen two men and a woman leave the El Floridita Hotel within seconds of each other. The first man was described as being very big and a gun was seen tucked in his belt as he ran by them. Undoubtedly, he is the man that Mr. Hilsman alluded to as Bannister. A search for this man has so far produced nothing, but Mr. President, I have decided to release your man from all suspicion. He is no longer a suspect.

It will be unfortunate if this man Bannister is not found. However, we will continue our search and I will keep you informed of our progress.

Sincerely and best regards,
Fidel Castro

"Well, that certainly is encouraging." The President folded the telegram and placed it in the top drawer of his desk. "Okay Miss Lincoln, before I begin dictation there is one other thing to make note of. At the White House Christmas party…let's see that's Saturday the 19th…I would like to honor all those involved in the Dallas operation. Roger, Chief Malinsky and their men…all of them…my brother, the two reporters, Mr. Scali, Mr. Cappetta…although I doubt he'll be able to attend…all of their names should appear on the invitation…honoring them. You'll have to get the names from Roger and the Chief…but don't tell them what I'm planning…and Miss Lincoln, I want your name on it as well."

"Thank you Mr. President."

"You're welcome Miss Lincoln. Roger told me about your performance right here at my desk."

"It was a wonderful team effort sir that I was glad to participate in. It's something I'll never forget!"

"Me too Miss Lincoln…now that letter to Mr. Castro."

LXII

At 3:00pm, Roger Hilsman, the Vice-President, Secretary of State Dean Rusk, Jim Flannery, Susan McNeil, General Maxwell Taylor, Chief Malinsky, the new Foreign Security advisor Sy Stern, the head of intelligence at the State Department Colonel L. Fletcher Prouty, John Scali and the President, all gathered in the main conference room off the Oval Office.

"Gentleman…and Miss McNeil, welcome. There are a number of issues that I would like to go over with you today that are of importance to the future of this administration. First, I introduce you to Mr. Sy Stern. Mr. Stern has taken over the duties of McGeorge Bundy who as you all know was uh…cut from the team, to put it mildly. Second, my visit to Havana was very encouraging. I fully expect to be working closely with Mr. Castro along with Chairman Khrushchev. The Cuban report is there in your packets and uh…we are presently putting together with the Soviets and Cuba, a summit to be hosted by Prime Minister Macmillan in Great Britain. I realize that a neutral site is the tradition here and with Great Britain our ally, Khrushchev and Castro may turn down the idea. We'll see soon enough, I've sent out letters today to both. Anyway, we're looking at an early spring date."

"Timing couldn't be better with the campaign and all sir."

"Yes Roger and before we begin our discussion on the campaign...with General Taylor's assistance, I've made my selection for the vacated top post at the Pentagon. General Frank Stratton will assume the duties as the Chairman of the Joint Chiefs of Staff."

"Good choice Mr. President."

"Thank you Dean. General Stratton never believed in the code of the industrial military complex. He told me many times that the Pentagon and the military hardware makers were gaining too much power and that when Eisenhower lost control of them, they became detrimental to the American way of life. Their code revolved around American involvement in confiicts around the world. This administration will have none of it...I promise you. Now, if there are no objections...the campaign. Mr. Vice-President, I'd like you to put together a list of cities that you believe are important. Cities that we had difficulty with in 1960 along with those that we did well with."

"Right Mr. President. Is your plan to have us, meaning you and I split up these cities for speaking engagements?"

"Yes. We'll be very busy traveling around the country...so let's prepare our strategy to cover as much ground in as little time as possible. I also want to spend a good deal of time on foreign affairs. My targets have increased in size since the talks with Mr. Castro."

"And Mr. President sir, what targets do you have in mind?"

"Well Dean, outside of Vietnam it's time that I approach Mr. Khrushchev about removing that uh...that Wall."

"In Berlin sir?"

"Yes, it's time to remove any obstacles that threaten peace and freedom anywhere in the world."

"Mr. Khrushchev's not likely to budge on that one sir."

"I feel differently about that Roger. When the Kremlin sees my entire Vietnam withdrawal plan at our next summit, my belief is that they will get the full picture of the American effort toward peace. And in order for the Soviets to participate in the peace process which Mr. Khrushchev has already supported, then they will have to make consessions of their own. That's when I'll raise the issue of the Berlin Wall."

"I like your plan sir. But in the event that Khrushchev resists, a good backup may be the presentation of a joint space program...you know, work together to put a man on the moon...it's possible sir."

"That's a brilliant idea Mr. Stern. I like it...I like it a lot. Please, outline your idea and we'll discuss it further......and uh...we seem to have gotten off the campaign track. Jim and Susan, I've asked you here today to get your feelings on traveling with the Vice-President and I on the campaign trail. I've already spoken to your editor and he's all for it. How does that sound to the two of you?"

"We're ready Mr. President."

"Good Susan. Jim, when we adjourn would you spend a little time filling in Chief Malinsky on your ordeal last night?"

"Of course Mr. President."

"Now, considering that the Republicans are in complete disarray at the moment, the candidates that show the most strength are Governor Rockefeller and Senator Goldwater. In my eyes neither presents much of a challenge. The Governor lacks the fortitude and spirit to run this office, while the Senator's ideas concerning the eradication of North Vietnam, lead me to believe that he has a serious shortage of gray matter."

Everyone in the room laughed out loud.

"So, with those two as the strength of the party...I believe the Republican Convention, although over six months away will be a real dogfight with Governor Rockefeller and Senator Goldwater falling by the wayside. The only serious challenger will rise from the ashes and give us one hell of a fight."

"Who are you speaking of Mr. President?"

"The man who gave us fits the last time…Richard Nixon."

LXIII

Arrangements were made, invitations went out and all who participated in the Dallas operation were honored at the White House Christmas Party. All with the exception of one. At Arlington Hospital, Peter Cappetta was still recovering. After a series of setbacks including internal bleeding and a mysterious infection that had all the doctors baffled, the patient was eventually stabilized and scheduled for release shortly after the holidays.

About the time of Cappetta's release, the first part of the President's Vietnam plans were underway. A little over one thousand troops were back on U.S. soil, while the remaining fourteen thousand continued training the South Vietnamese Army for their struggle against the North. In a little over a year all U.S. troops would be shipped home and the American involvement in Southeast Asia would come to an end. And with the Soviets following the American lead by halting their military supply flow to the North, peace appeared a viable entity. The only stumbling block to arise was Red China. They became a huge obstacle. Chinese leader

Mao Tse-tung balked at the American President's peace plan and then broke communist ties with the Soviet Union. Mao continued to support the communist North with military supplies and the Vietnam struggle continued. Still, during the first six months of 1964, correspondence between the United States, the Soviet Union and Red China continued in an effort to bring peace to the tiny but volatile country of Vietnam.

Before beginning the campaign tour, the President created a new department in the administration to deal solely with the Civil Rights issues. He asked his good friend Martin Luther King to head up the department which the Reverend gladly accepted with one stipulation. He insisted that any salary associated with the post, be given to organizations in the south that would benefit the advancement of all Black Americans. The President of course agreed and Reverend King was quickly at work in the White House with his number one assistant John Nash at his side. The pair worked closely with Vice-President Bobby Kennedy in tackling issues of importance, which resulted in a welcomed atmosphere of calm in American race relations.

During that first six months of 1964, the President and the Vice-President traversed the country with stops in Boston, New York City, Pittsburgh, Richmond, Charlotte, Charleston, Atlanta, Montgomery, Memphis, Louisville, Dayton, Chicago, Detroit, Milwaukee, St. Louis, Rapid City, Omaha, Topeka, Little Rock, Tulsa, Denver, Helena, Salt Lake City, Seattle, Los Angeles, Phoenix and Santa Fe. Missing from the stops were cities in Louisiana and Texas for obvious reasons. The President had already made his campaign swing through the Lone Star state. He saw no reason to return…ever.

Mixed into the hectic schedule in early April was the three day summit in Great Britain. Everyone involved agreed that a break from tradition was refreshing in having the English host the talks. Chairman Mao declined his invitation.

At the summit, again the President was right on the money.

After a discussion involving United States intentions in Southeast Asia, the President pressed the Berlin issue. The Soviet Premier treated the situation very matter of factly. He gave the impression that it was something the Kremlin felt necessary if the present plans for peace were to be successful. He gave a mid summer date to begin demolition of the wall and the President still had the space program ace up his sleeve.

Also during this politically bustling six months the trials began for the conspirators. In addition to those initially arrested, Chief Malinsky's investigation in New Orleans and into the Dallas Police Department turned up another half dozen dirty cops and the head of New Orleans underworld activities Carlos Marcello. Along with Marcello a flunky by the name of Hank Ripperton was also collared. Sam Giancana and Santos Trafficante were also snared in Malinsky's net. Vice-President Johnson's involvement was detailed in testimony given by all four Generals in an effort toward leniency. When the trials ended in mid June, there would be no leniency. Each conspirator was rewarded for their efforts with nothing less than life imprisonment.

The book was closed on the havoc in Dallas just as the President geared up for re-election. The Democratic convention produced no surprises. The very popular incumbent President went uncontested as opposed to the Republican debacle. At their convention, Goldwater and Rockefeller destroyed each other in a head to head drawn out battle, while Richard Nixon slipped in on the third ballot. The slate was set. After beating the Republican by a mere one tenth of one percent in 1960, the President's worst fears were realized. The never say die Nixon was intent on gaining the seat he so desired. In his mind that seat was a throne, the throne of the King and Richard Nixon would spare no one in his quest for that majestic power.

LXIV

As promised by the Soviet Premier the Berlin Wall came down. It came down to the absolute delight of all Berliners. It was late September and a bit later than originally pledged but Khrushchev planned it that way. He wanted the American public to see President Kennedy's efforts in the homestretch of the Presidential campaign. Working with Richard Nixon the communist hater, he knew would be an impossibility, so he did everything he could to assist the President's bid for re-election.

It was at this time that the mud slinging began. The Republican candidate attacked the President's meetings with the communist leaders calling them a prelude to communism manipulating its way into the mainstream of the American system. The majority of Americans considered Nixon's attacks as foolish and placed little stock in his approach. He began the process of burying himself.

The death blow to his aspirations was delivered when he challenged the President to a return to the famous 1960 Great Debates. In a paid television announcement, the President answered the Nixon challenge with the following:

"When you Mr. Nixon have something intelligent to say in this campaign, concerning the issues of importance to all Americans, THEN I will gladly meet you face to face in the forum of your choice. However, as long as you continue in your efforts to deceive the American public with your mud slinging lies, one cannot help but believe that whatever issues are chosen to debate, your answers will be filled with more deception. For this reason I have to decline."

This was a complete departure from 1960 when then Senator Kennedy challenged Vice-President Nixon to a series of debates. Nixon was then urged by President Eisenhower to decline. Going against Eisenhower's recommendation, Nixon accepted the Senator's challenge and the rest is history.

After viewing the President's television response, Nixon dug himself deeper by continuing his attacks, completely avoiding the issues of importance on the minds of the voting public. The President's strategy had worked. The polls showed the incumbent ahead by an overwhelming margin.

Even though the polls heavily favored the President, no one expected what occurred on election night, November 3rd, 1964. American voters turned out in record numbers in support of their President, producing the landslide of the century. It was more than a landslide, it was a complete demolition of the Republican candidate Richard Nixon. Even the state of California voted against its favorite son by a margin of 4 to 1.

When all the votes were tallied, the President pulled in a whopping 82% of the popular vote. Nixon was devastated. He refused to concede and left his headquarters in Los Angeles without acknowledging his staff or his opponent's victory. Despondent and depressed, he immediately returned to his San Clemente compound and spoke with no one. His dream was shattered.

The Saturday after the election Susan McNeil became Mrs.

James Flannery in a ceremony hosted by the President and First Lady in the White House dining hall. The President's election victory and the marriage of the two reporters, who one year earlier were instrumental in saving the life of the President, were both celebrated in a grand and glorious style. Serving as Jim Flannery's best man was the unassuming Peter Cappetta, the man who not only saved the President, but also the young couple from a certain death.

Sunday morning the newlyweds left on a one week honeymoon to Bermuda while in San Clemente, a despondent Richard Nixon paced his study. He was haunted by his inability to address the issues. The issues that his opponent flawlessly dealt with. In his tortured mind, his only hope was to attack and whatever approach he took, it failed. He thought – "The throne will never be mine."

He then walked slowly to his desk. The top drawer was open. He stared down on the snub nosed .38 sitting in the open drawer, just as he had done every night since the election. This time he lifted it and placed it to his temple. He closed his eyes and whispered softly – "God forgive me." He then squeezed the trigger.

LXV

By early Sunday evening, the news from San Clemente flooded the airwaves from California to Connecticut. The major television networks worked feverishly compiling footage on the life of Richard Nixon. His years in the House, the Senate, the two terms as the Vice-President and the three bitter losses.

The first loss produced the closest Presidential race in history. The second was a tough pill to swallow. His bid for the Governorship of his home state ended the same way. In a press conference following that defeat, his words were – "You won't have Nixon to kick around anymore, because gentlemen, this is my last press conference."

However, Nixon just couldn't stay away. His lust for power propelled him to the top of the party ticket in the Republican drive to regain the White House. But again, it wasn't meant to be. In the most lopsided election in history, Richard Nixon emerged the loser. Three major elections, three heartbreaking losses tortured the mind of the one time great politician.

President Kennedy's observations of the death of Allen Dulles were that "…tortured minds present drastic choices…and more often than not…make rash decisions." Once again those words rang true. This time for Richard Nixon.

When the news hit Washington D.C., a dark cloud fell over the White House. The President always considered his rival a tough and worthy opponent. He had great respect for his years of service to the American political system and, for those reasons, the President asked Congress to erect a memorial in Nixon's honor. Congress agreed and plans were quickly underway to pay homage to the fallen leader.

As the weeks rolled by, the gloom that encompassed the White house had lifted and the President began work on his Inaugural Address. He wanted it to be his best. Along with the administration's plans for the future, he would recognize those who unselfishly made contributions during the turbulent year that just passed.

On Inauguration Day January 20th, 1965, President John F. Kennedy gave his most moving speech.

In the frigid air on that winter day, the President outlined his domestic plans for the next four years. He then honored the fallen leader of the past election. He honored the man who saved his life in Dallas with the Medal of Freedom and he honored the efforts of those communist leaders who had moved toward peace.

The President's eloquence resonated across the country as he spoke of Berlin, Cuba, the Soviet Union, Vietnam and Civil Rights.

He spoke of the new found freedom without the Wall. He spoke of the lifted embargo and how those in need on that tiny island, were already benefitting. He spoke of the working relationship with America's chief rival since World War II. He spoke of the end of an American involvement in a conflict that needed to be settled by its own people. And finally he spoke of the improving relations of all ethnic groups within the confines of the shores of the United States.

The nightmares of the past were gone. Now, with the President's vision of peace and equality, America was on the path of setting the example for all to follow.

He also let it be known that although great strides had been made, hard work and perseverance were the key elements in maintaining the American position in the global arena. However, there was still the problem of Red China to be dealt with. Speaking of Red China, in 1964 a song was written about war and devastation. The name of that song was 'On the Eve of Destruction.' The words of war no longer held truth. The one line of significance went as follows – "Think of all the hate…there is in Red China…" The song was never released. There was no war, no marches, no demonstrations and no divisions among the people. It was 1965 and America was at peace. A pleasant thought.

Could it have come to pass in the manner presented on these pages? The possibilities extend far beyond this study. However, all chances for a peaceful America were inexorably crushed, when the assassin's bullets rained down on our young President. Although the sun was shining, it may have been one of the darkest days in American history. It was Friday, November 22nd, 1963.

On that day, it rained in Dallas.

It Rained In Dallas